O9-AIF-613

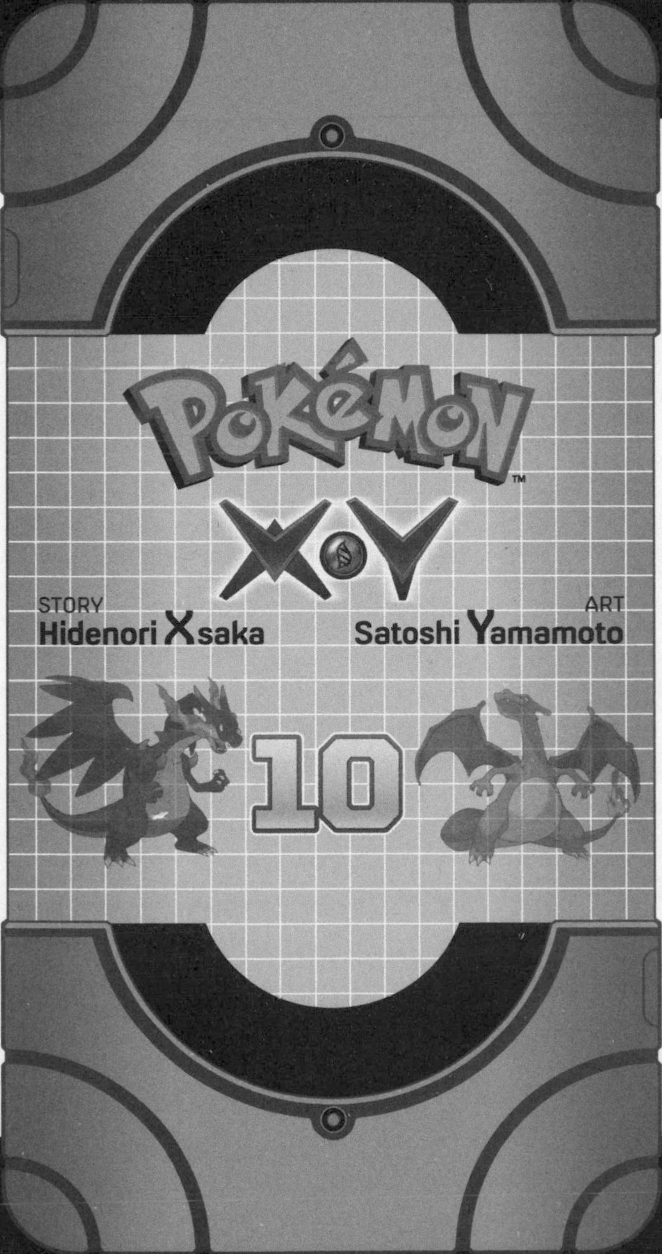
POKÉMON™
X•Y
STORY
Hidenori Xsaka
ART
Satoshi Yamamoto
10

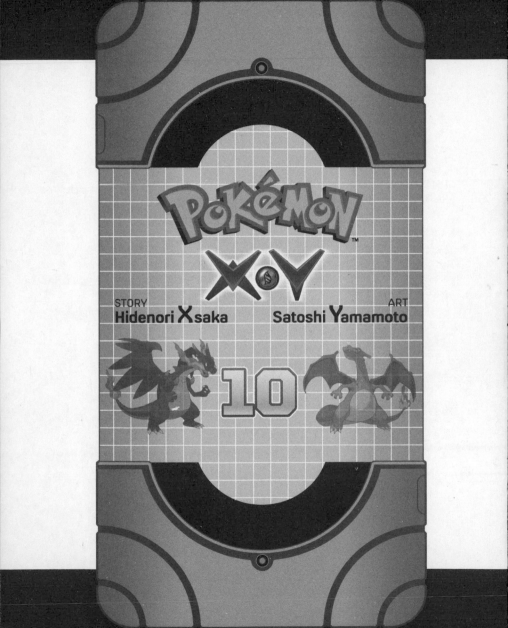

CHARACTERS

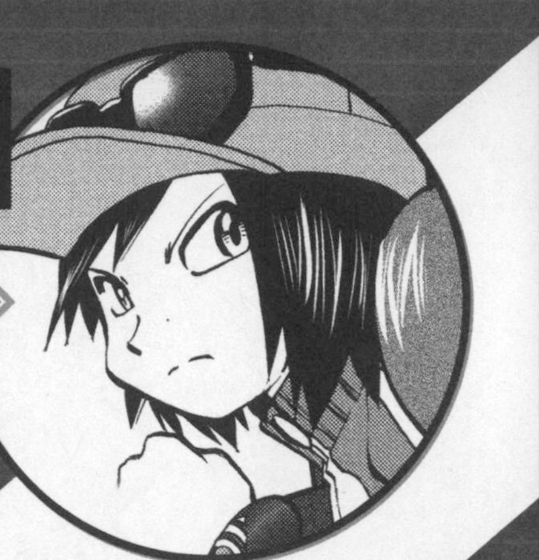

X

The main character of this chapter, and one of five close childhood friends. He was once a highly skilled Trainer who even won the Junior Pokémon Battle Tournament, but now...

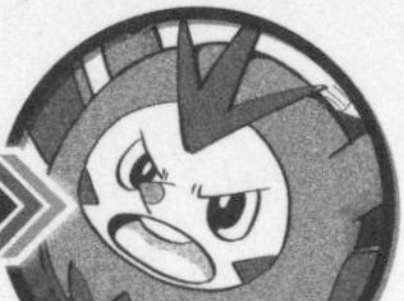

MARISSO

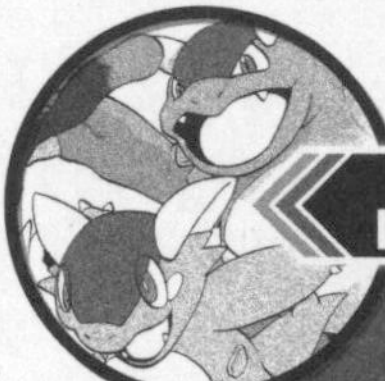

KANGA & LI'L KANGA

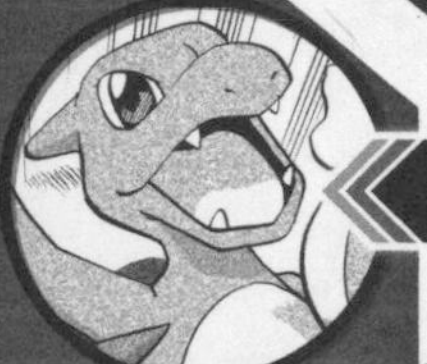

SALAMÈ

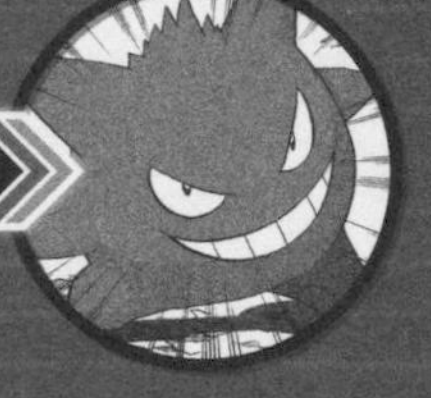

GARMA

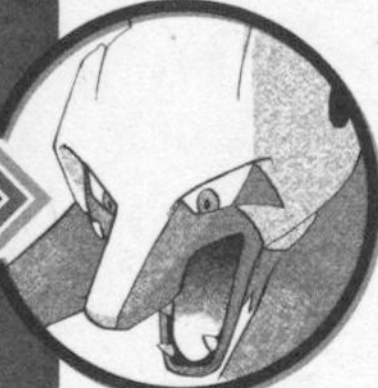

ÉLEC

OUR STORY THUS FAR...

In Vaniville Town in the Kalos region, X is a Pokémon Trainer child prodigy. But then he falls into a depression. A sudden attack by the legendary Pokémon Xerneas and Yveltal, controlled by Team Flare, forces X out into the world. He and his closest childhood friends—Y, Trevor, Tierno and Shauna—are now on the run. Turns out Team Flare has a nefarious plan to fire an ancient artifact called the Ultimate Weapon and destroy the Kalos region. Xerneas allies itself with Y and Yveltal allies itself with Team Flare's Malva. How will X and his friends increase their power to have a chance of winning the next battle and saving Kalos...?! And how does Mega Evolution fit into all this?!

MEET THE

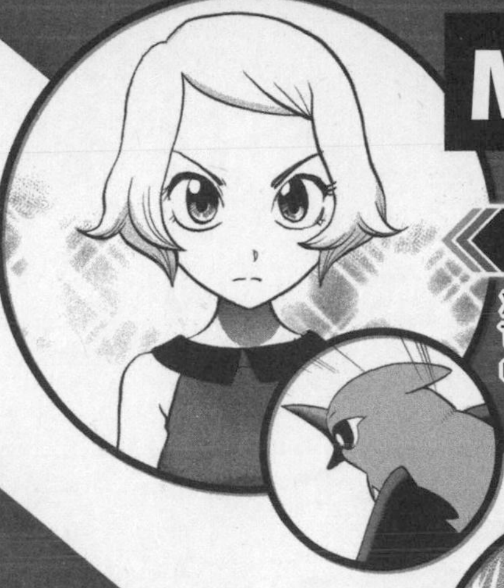

Y

X's best friend, a Sky Trainer trainee. Her full name is Yvonne Gabena.

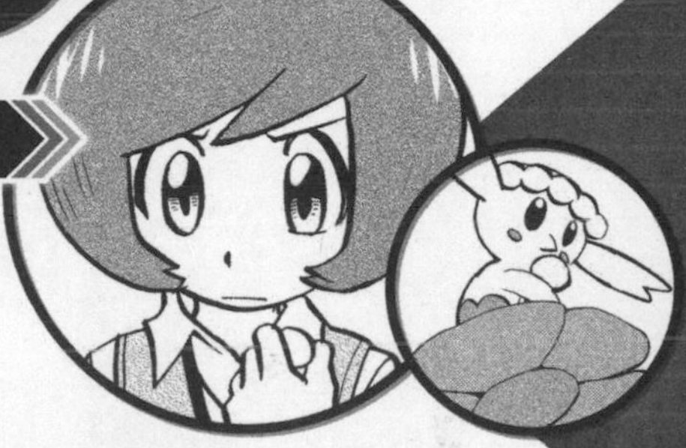

TREVOR

One of the five friends. A quiet boy who hopes to become a fine Pokémon Researcher one day.

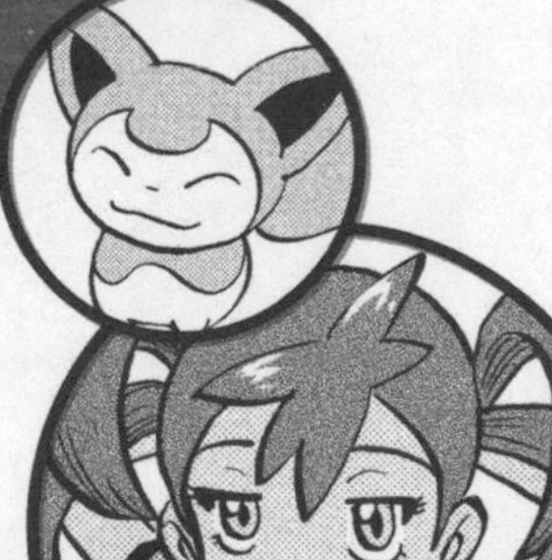

SHAUNA

One of the five friends. Her dream is to become a Furfrou Groomer. She is quick to speak her mind.

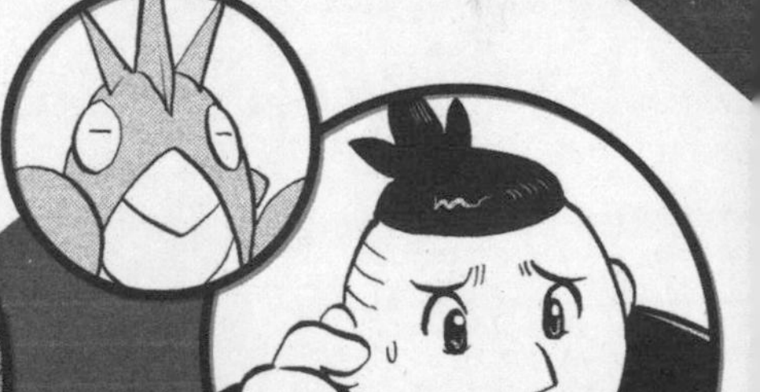

TIERNO

One of the five friends. A big boy with an even bigger hear He is currently training to become a dancer.

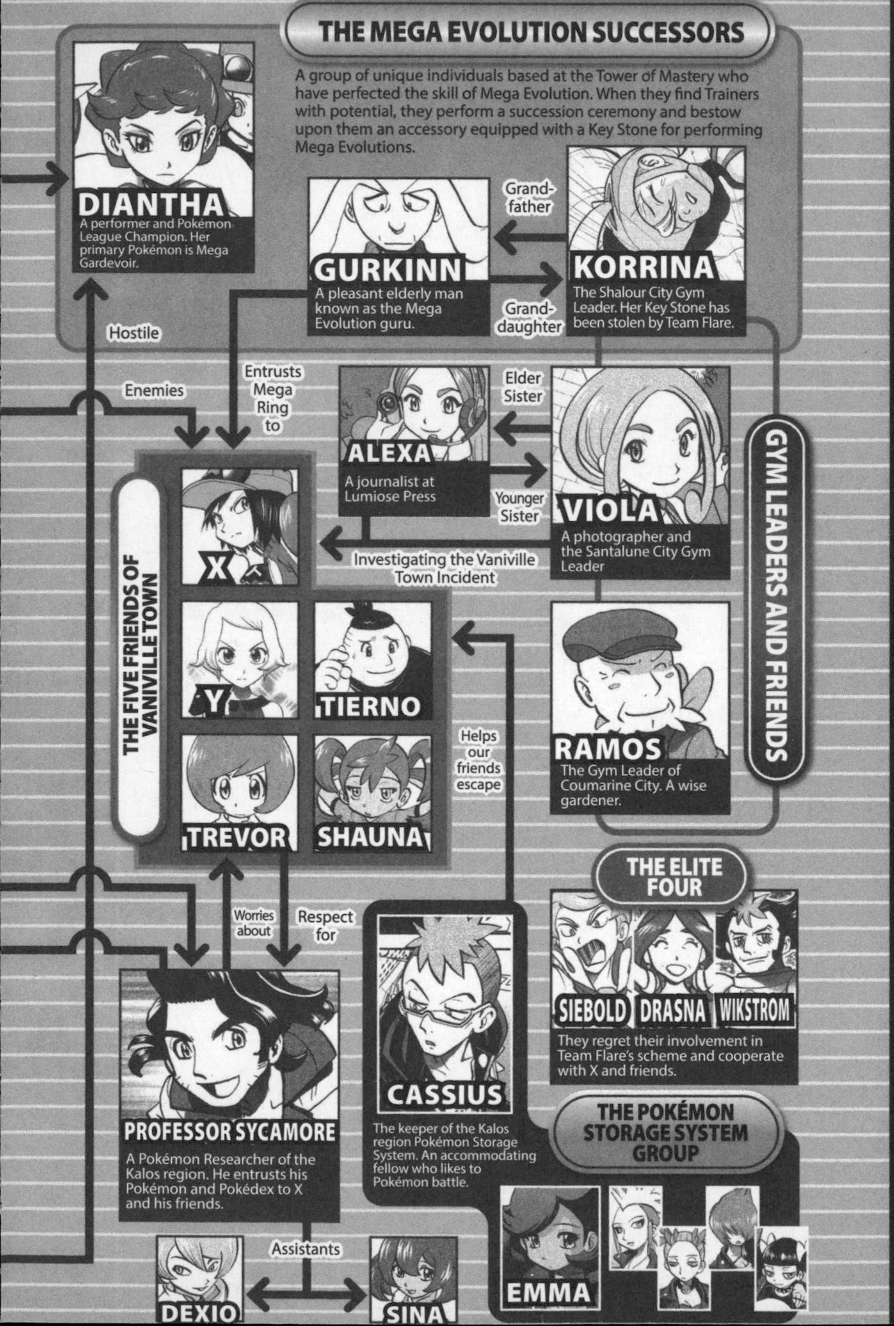
THE MEGA EVOLUTION SUCCESSORS
A group of unique individuals based at the Tower of Mastery who have perfected the skill of Mega Evolution. When they find Trainers with potential, they perform a succession ceremony and bestow upon them an accessory equipped with a Key Stone for performing Mega Evolutions.
DIANTHA
A performer and Pokémon League Champion. Her primary Pokémon is Mega Gardevoir.
Grand-father
GURKINN
A pleasant elderly man known as the Mega Evolution guru.
Grand-daughter
KORRINA
The Shalour City Gym Leader. Her Key Stone has been stolen by Team Flare.
Hostile
Enemies
Entrusts Mega Ring to
Elder Sister
ALEXA
A journalist at Lumiose Press
Younger Sister
VIOLA
A photographer and the Santalune City Gym Leader
Investigating the Vaniville Town Incident
GYM LEADERS AND FRIENDS
THE FIVE FRIENDS OF VANIVILLE TOWN
X
Y
TIERNO
TREVOR
SHAUNA
Helps our friends escape
RAMOS
The Gym Leader of Coumarine City. A wise gardener.
THE ELITE FOUR
SIEBOLD
DRASNA
WIKSTROM
They regret their involvement in Team Flare's scheme and cooperate with X and friends.
Worries about
Respect for
PROFESSOR SYCAMORE
A Pokémon Researcher of the Kalos region. He entrusts his Pokémon and Pokédex to X and his friends.
CASSIUS
The keeper of the Kalos region Pokémon Storage System. An accommodating fellow who likes to Pokémon battle.
THE POKÉMON STORAGE SYSTEM GROUP
EMMA
Assistants
DEXIO
SINA

CHARACTER CORRELATION CHART

Track the connections between the people revolving around X.

TEAM FLARE

An organization identifiable by their red uniforms that has been scheming behind the scenes in the Kalos region. They successfully obtained the Legendary Pokémon Xerneas and the power of Mega Evolution and just stole Korrina's Key Stone. Now they are ready to put their evil plan in motion...!

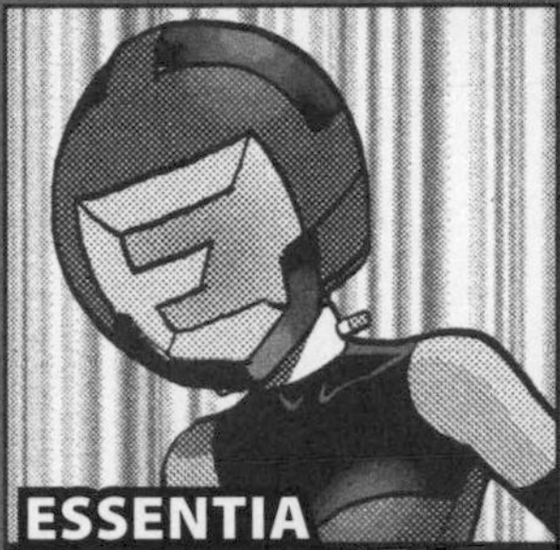

ESSENTIA

A mysterious Trainer who wears an Expansion Suit.

Development

Obedience to

TEAM FLARE'S SCIENTIFIC TEAM

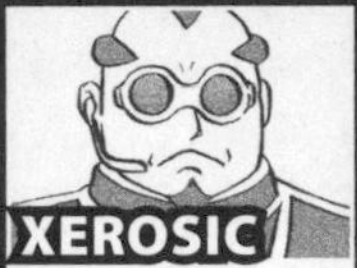

XEROSIC

Member of Unit A. Developed Team Flare's gadgets and the Expansion Suit.

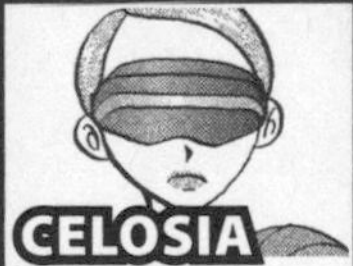

CELOSIA

Member of Unit A. A vengeful woman who somehow always bounces back from failure.

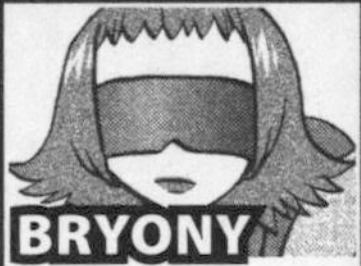

BRYONY

Member of Unit A. A quiet bookworm and military scientist who studies battles.

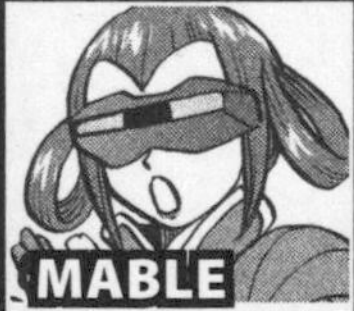

MABLE

Member of Unit B. Outspoken and emotional.

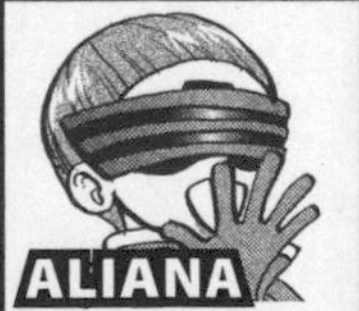

ALIANA

Member of Unit B. Charged with obtaining the Mega Ring.

Old Friends

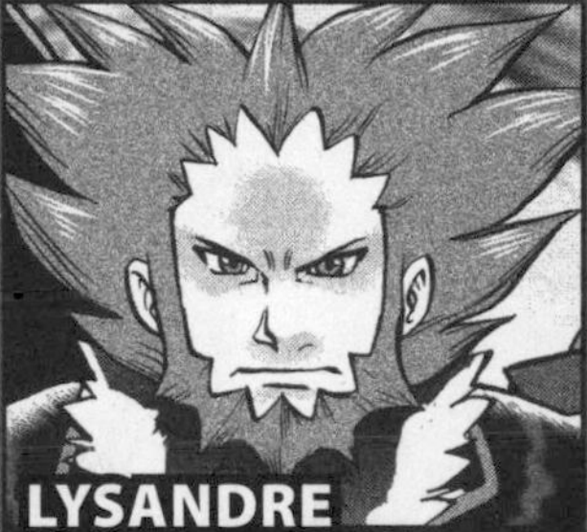

LYSANDRE

The developer of the Holo Caster. He has a reputation for charitable acts but is secretly the boss of Team Flare. He plans to destroy the world and rebuild it from scratch.

Loyalty

Trust

Support

Reports on his research

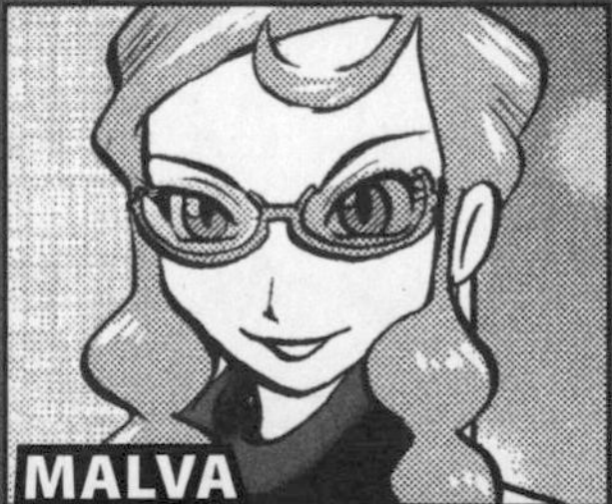

MALVA

A member of the Kalos Elite Four and also secretly a member of Team Flare. Often works as a news reporter and manipulates the media to the benefit of Team Flare.

Proposes plans, assists others

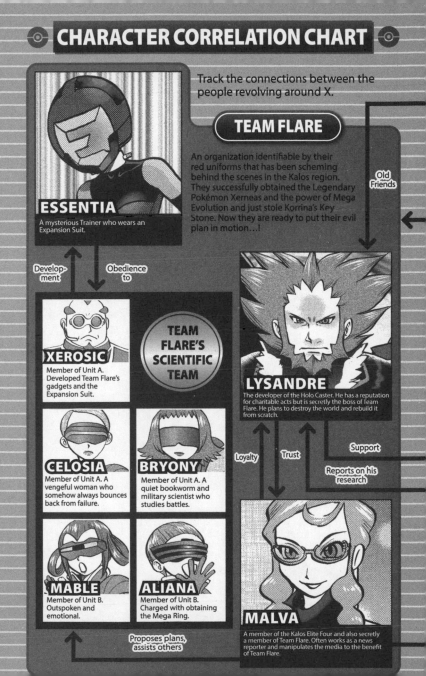

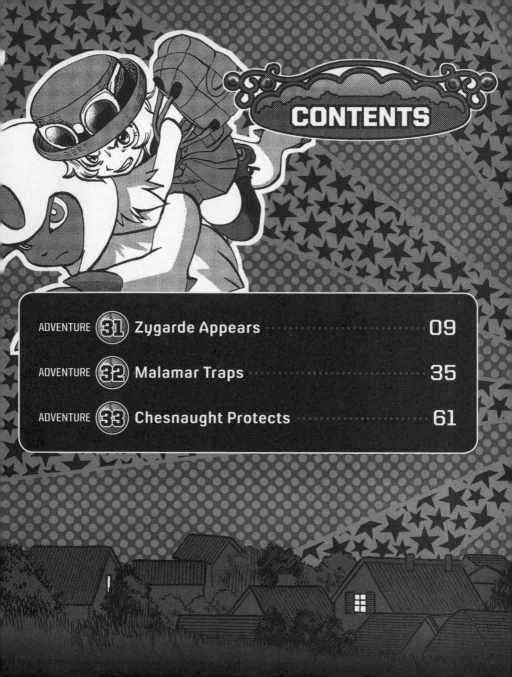

CONTENTS

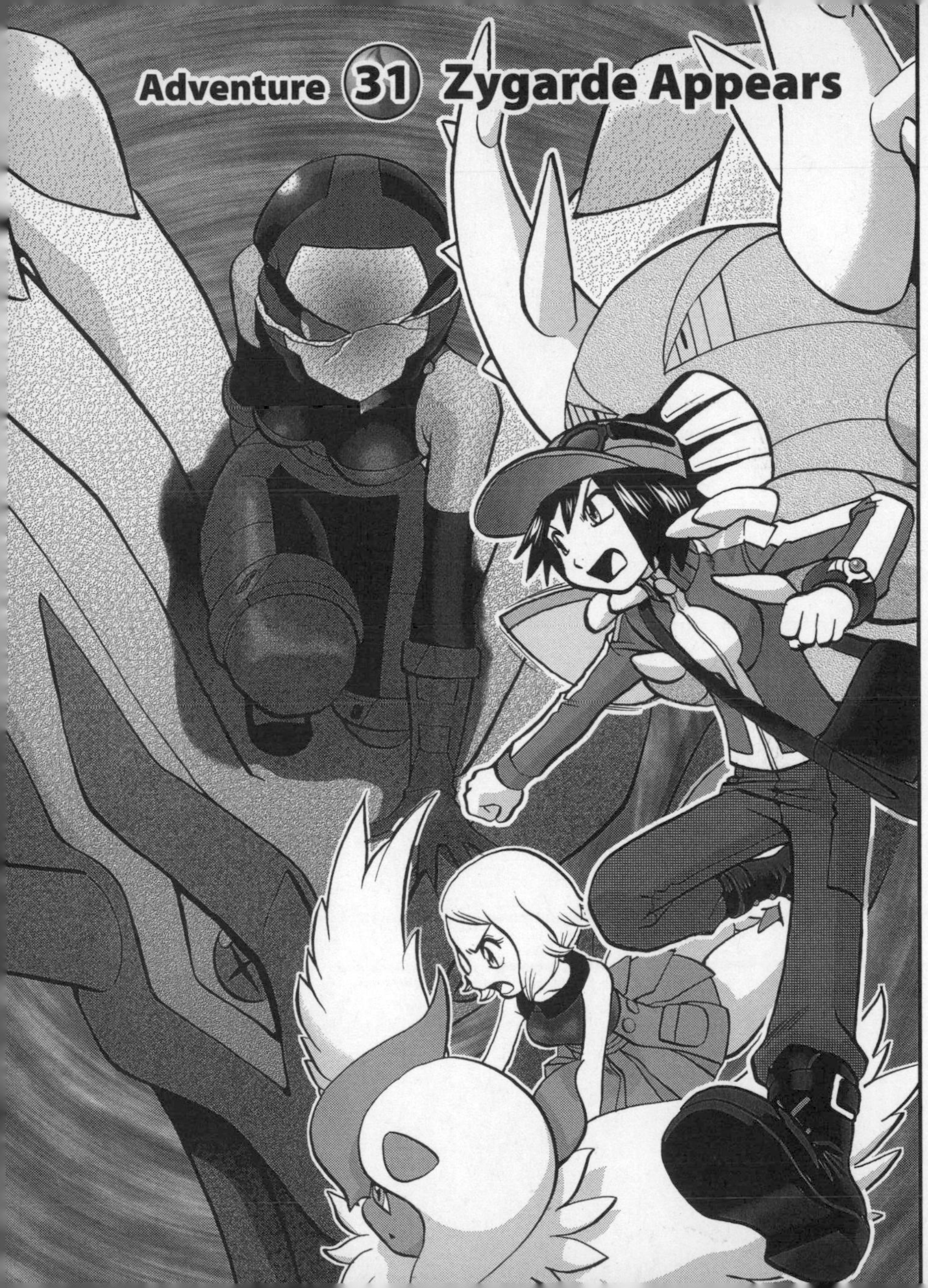
Adventure 31 Zygarde Appears

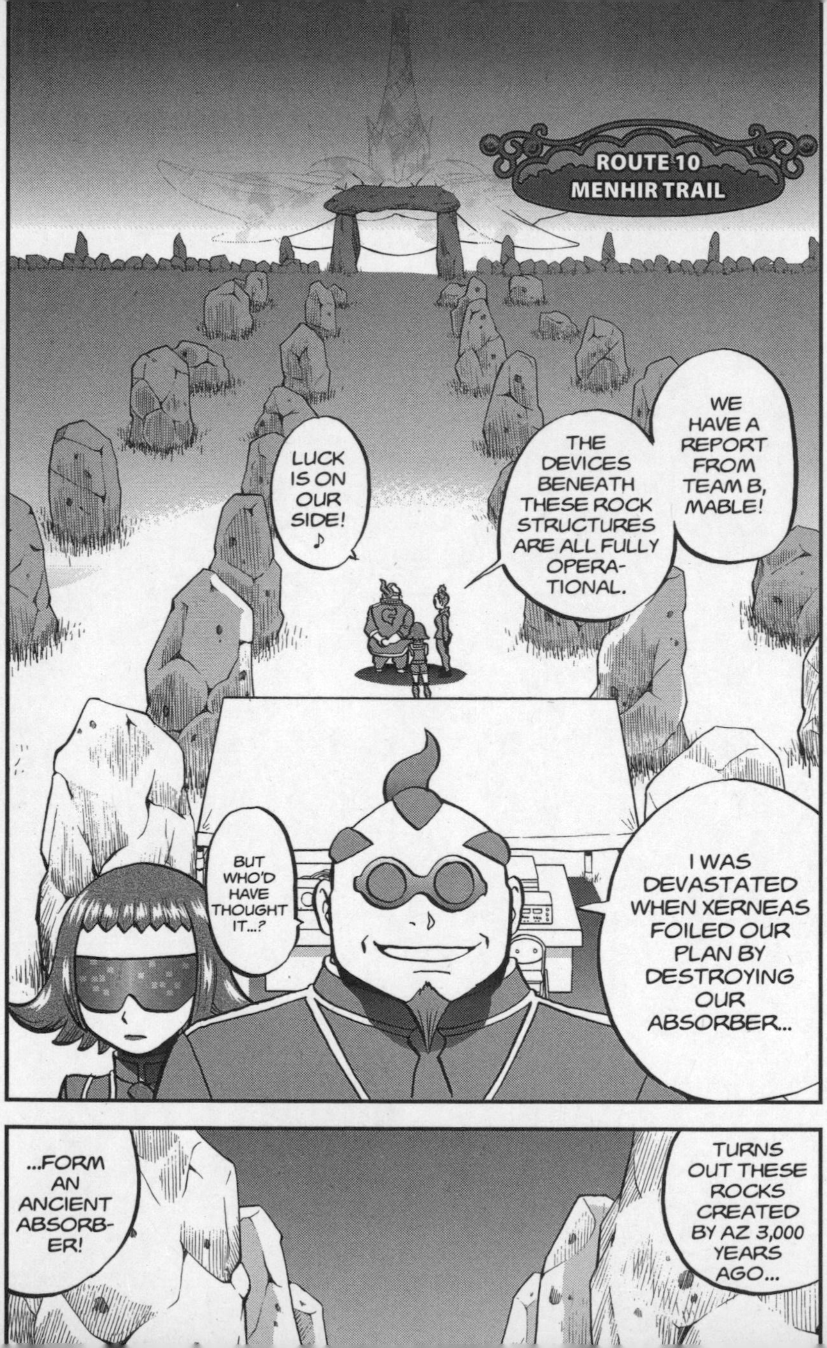
ROUTE 10 MENHIR TRAIL
WE HAVE A REPORT FROM TEAM B, MABLE!
THE DEVICES BENEATH THESE ROCK STRUCTURES ARE ALL FULLY OPERA-TIONAL.
LUCK IS ON OUR SIDE! ♪
I WAS DEVASTATED WHEN XERNEAS FOILED OUR PLAN BY DESTROYING OUR ABSORBER...
BUT WHO'D HAVE THOUGHT IT...?
TURNS OUT THESE ROCKS CREATED BY AZ 3,000 YEARS AGO...
...FORM AN ANCIENT ABSORB-ER!

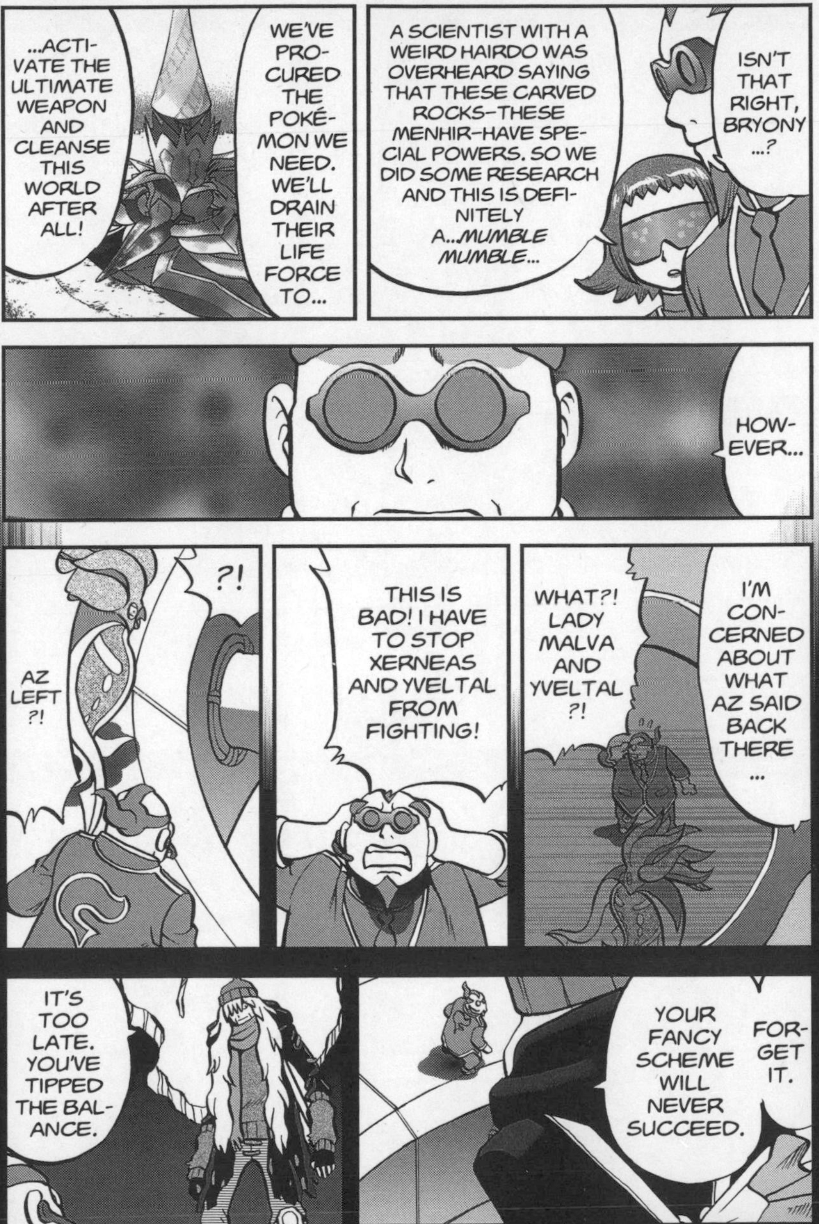
ISN'T THAT RIGHT, BRYONY ...?
A SCIENTIST WITH A WEIRD HAIRDO WAS OVERHEARD SAYING THAT THESE CARVED ROCKS—THESE MENHIR—HAVE SPECIAL POWERS. SO WE DID SOME RESEARCH AND THIS IS DEFINITELY A...*MUMBLE MUMBLE*...
WE'VE PROCURED THE POKÉMON WE NEED. WE'LL DRAIN THEIR LIFE FORCE TO...
...ACTIVATE THE ULTIMATE WEAPON AND CLEANSE THIS WORLD AFTER ALL!
HOWEVER...
I'M CONCERNED ABOUT WHAT AZ SAID BACK THERE ...
WHAT?! LADY MALVA AND YVELTAL ?!
THIS IS BAD! I HAVE TO STOP XERNEAS AND YVELTAL FROM FIGHTING!
?!
AZ LEFT ?!
FORGET IT.
YOUR FANCY SCHEME WILL NEVER SUCCEED.
IT'S TOO LATE. YOU'VE TIPPED THE BALANCE.

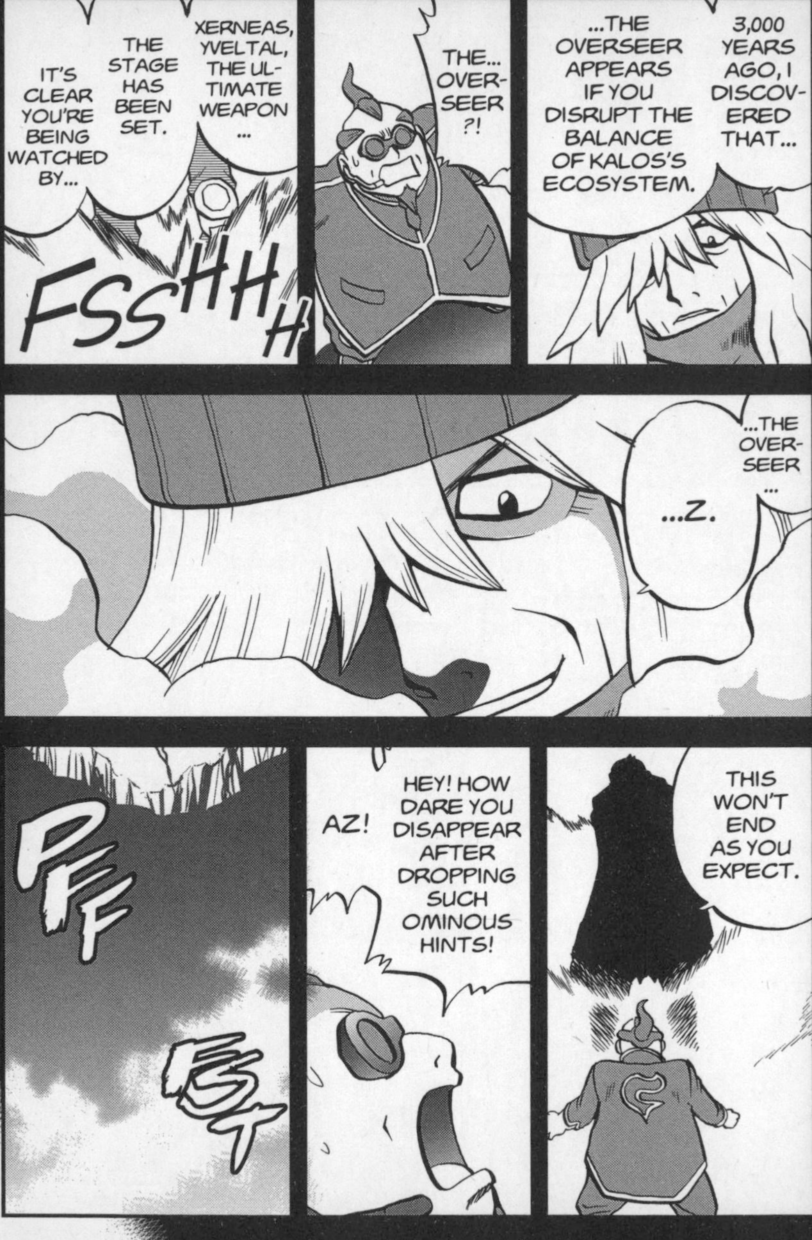
3,000 YEARS AGO, I DISCOVERED THAT...
...THE OVERSEER APPEARS IF YOU DISRUPT THE BALANCE OF KALOS'S ECOSYSTEM.
THE... OVERSEER?!
XERNEAS, YVELTAL, THE ULTIMATE WEAPON...
THE STAGE HAS BEEN SET.
IT'S CLEAR YOU'RE BEING WATCHED BY...
FSSHHHH
...THE OVERSEER...
...Z.
THIS WON'T END AS YOU EXPECT.
HEY! HOW DARE YOU DISAPPEAR AFTER DROPPING SUCH OMINOUS HINTS!
AZ!
PFFF
FST

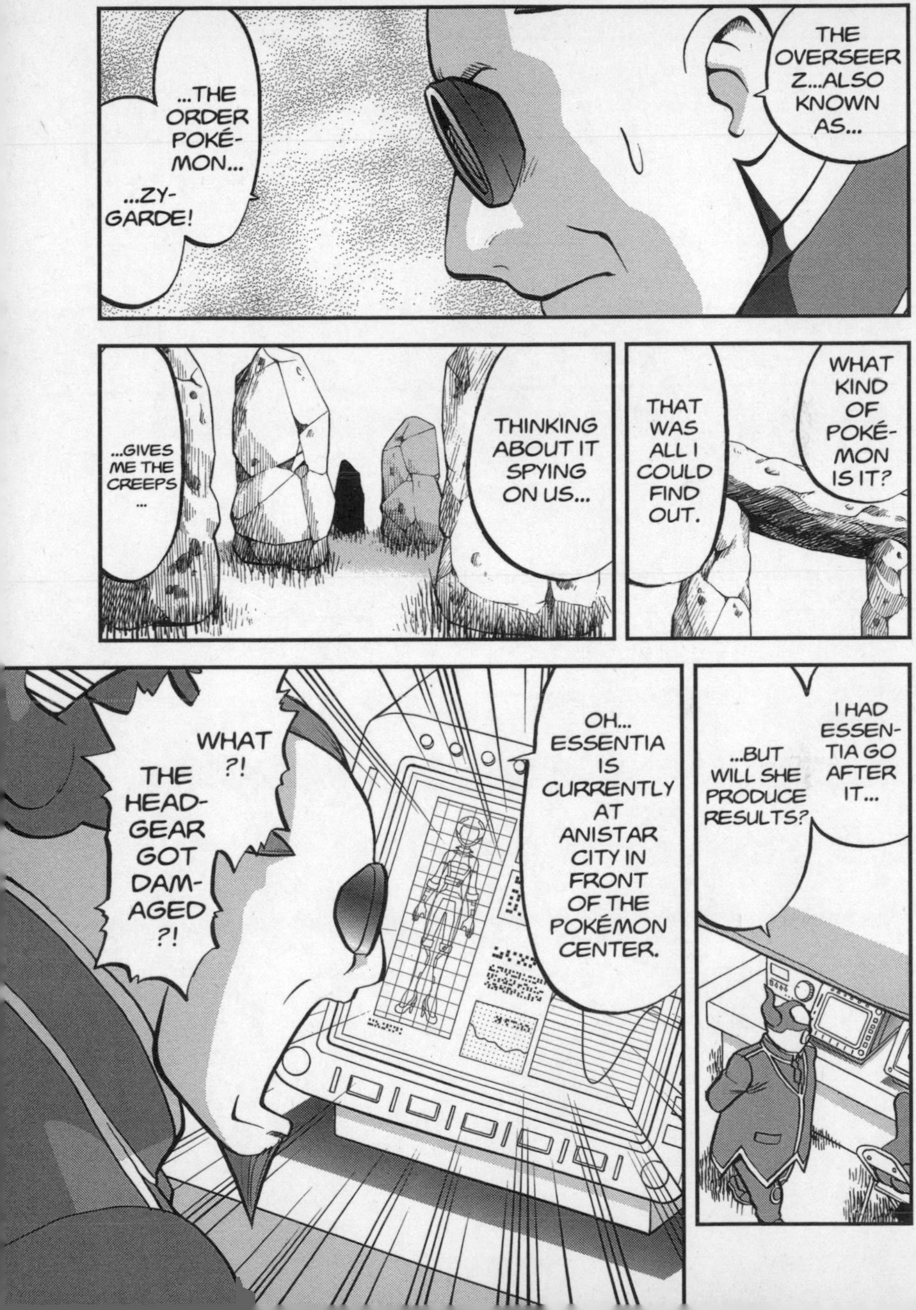
THE OVERSEER Z...ALSO KNOWN AS...
...THE ORDER POKÉMON...
...ZYGARDE!
WHAT KIND OF POKÉMON IS IT?
THAT WAS ALL I COULD FIND OUT.
THINKING ABOUT IT SPYING ON US...
...GIVES ME THE CREEPS...
I HAD ESSENTIA GO AFTER IT...
...BUT WILL SHE PRODUCE RESULTS?
OH... ESSENTIA IS CURRENTLY AT ANISTAR CITY IN FRONT OF THE POKÉMON CENTER.
WHAT?!
THE HEADGEAR GOT DAMAGED?!

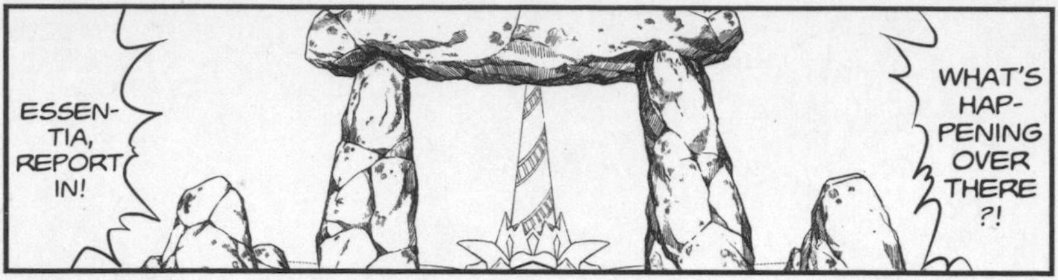
WHAT'S HAP-PENING OVER THERE?!
ESSEN-TIA, REPORT IN!

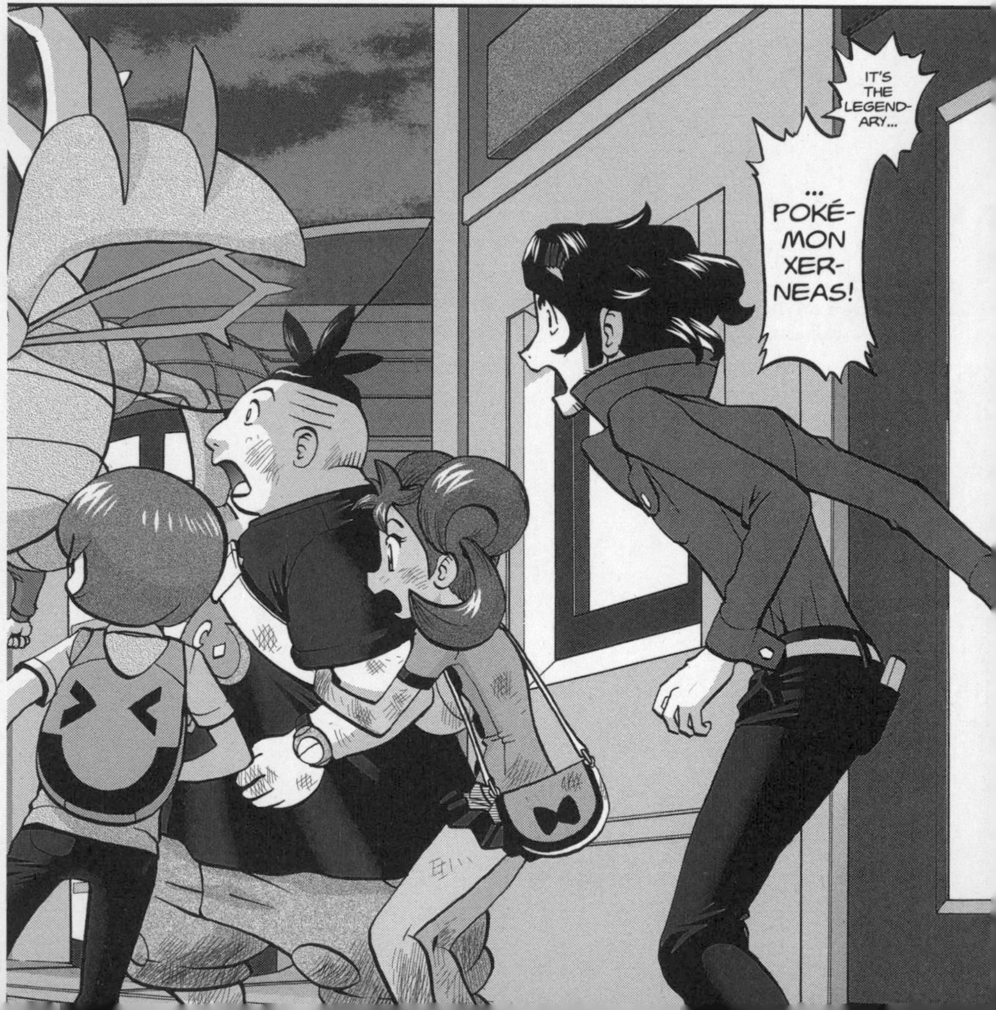
IT'S THE LEGEND-ARY...
...POKÉ-MON XER-NEAS!

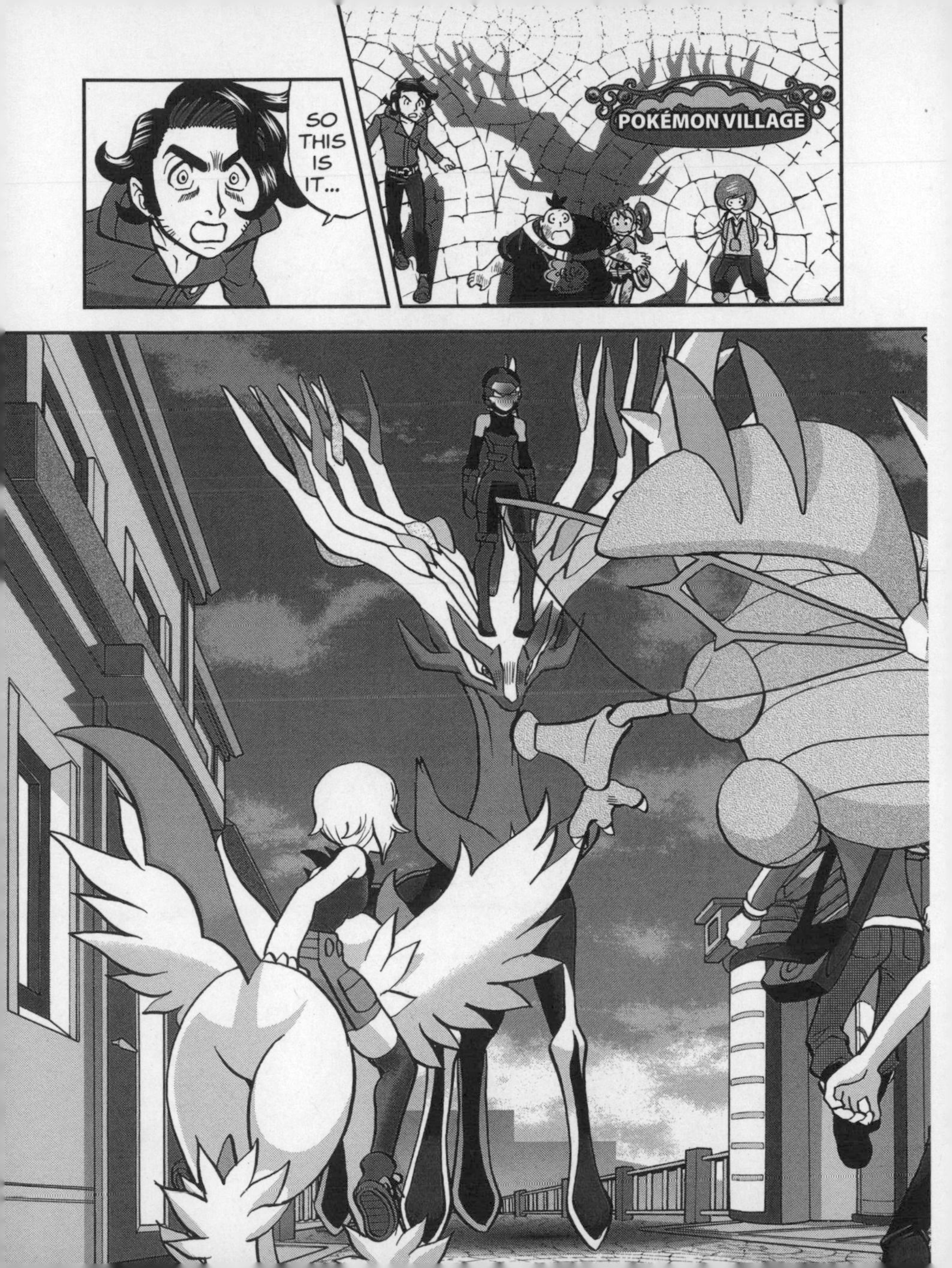
POKÉMON VILLAGE
SO THIS IS IT...

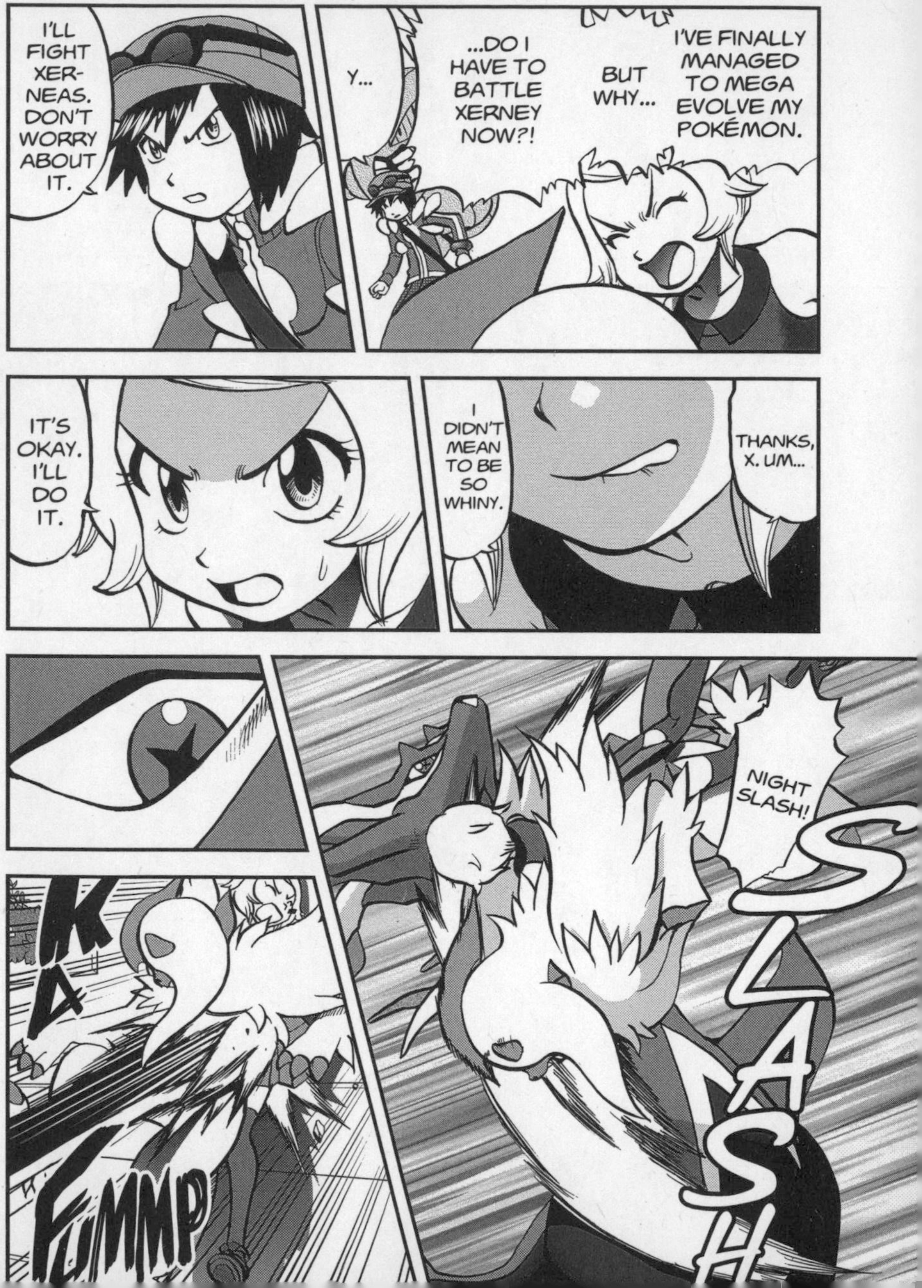
I'VE FINALLY MANAGED TO MEGA EVOLVE MY POKÉMON.
BUT WHY...
...DO I HAVE TO BATTLE XERNEY NOW?!
Y...
I'LL FIGHT XER-NEAS. DON'T WORRY ABOUT IT.
THANKS, X. UM...
I DIDN'T MEAN TO BE SO WHINY.
IT'S OKAY. I'LL DO IT.
NIGHT SLASH!
SLASH
KA
FUMMP

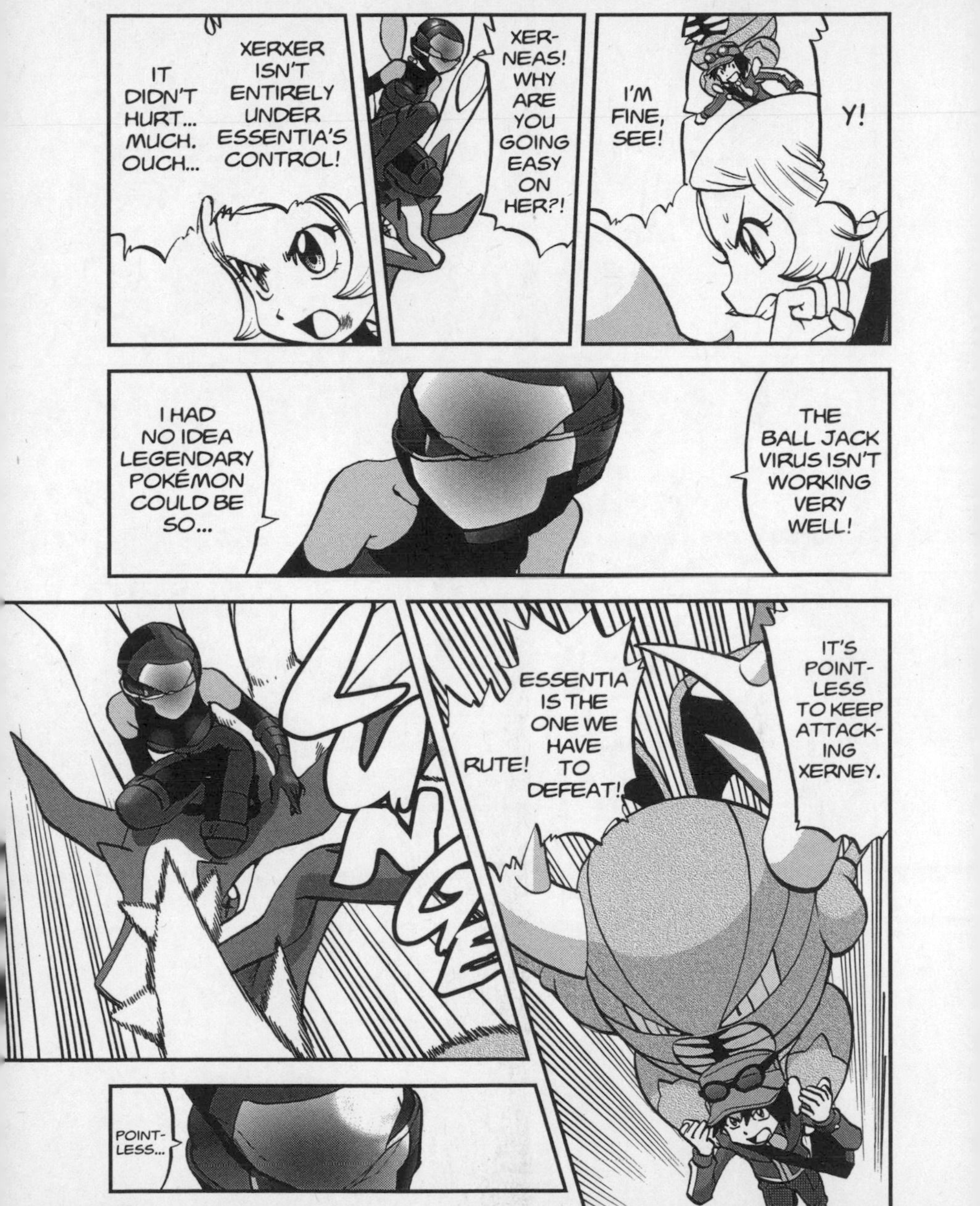
Y!
I'M FINE, SEE!
XER-NEAS! WHY ARE YOU GOING EASY ON HER?!
XERXER ISN'T ENTIRELY UNDER ESSENTIA'S CONTROL!
IT DIDN'T HURT... MUCH. OUCH...
THE BALL JACK VIRUS ISN'T WORKING VERY WELL!
I HAD NO IDEA LEGENDARY POKÉMON COULD BE SO...
IT'S POINT-LESS TO KEEP ATTACK-ING XERNEY.
ESSENTIA IS THE ONE WE HAVE TO DEFEAT!
RUTE!
POINT-LESS...

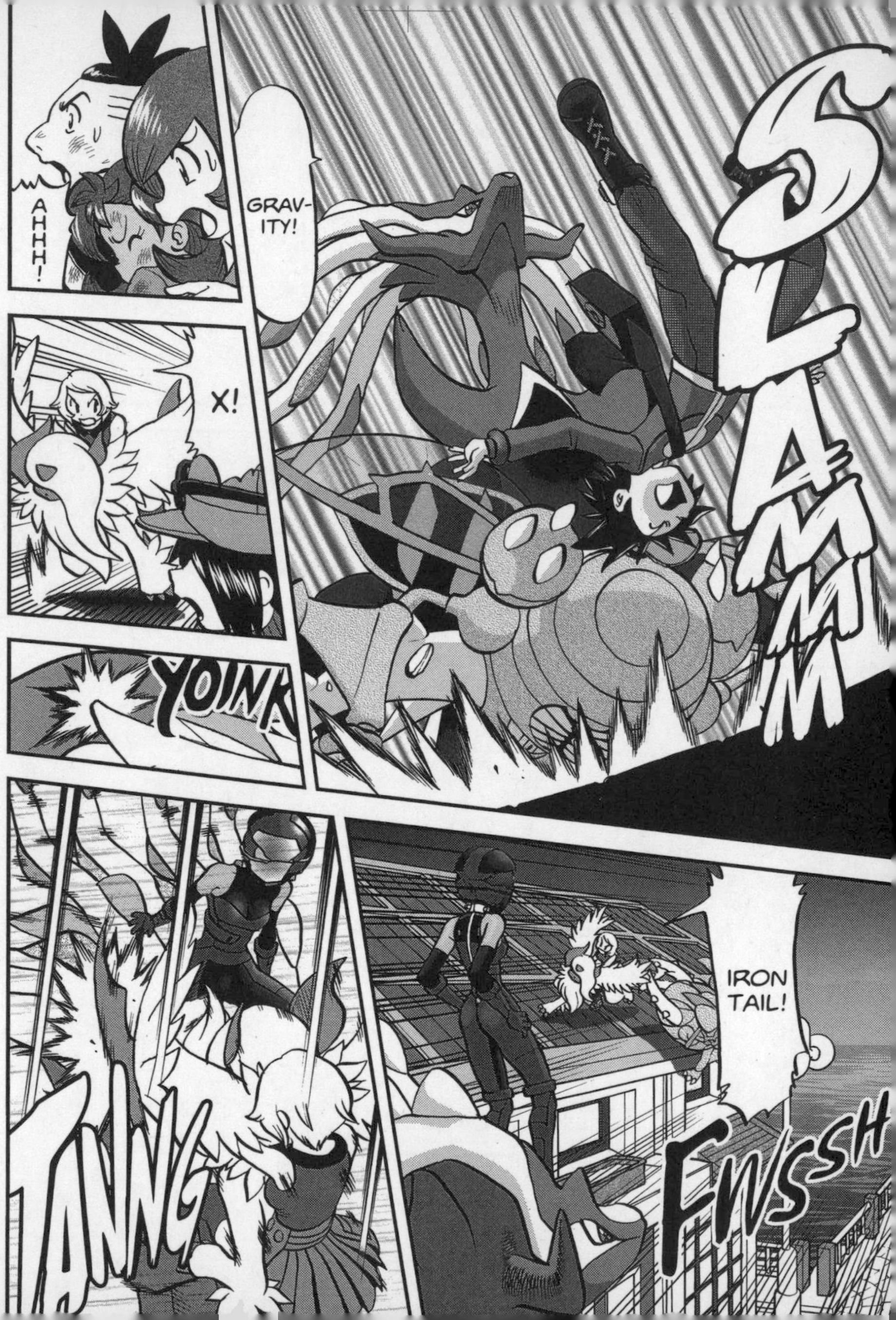
GRAV-
ITY!
SLAMMM
AHHHH!
X!
YOINK
IRON
TAIL!
FWSSH
TANNG

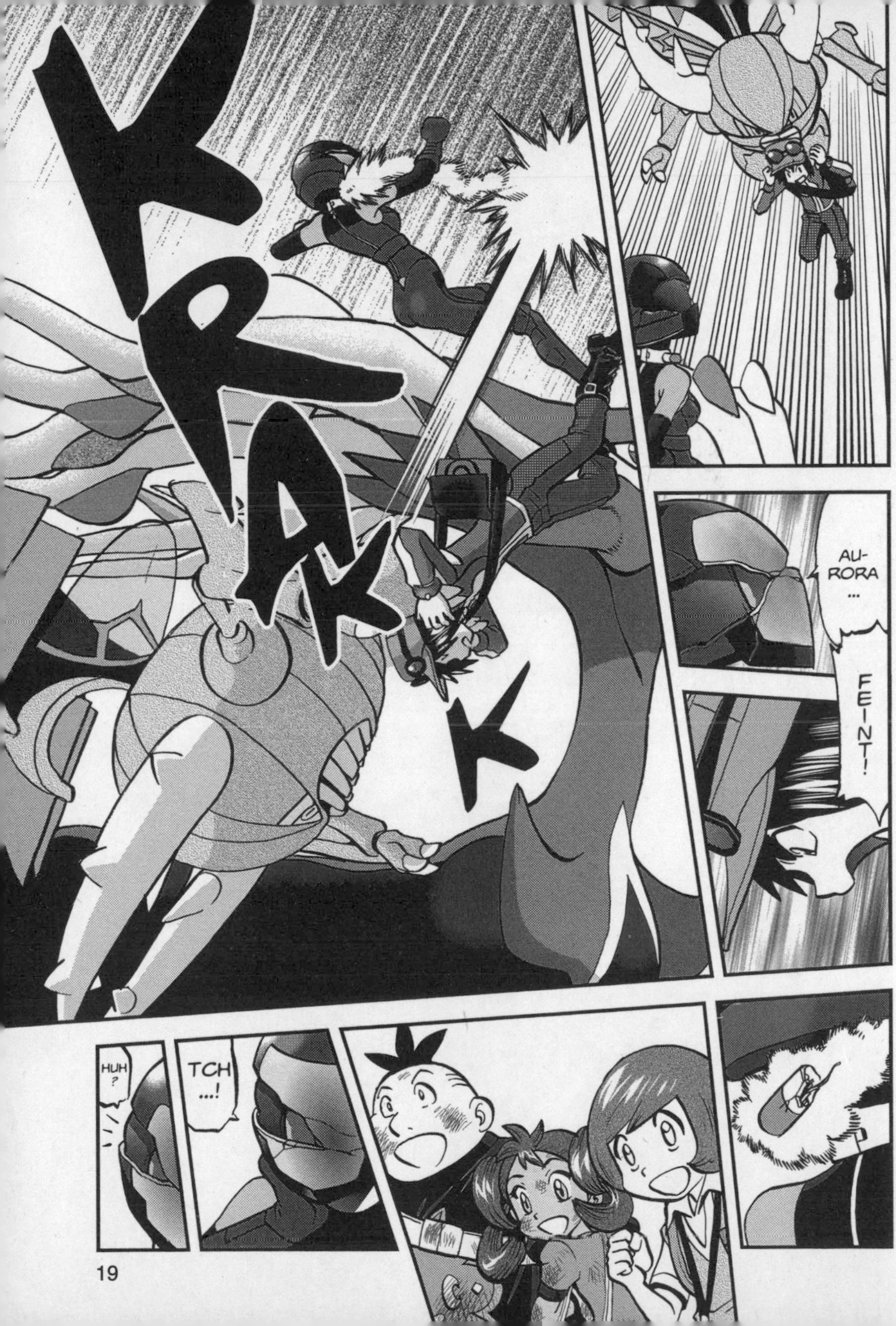
AU-RORA ...
FEINT!
KRAKK
TCH ...!
HUH ?

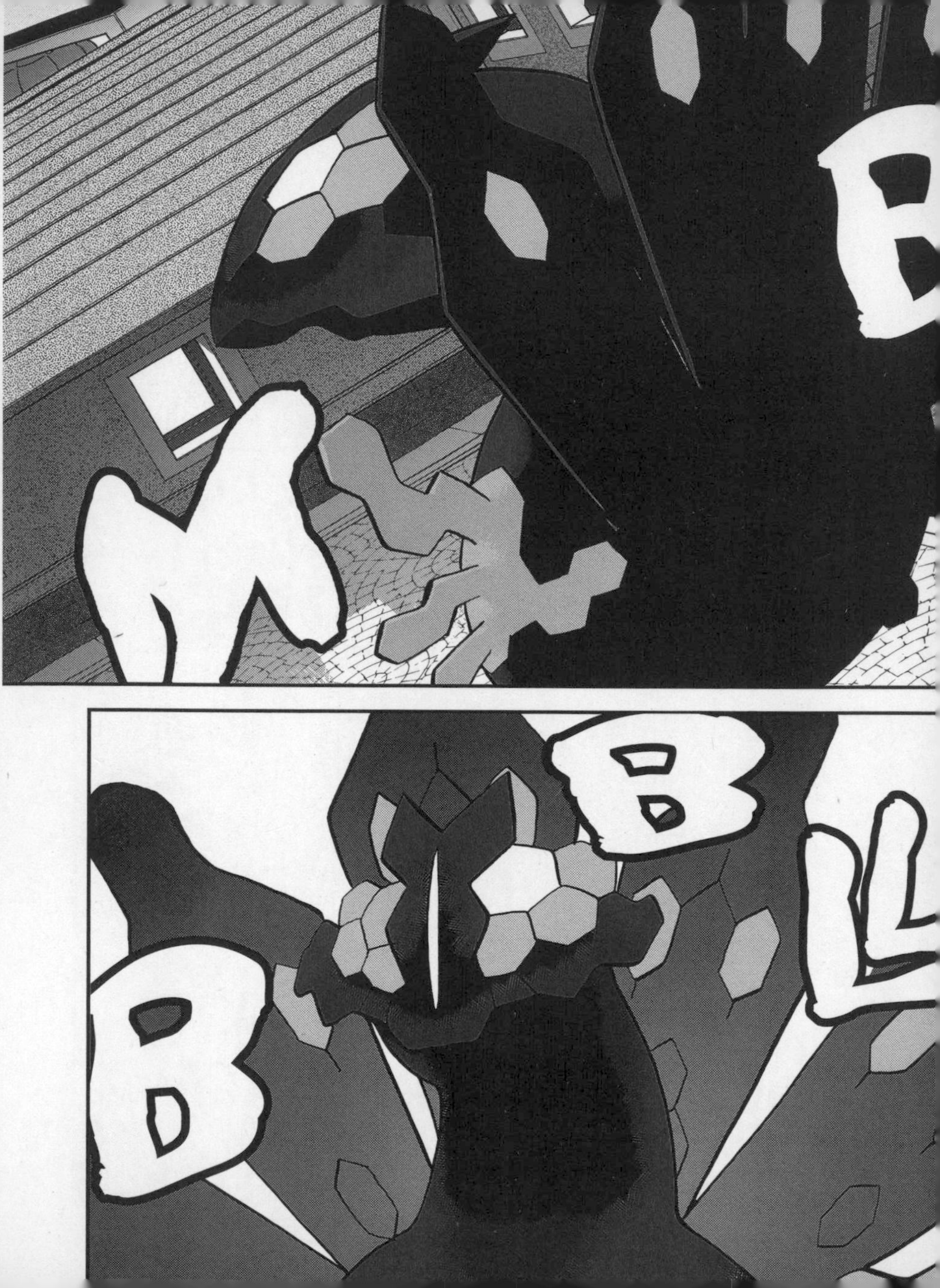
B
M
B
L
B

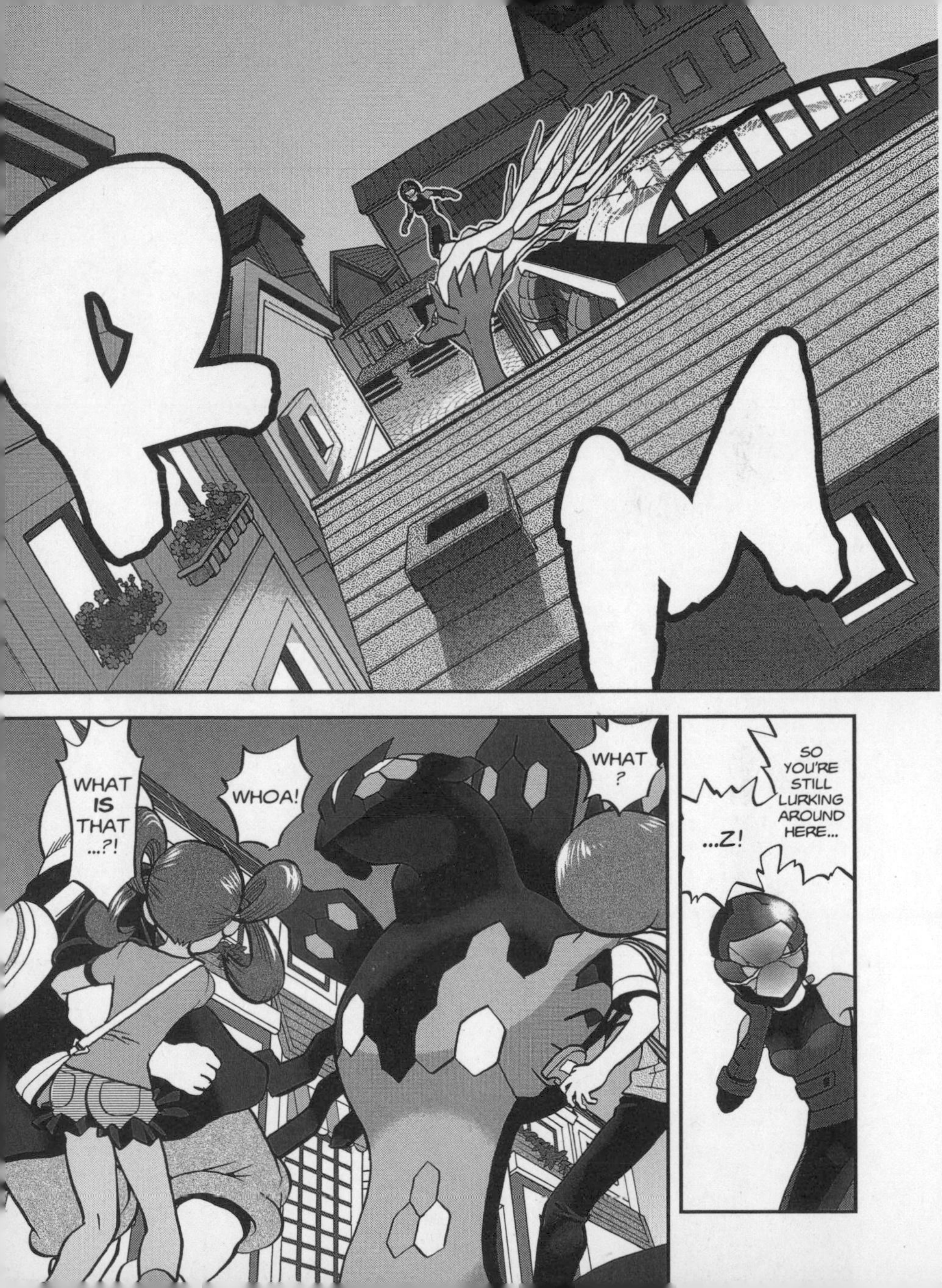
SO YOU'RE STILL LURKING AROUND HERE...
...Z!
WHAT?
WHOA!
WHAT IS THAT ...?!

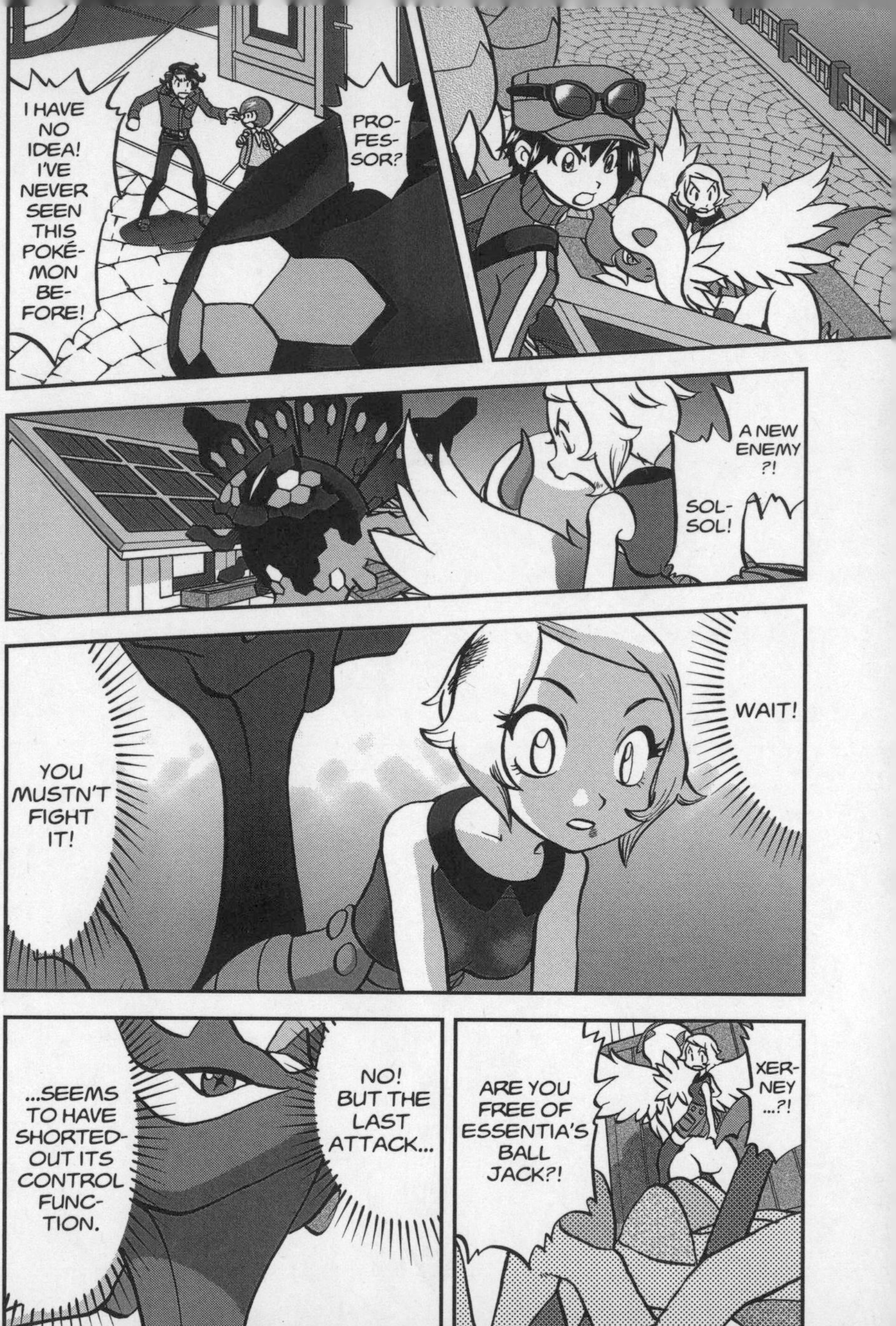
PRO-FES-SOR?
I HAVE NO IDEA! I'VE NEVER SEEN THIS POKÉ-MON BE-FORE!
A NEW ENEMY?!
SOL-SOL!
WAIT!
YOU MUSTN'T FIGHT IT!
XER-NEY...?!
ARE YOU FREE OF ESSENTIA'S BALL JACK?!
NO! BUT THE LAST ATTACK...
...SEEMS TO HAVE SHORTED-OUT ITS CONTROL FUNC-TION.

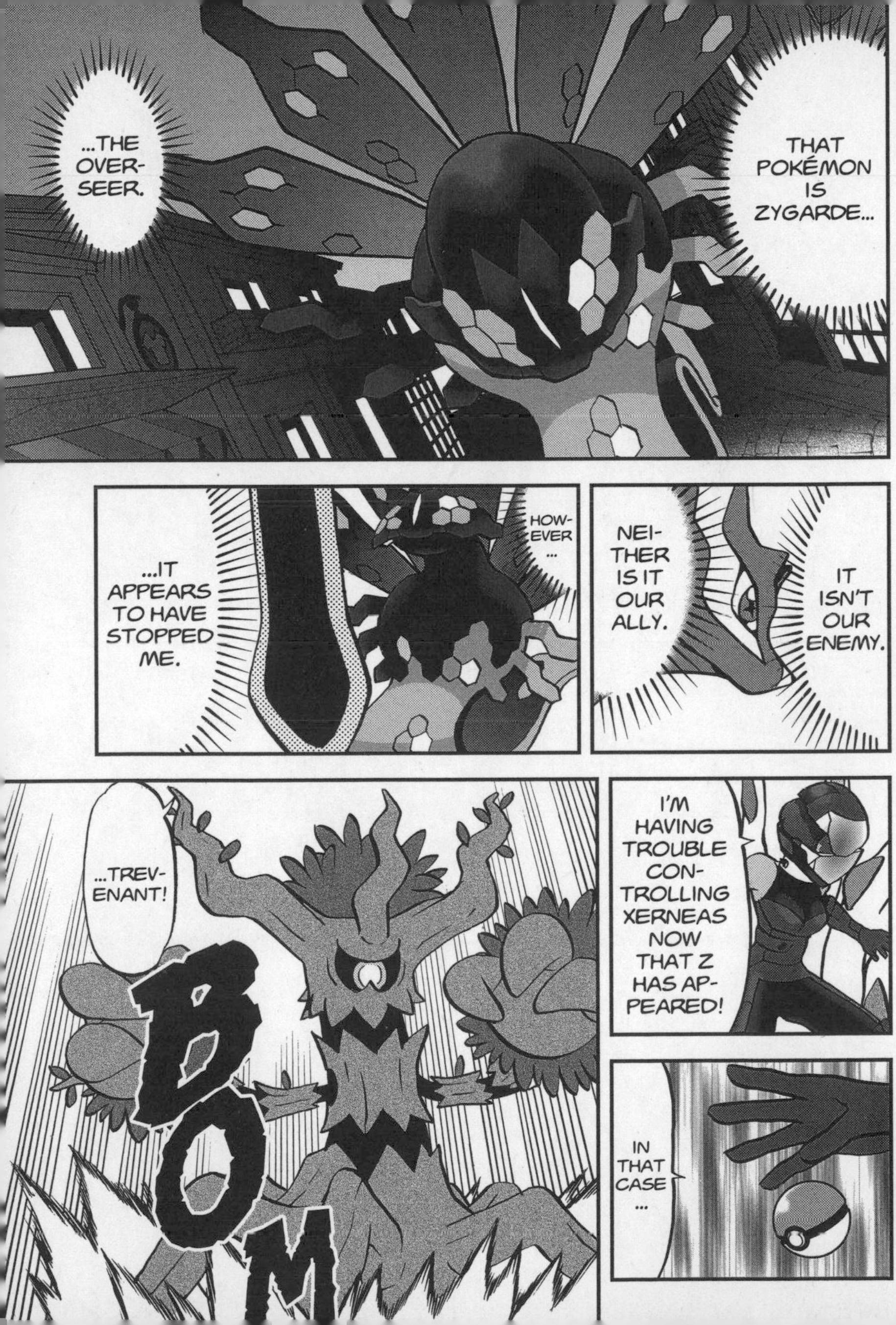
THAT POKÉMON IS ZYGARDE...
...THE OVERSEER.
IT ISN'T OUR ENEMY.
NEITHER IS IT OUR ALLY.
HOWEVER...
...IT APPEARS TO HAVE STOPPED ME.
I'M HAVING TROUBLE CONTROLLING XERNEAS NOW THAT Z HAS APPEARED!
IN THAT CASE...
...TREVENANT!
BOOM

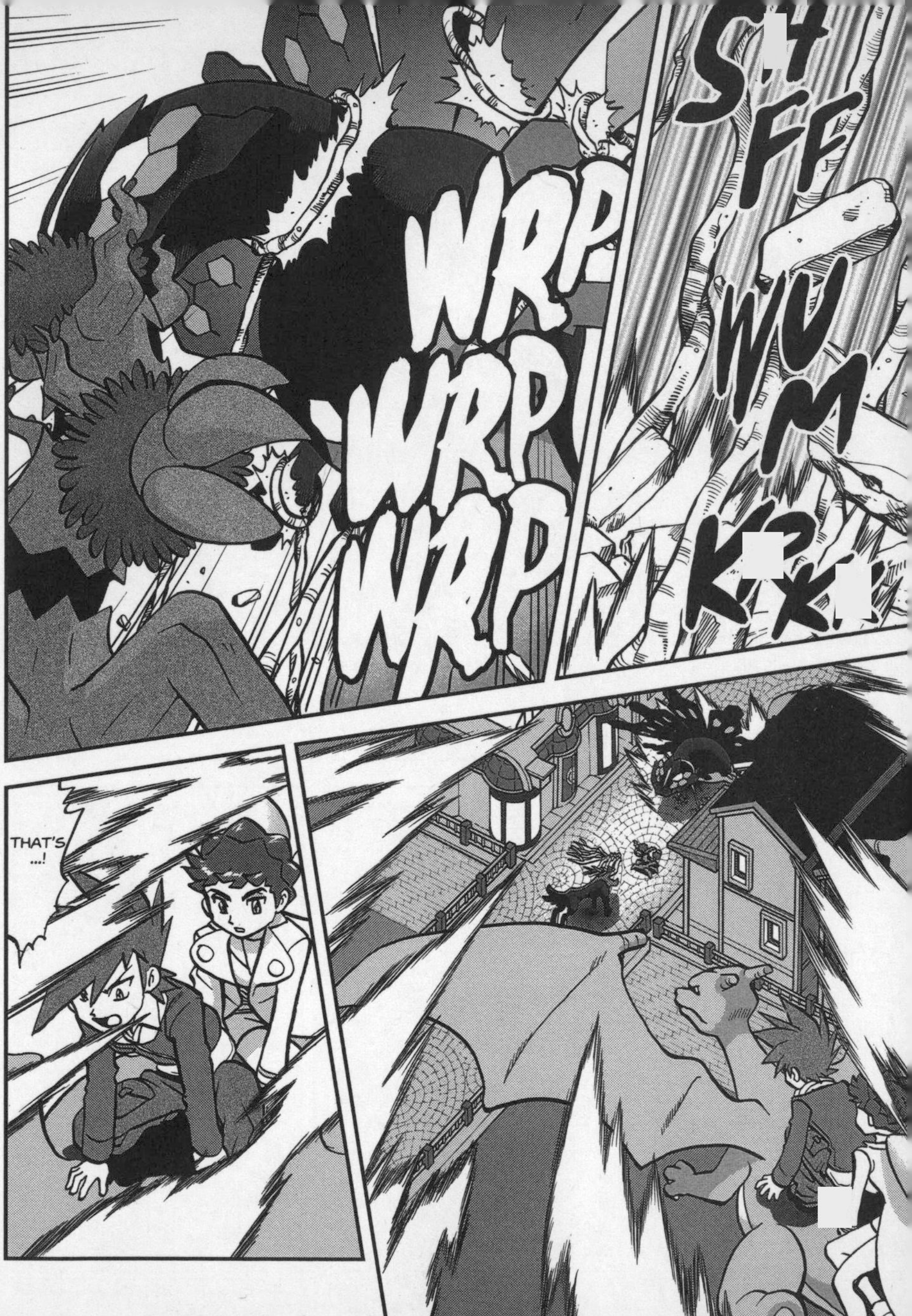
SHFF
WUM
KRK
WRP WRP WRP
THAT'S ...!

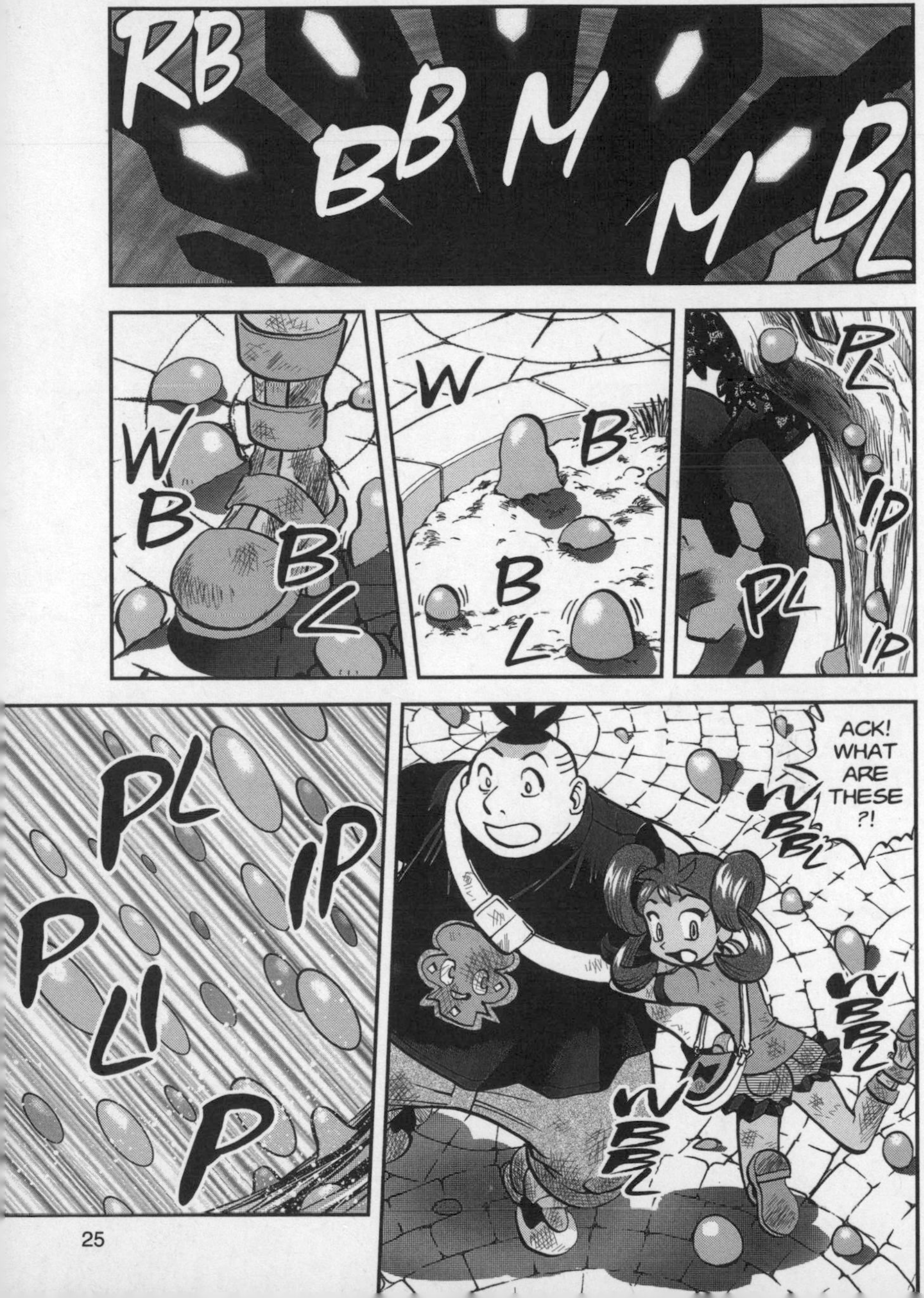

RBBBMMBL
PLIP
PLIP
WBBL
WBBL
ACK! WHAT ARE THESE?!
WBBL
WBBL
WBBL
PLIP
PLIP

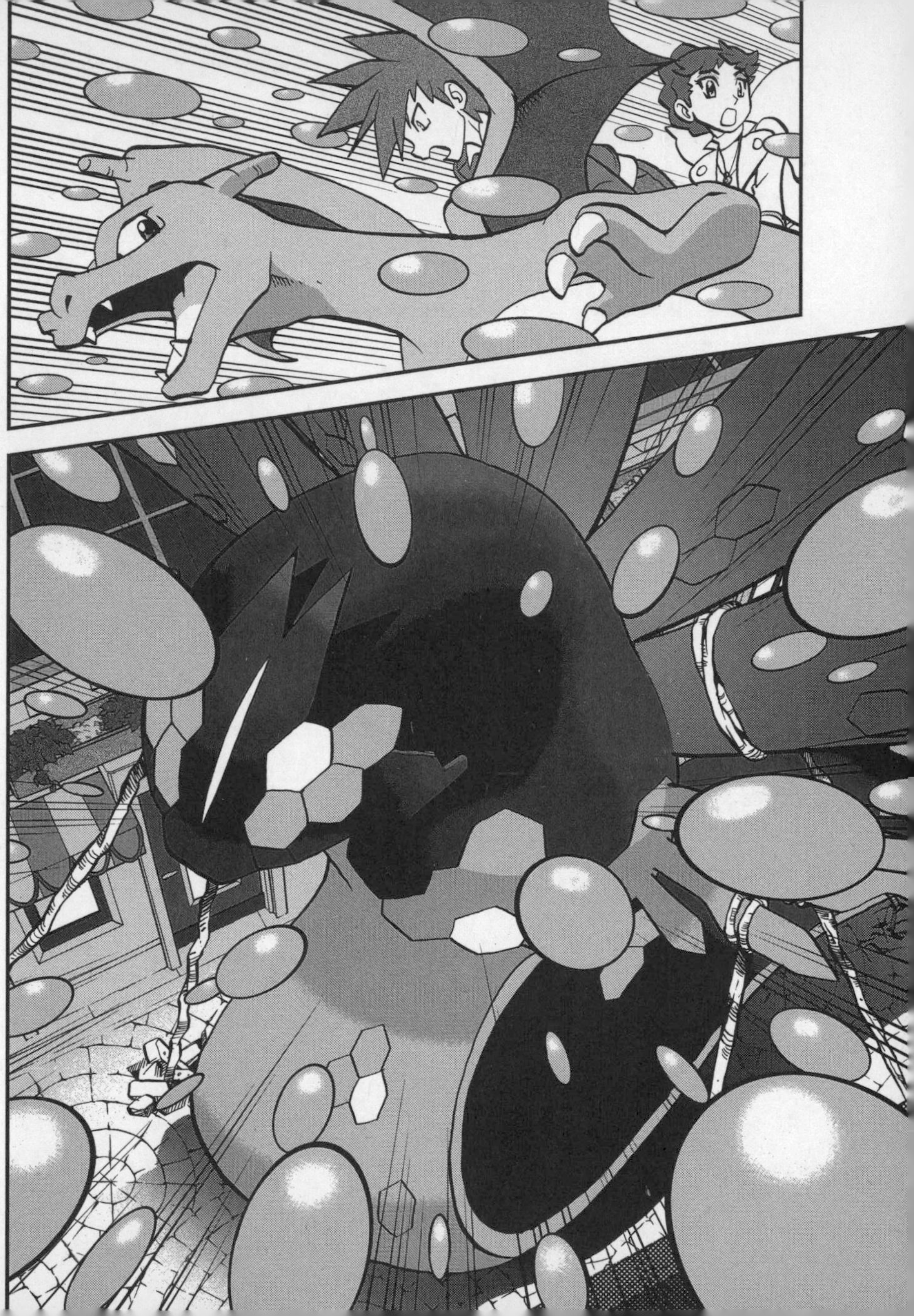

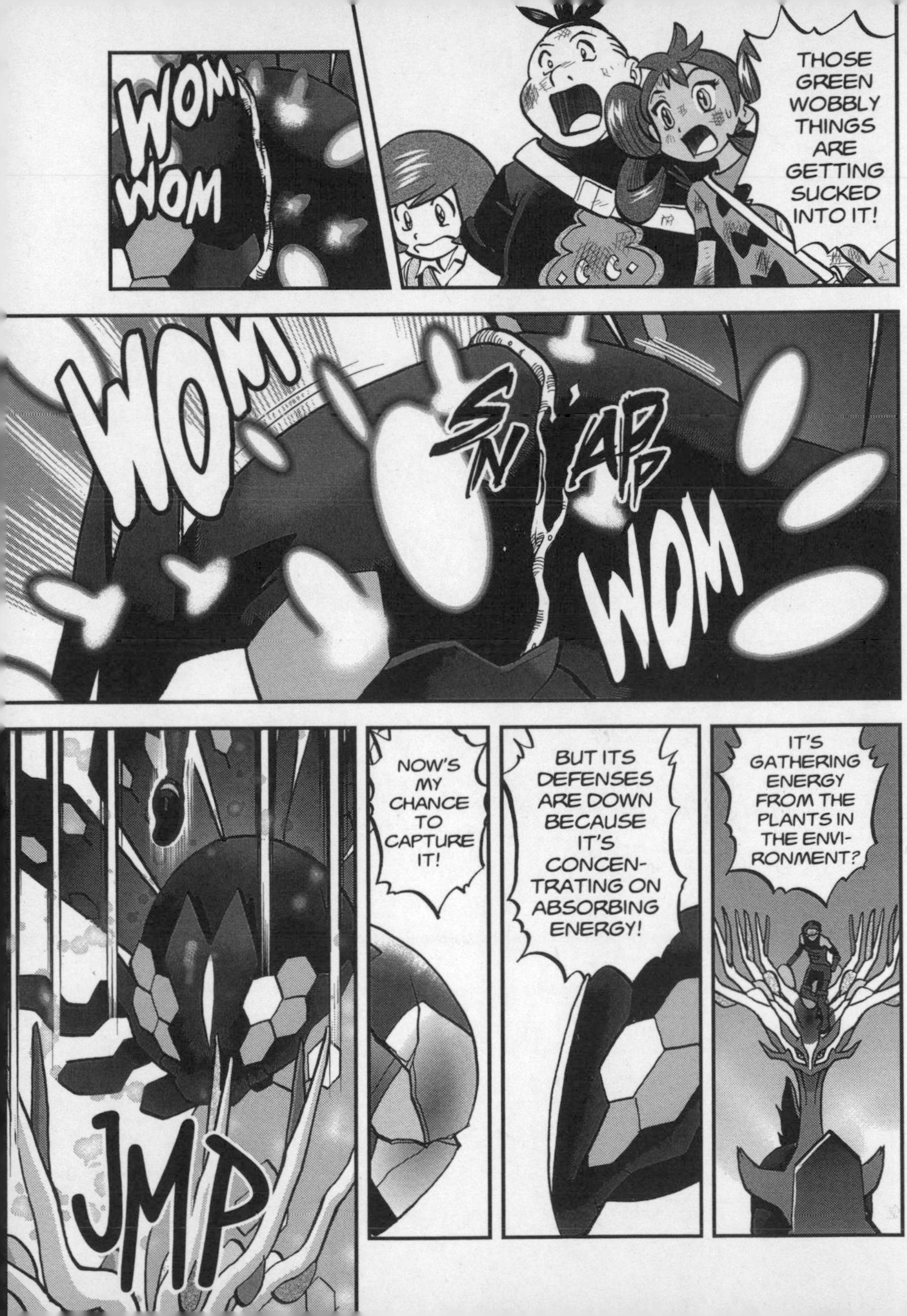
THOSE GREEN WOBBLY THINGS ARE GETTING SUCKED INTO IT!
WOM WOM
WOM
SNAP
WOM
IT'S GATHERING ENERGY FROM THE PLANTS IN THE ENVI-RONMENT?
BUT ITS DEFENSES ARE DOWN BECAUSE IT'S CONCEN-TRATING ON ABSORBING ENERGY!
NOW'S MY CHANCE TO CAPTURE IT!
JMP

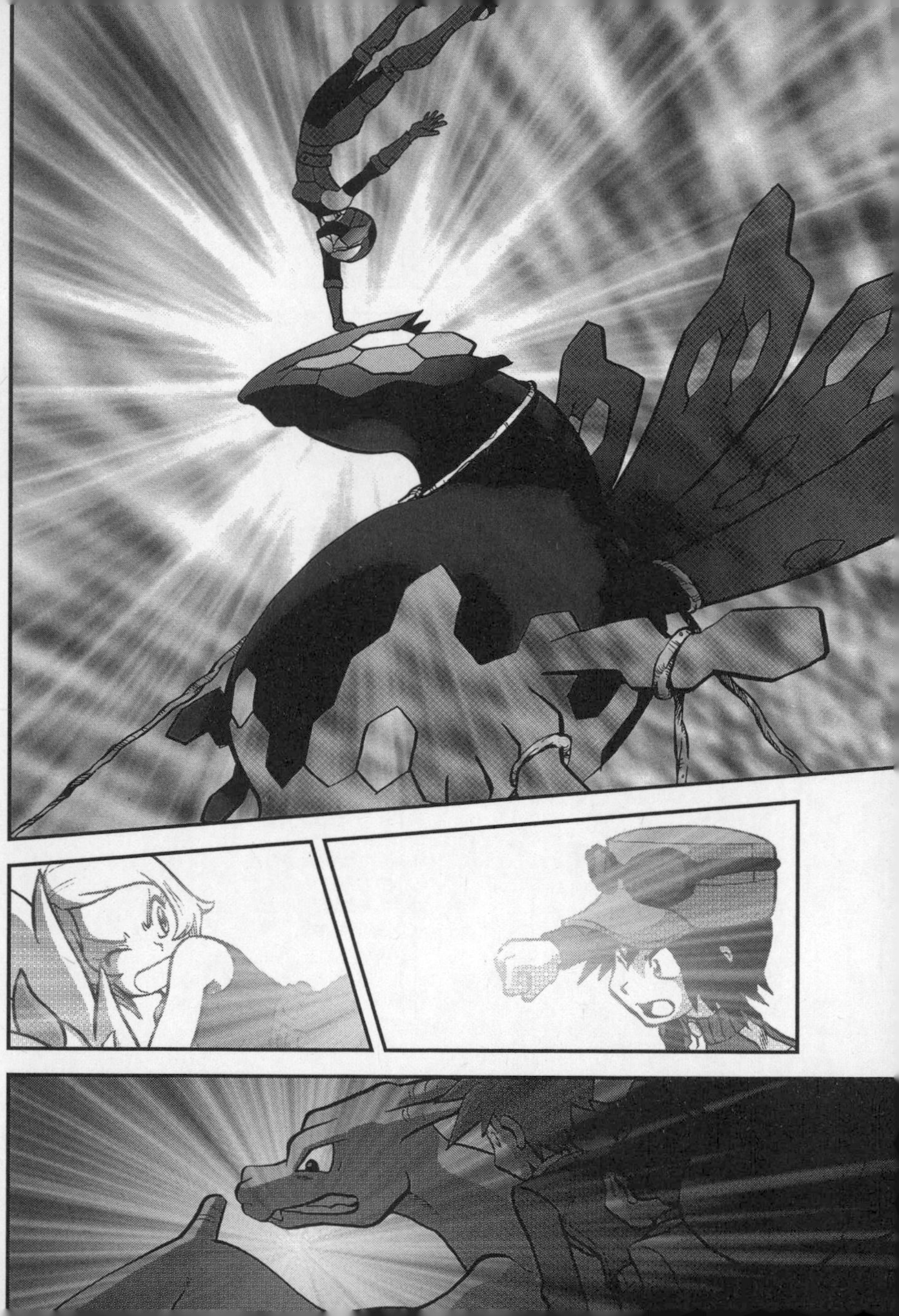

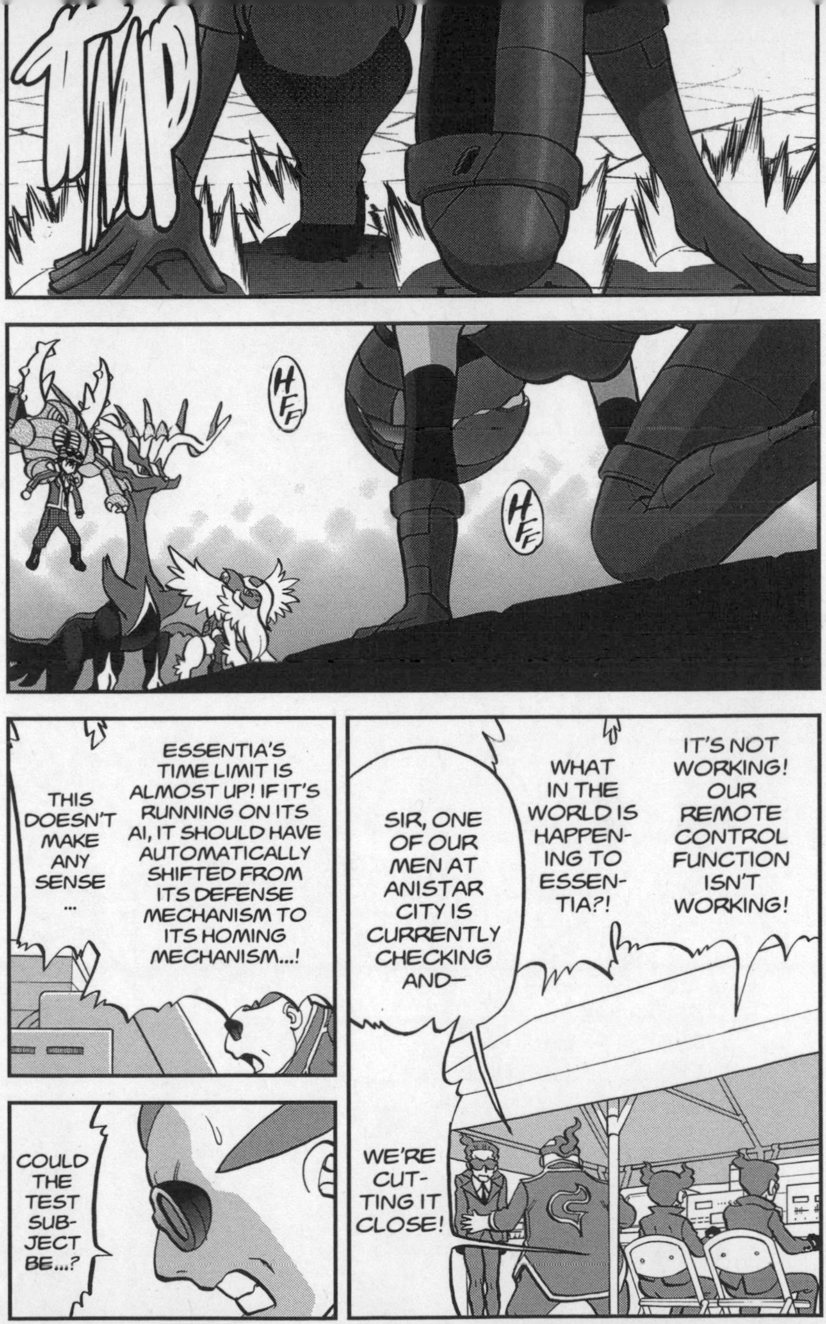
TMP
HFF
HFF
IT'S NOT WORKING! OUR REMOTE CONTROL FUNCTION ISN'T WORKING!
WHAT IN THE WORLD IS HAPPENING TO ESSENTIA?!
SIR, ONE OF OUR MEN AT ANISTAR CITY IS CURRENTLY CHECKING AND—
WE'RE CUTTING IT CLOSE!
ESSENTIA'S TIME LIMIT IS ALMOST UP! IF IT'S RUNNING ON ITS AI, IT SHOULD HAVE AUTOMATICALLY SHIFTED FROM ITS DEFENSE MECHANISM TO ITS HOMING MECHANISM...!
THIS DOESN'T MAKE ANY SENSE...
COULD THE TEST SUBJECT BE...?

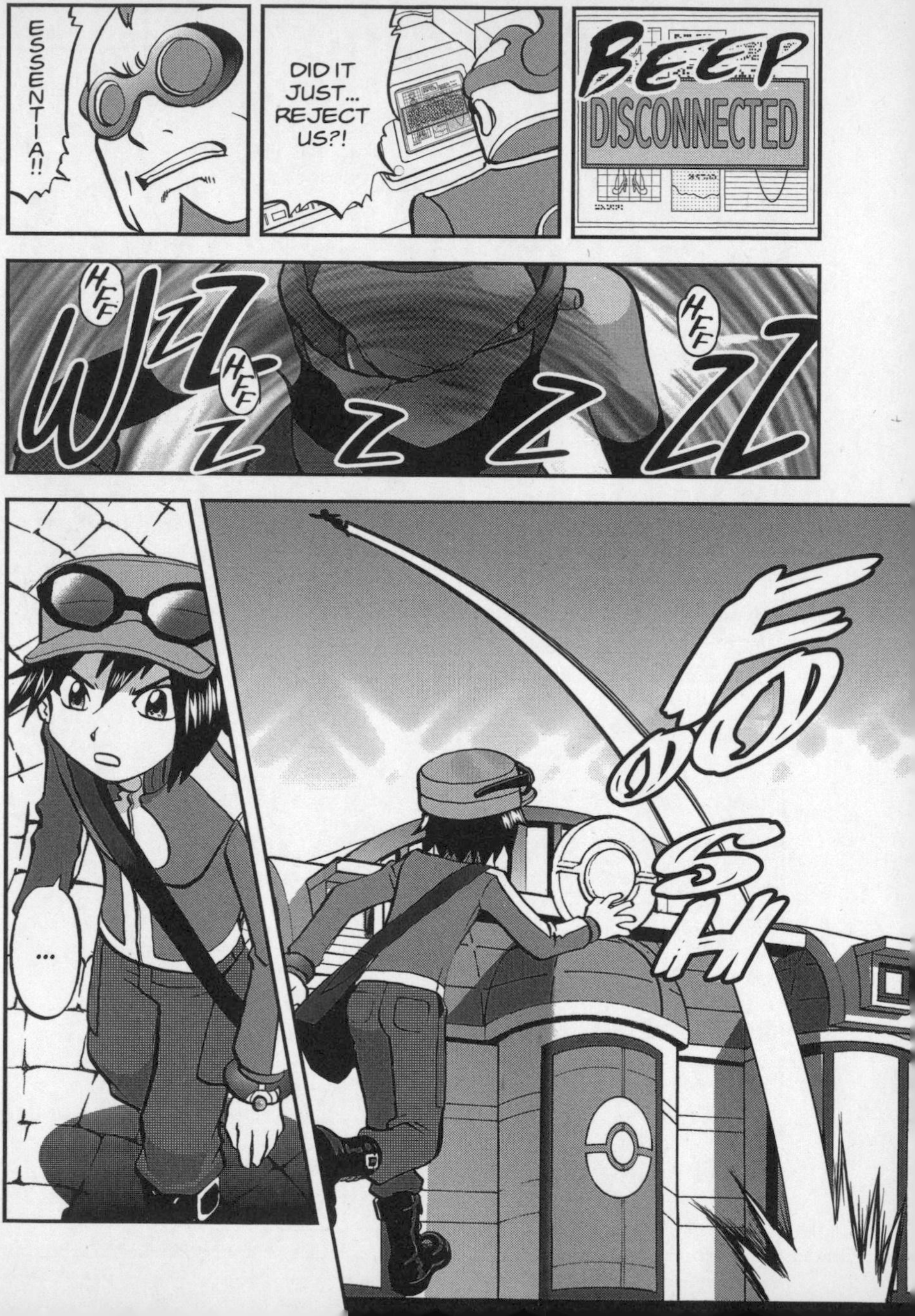
BEEP
DISCONNECTED
DID IT JUST... REJECT US?!
ESSENTIA!!
HFF
HFF
HFF
WZZZZZZ
FOOOSH
...

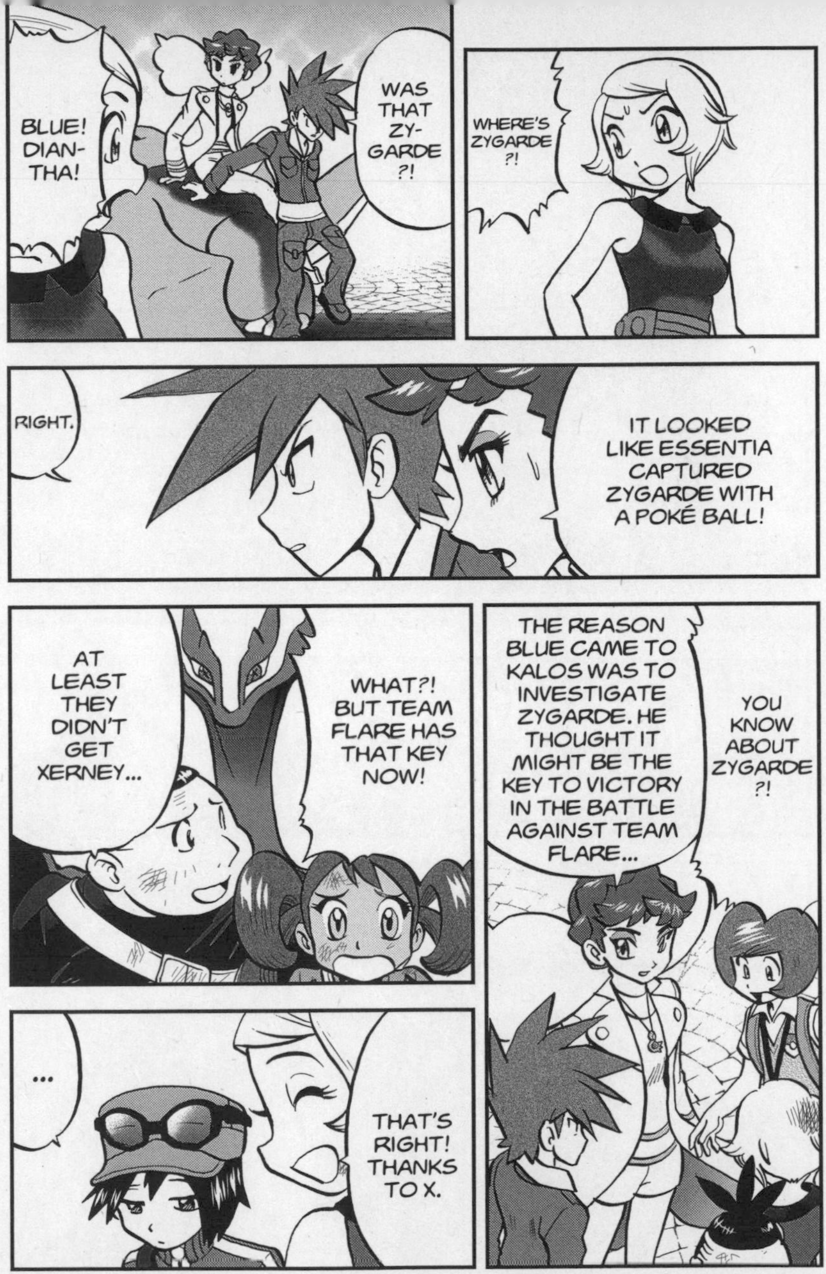
WHERE'S ZYGARDE ?!
WAS THAT ZY-GARDE ?!
BLUE! DIAN-THA!
IT LOOKED LIKE ESSENTIA CAPTURED ZYGARDE WITH A POKÉ BALL!
RIGHT.
YOU KNOW ABOUT ZYGARDE ?!
THE REASON BLUE CAME TO KALOS WAS TO INVESTIGATE ZYGARDE. HE THOUGHT IT MIGHT BE THE KEY TO VICTORY IN THE BATTLE AGAINST TEAM FLARE...
WHAT?! BUT TEAM FLARE HAS THAT KEY NOW!
AT LEAST THEY DIDN'T GET XERNEY...
THAT'S RIGHT! THANKS TO X.
...

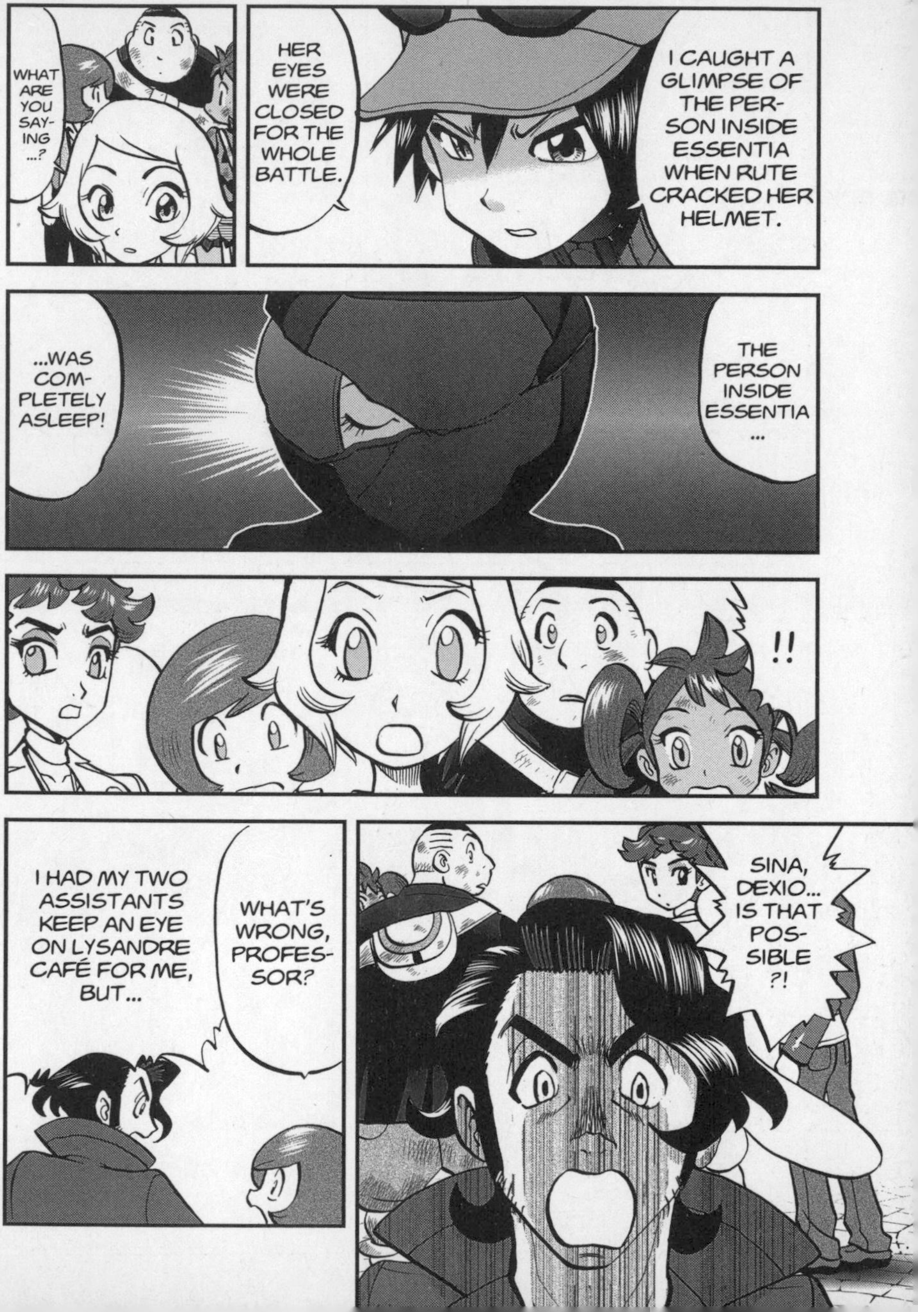
I CAUGHT A GLIMPSE OF THE PER-SON INSIDE ESSENTIA WHEN RUTE CRACKED HER HELMET.
HER EYES WERE CLOSED FOR THE WHOLE BATTLE.
WHAT ARE YOU SAY-ING ...?
THE PERSON INSIDE ESSENTIA ...
...WAS COM-PLETELY ASLEEP!
!!
SINA, DEXIO... IS THAT POS-SIBLE ?!
WHAT'S WRONG, PROFES-SOR?
I HAD MY TWO ASSISTANTS KEEP AN EYE ON LYSANDRE CAFÉ FOR ME, BUT...

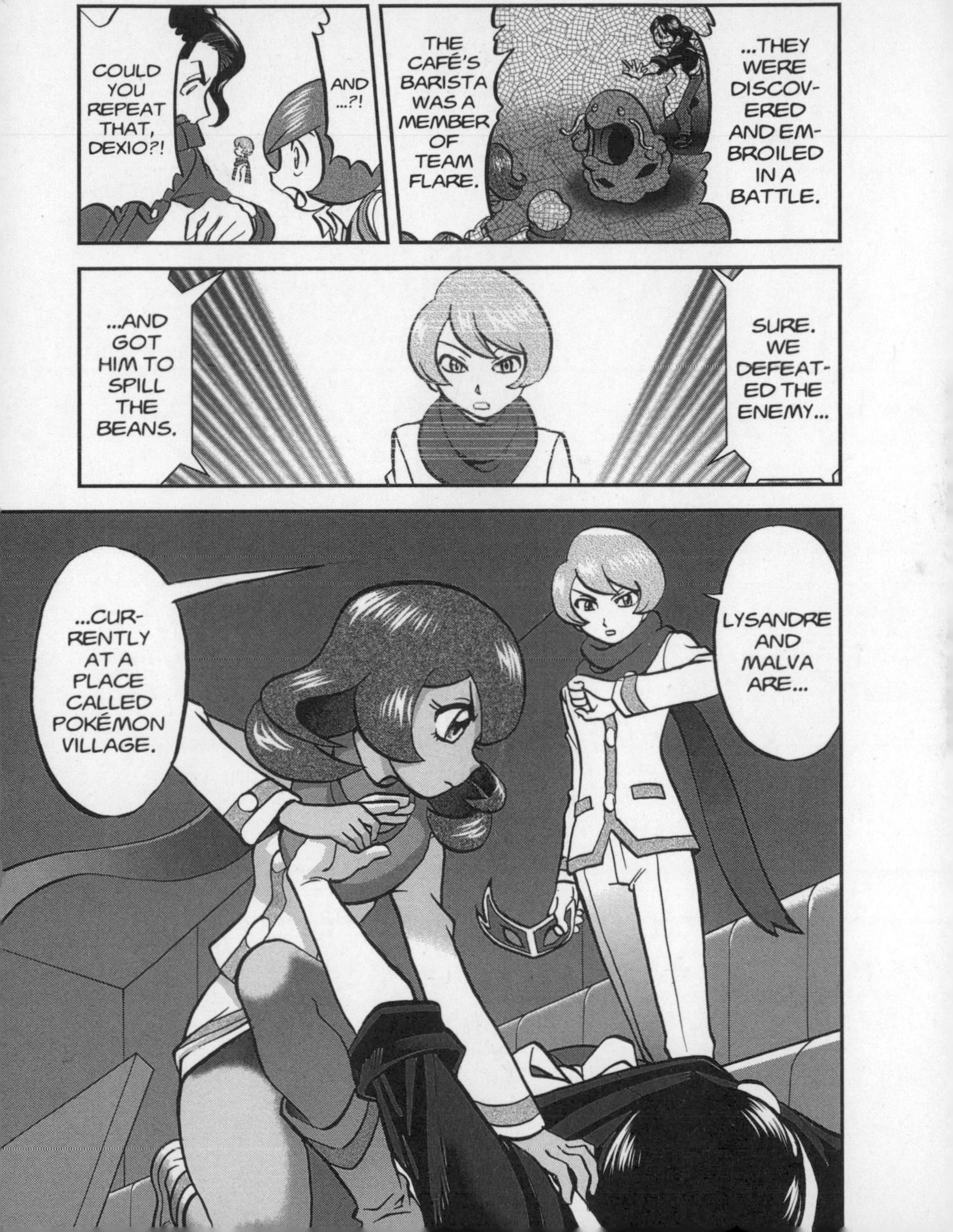
...THEY WERE DISCOVERED AND EMBROILED IN A BATTLE.
THE CAFÉ'S BARISTA WAS A MEMBER OF TEAM FLARE.
AND ...?!
COULD YOU REPEAT THAT, DEXIO?!
SURE. WE DEFEATED THE ENEMY...
...AND GOT HIM TO SPILL THE BEANS.
LYSANDRE AND MALVA ARE...
...CURRENTLY AT A PLACE CALLED POKÉMON VILLAGE.

Current Location

Anistar City

Some say the enigmatic device used as a sundial came from outer space.

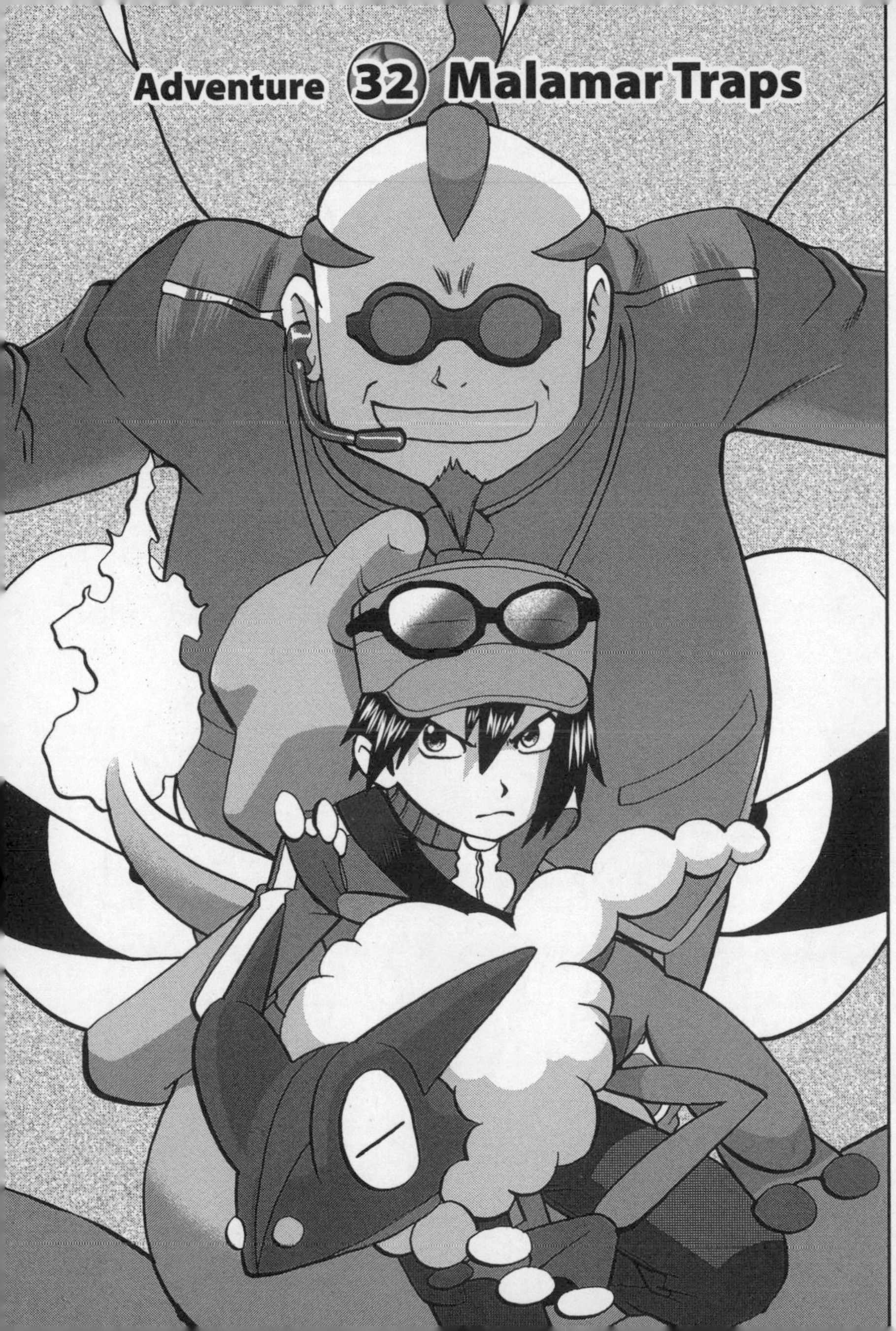
Adventure 32 Malamar Traps

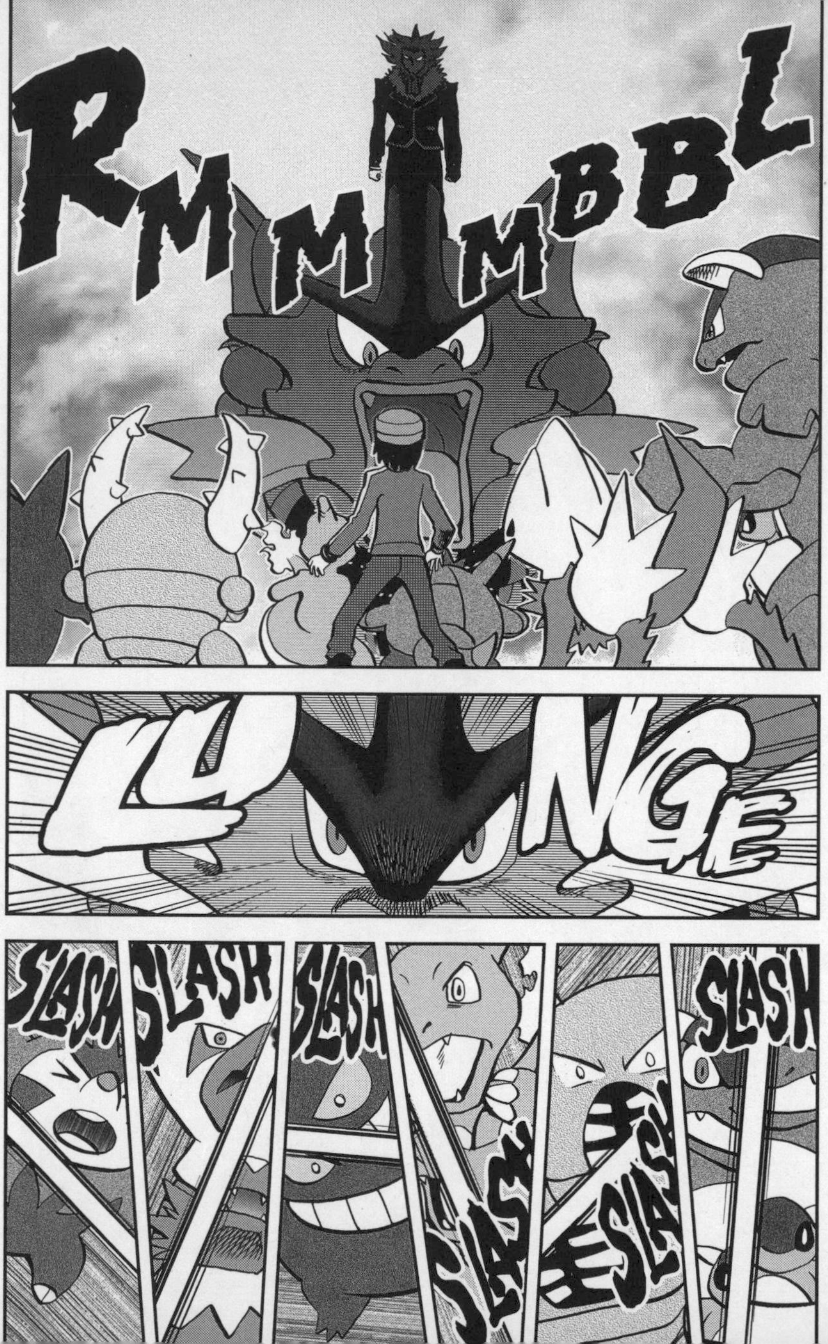

RMMMBBL
LUNGE
SLASH
SLASH
SLASH
SLASH
SLASH
SLASH
SLASH

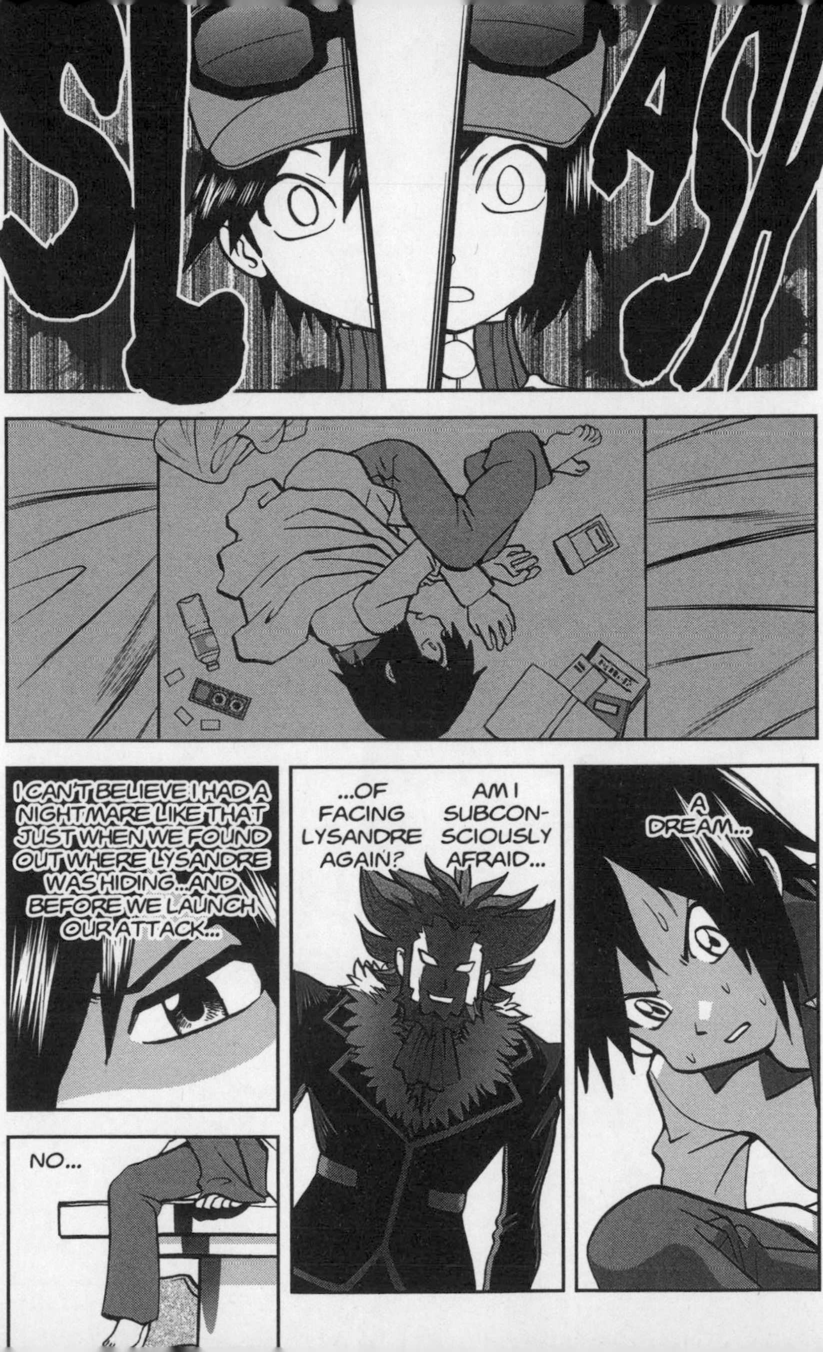
SLASH
A DREAM...
AM I SUBCON-SCIOUSLY AFRAID...
...OF FACING LYSANDRE AGAIN?
I CAN'T BELIEVE I HAD A NIGHTMARE LIKE THAT JUST WHEN WE FOUND OUT WHERE LYSANDRE WAS HIDING...AND BEFORE WE LAUNCH OUR ATTACK...
NO...

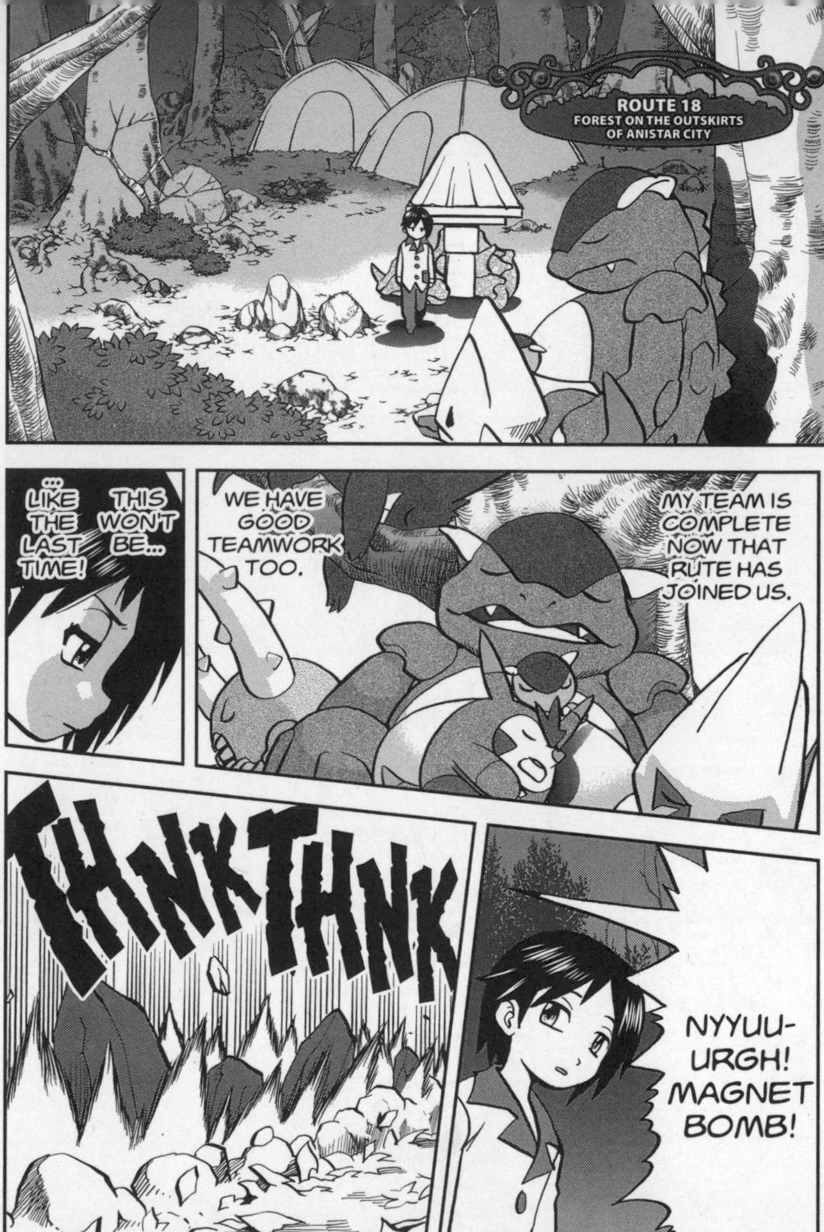
ROUTE 18
FOREST ON THE OUTSKIRTS OF ANISTAR CITY
MY TEAM IS COMPLETE NOW THAT RUTE HAS JOINED US.
WE HAVE GOOD TEAMWORK TOO.
THIS WON'T BE...
...LIKE THE LAST TIME!
NYYUU-URGH! MAGNET BOMB!
THNK THNK

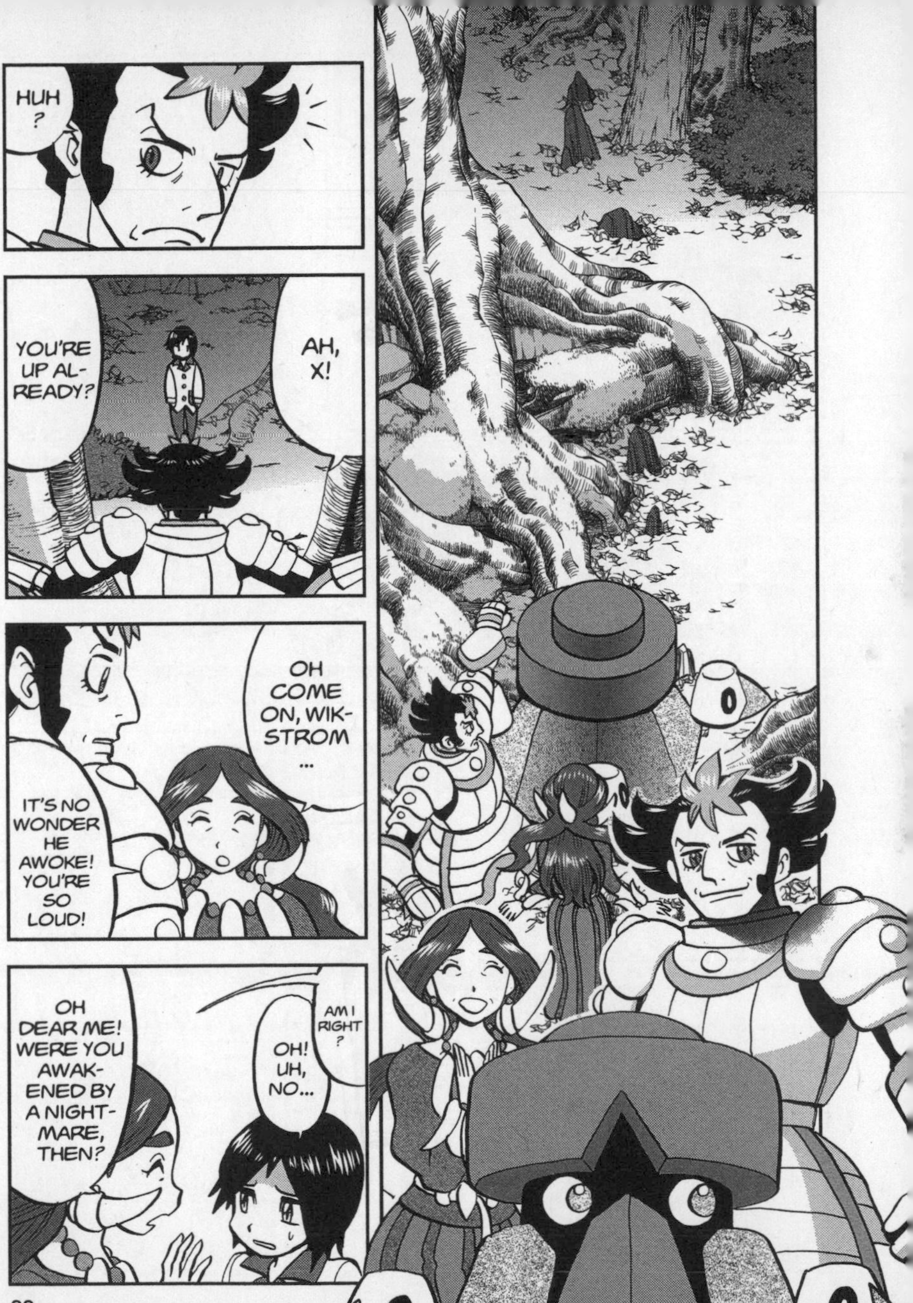
HUH?
AH, X!
YOU'RE UP ALREADY?
OH COME ON, WIKSTROM...
IT'S NO WONDER HE AWOKE! YOU'RE SO LOUD!
OH DEAR ME! WERE YOU AWAKENED BY A NIGHTMARE, THEN?
AM I RIGHT?
OH! UH, NO...

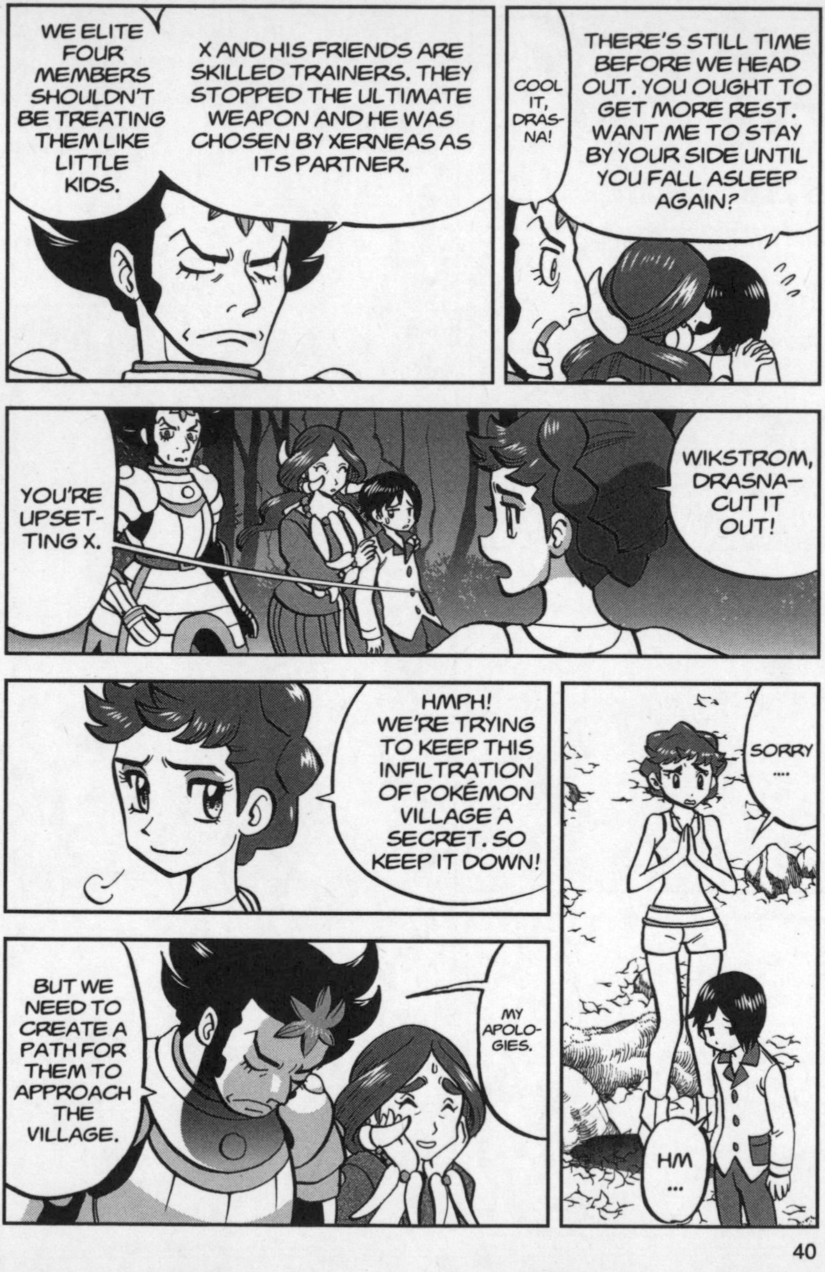
THERE'S STILL TIME BEFORE WE HEAD OUT. YOU OUGHT TO GET MORE REST. WANT ME TO STAY BY YOUR SIDE UNTIL YOU FALL ASLEEP AGAIN?
COOL IT, DRAS-NA!
X AND HIS FRIENDS ARE SKILLED TRAINERS. THEY STOPPED THE ULTIMATE WEAPON AND HE WAS CHOSEN BY XERNEAS AS ITS PARTNER.
WE ELITE FOUR MEMBERS SHOULDN'T BE TREATING THEM LIKE LITTLE KIDS.
WIKSTROM, DRASNA— CUT IT OUT!
YOU'RE UPSET-TING X.
SORRY ....
HM ...
HMPH! WE'RE TRYING TO KEEP THIS INFILTRATION OF POKÉMON VILLAGE A SECRET. SO KEEP IT DOWN!
MY APOLO-GIES.
BUT WE NEED TO CREATE A PATH FOR THEM TO APPROACH THE VILLAGE.

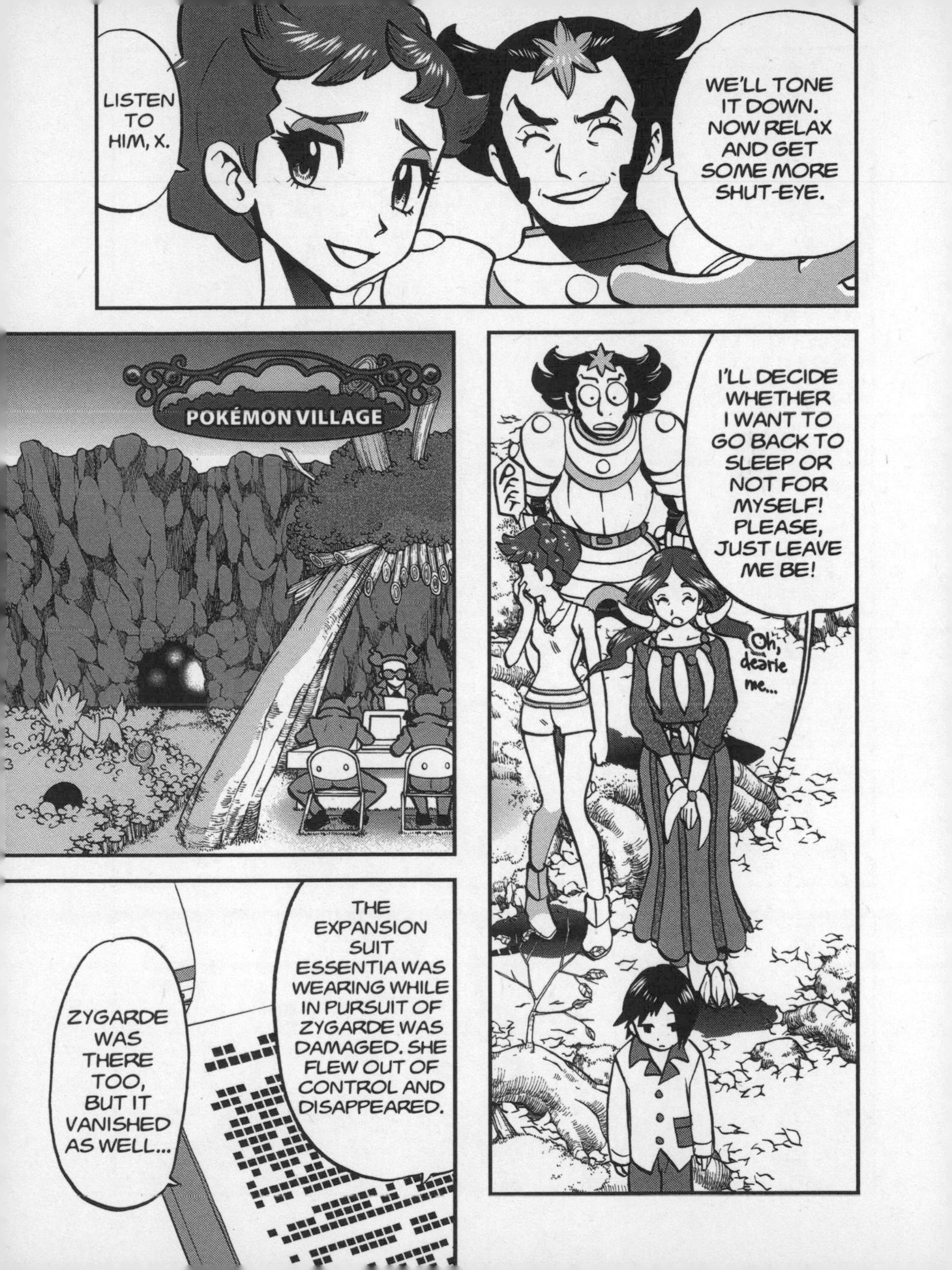
WE'LL TONE IT DOWN. NOW RELAX AND GET SOME MORE SHUT-EYE.
LISTEN TO HIM, X.
I'LL DECIDE WHETHER I WANT TO GO BACK TO SLEEP OR NOT FOR MYSELF! PLEASE, JUST LEAVE ME BE!
PFFT
Oh, dearie me...
POKÉMON VILLAGE
THE EXPANSION SUIT ESSENTIA WAS WEARING WHILE IN PURSUIT OF ZYGARDE WAS DAMAGED. SHE FLEW OUT OF CONTROL AND DISAPPEARED.
ZYGARDE WAS THERE TOO, BUT IT VANISHED AS WELL...

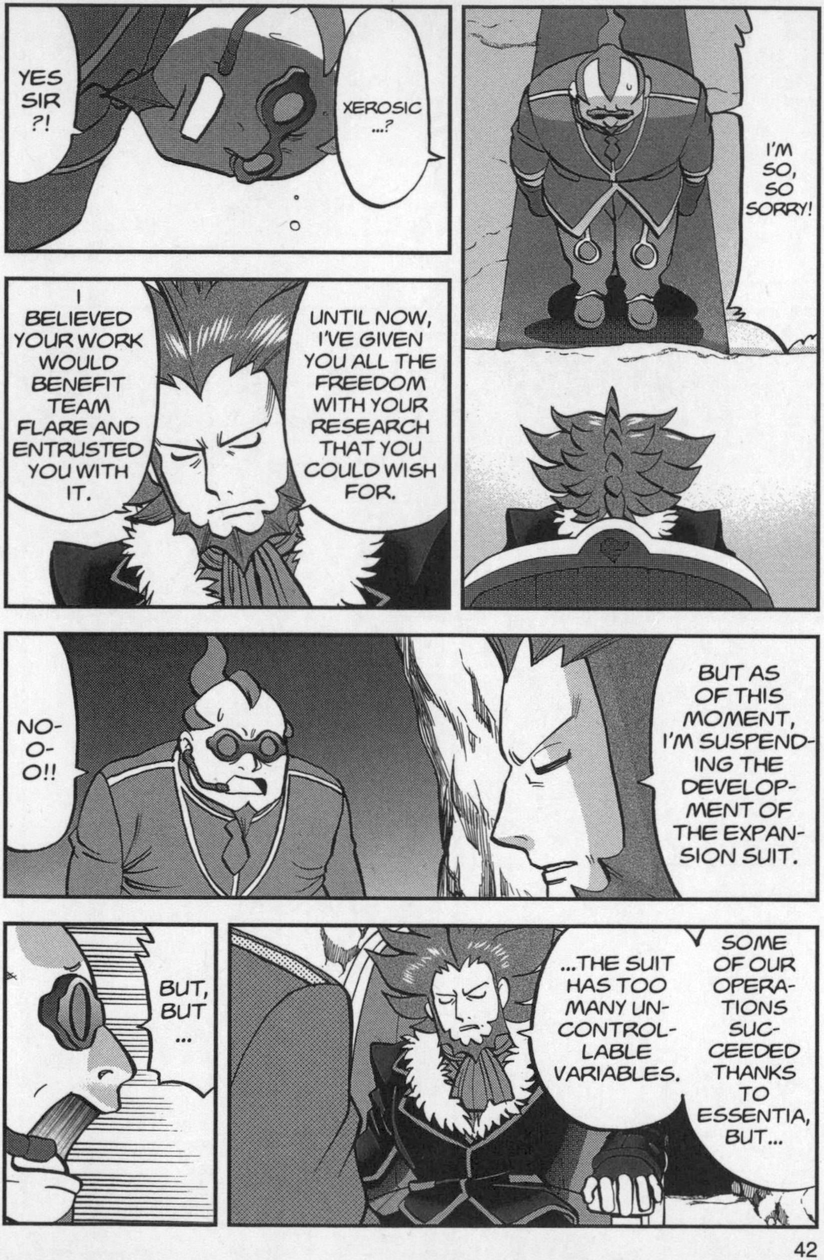

I'M SO, SO SORRY!
XEROSIC ...?
YES SIR ?!
UNTIL NOW, I'VE GIVEN YOU ALL THE FREEDOM WITH YOUR RESEARCH THAT YOU COULD WISH FOR.
I BELIEVED YOUR WORK WOULD BENEFIT TEAM FLARE AND ENTRUSTED YOU WITH IT.
BUT AS OF THIS MOMENT, I'M SUSPEND-ING THE DEVELOP-MENT OF THE EXPAN-SION SUIT.
NO-O-O!!
SOME OF OUR OPERA-TIONS SUC-CEEDED THANKS TO ESSENTIA, BUT...
...THE SUIT HAS TOO MANY UN-CONTROL-LABLE VARIABLES.
BUT, BUT ...

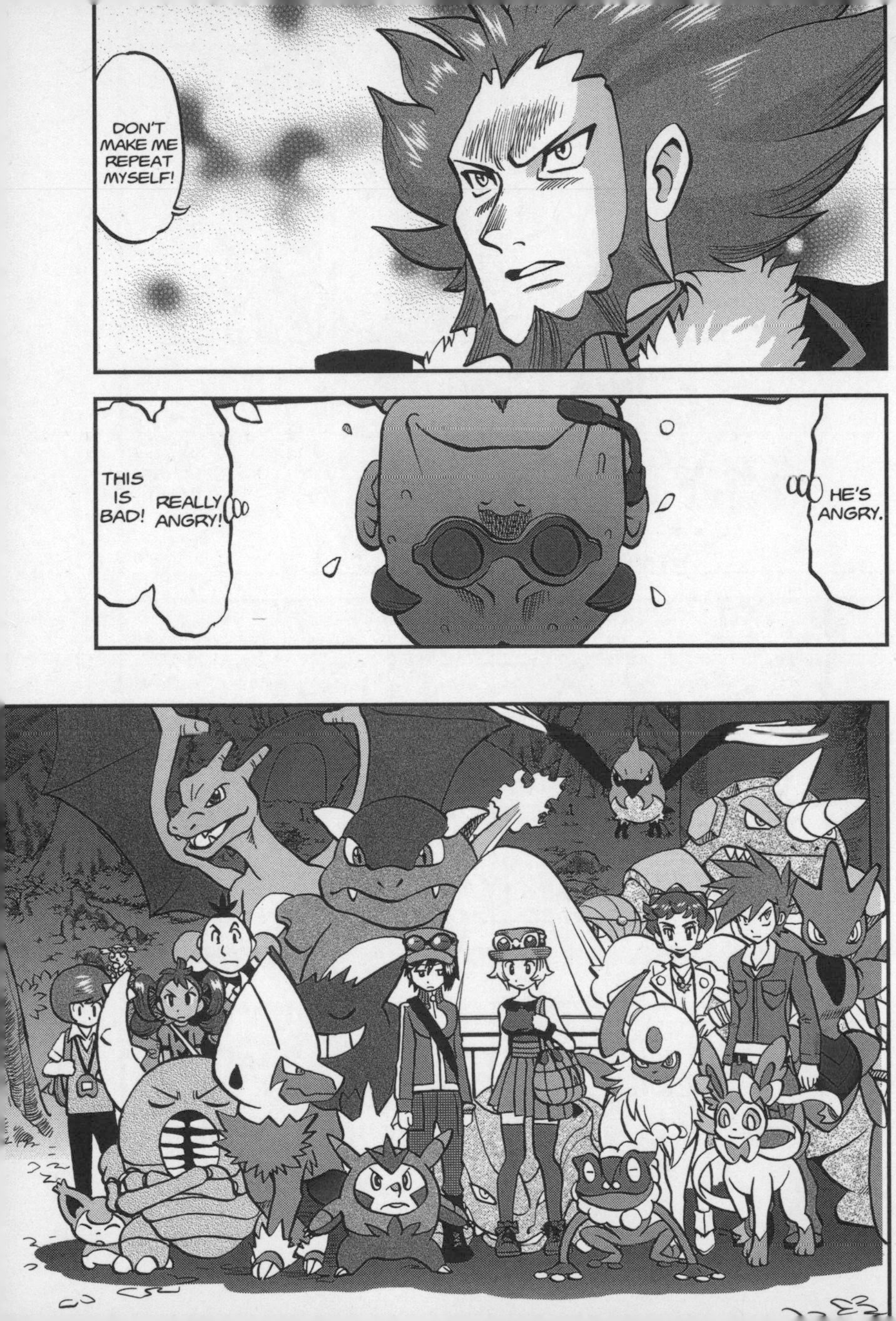
DON'T MAKE ME REPEAT MYSELF!
HE'S ANGRY.
REALLY ANGRY!
THIS IS BAD!

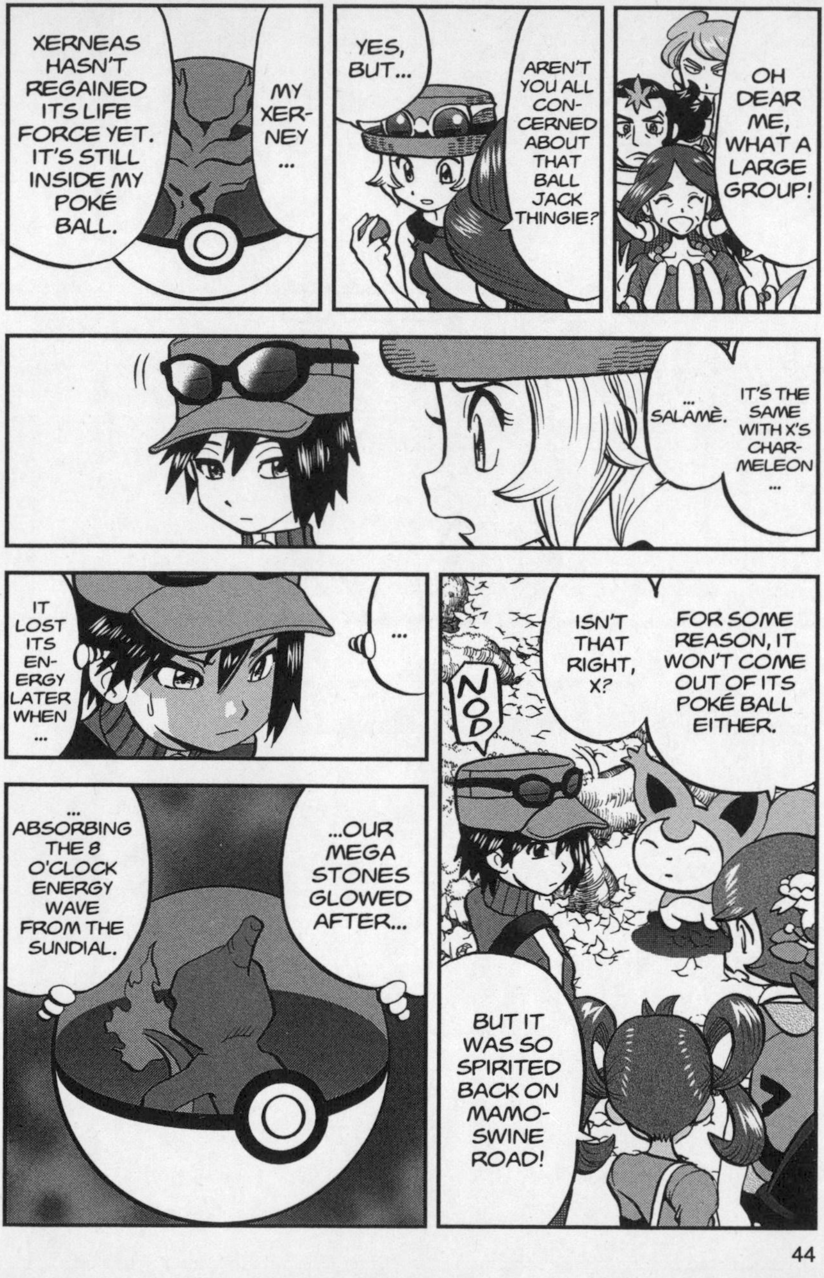
OH DEAR ME, WHAT A LARGE GROUP!
AREN'T YOU ALL CON-CERNED ABOUT THAT BALL JACK THINGIE?
YES, BUT...
MY XER-NEY ...
XERNEAS HASN'T REGAINED ITS LIFE FORCE YET. IT'S STILL INSIDE MY POKÉ BALL.
IT'S THE SAME WITH X'S CHAR-MELEON ...
... SALAMÈ.
FOR SOME REASON, IT WON'T COME OUT OF ITS POKÉ BALL EITHER.
ISN'T THAT RIGHT, X?
NOD
BUT IT WAS SO SPIRITED BACK ON MAMO-SWINE ROAD!
...
IT LOST ITS EN-ERGY LATER WHEN ...
...OUR MEGA STONES GLOWED AFTER...
... ABSORBING THE 8 O'CLOCK ENERGY WAVE FROM THE SUNDIAL.

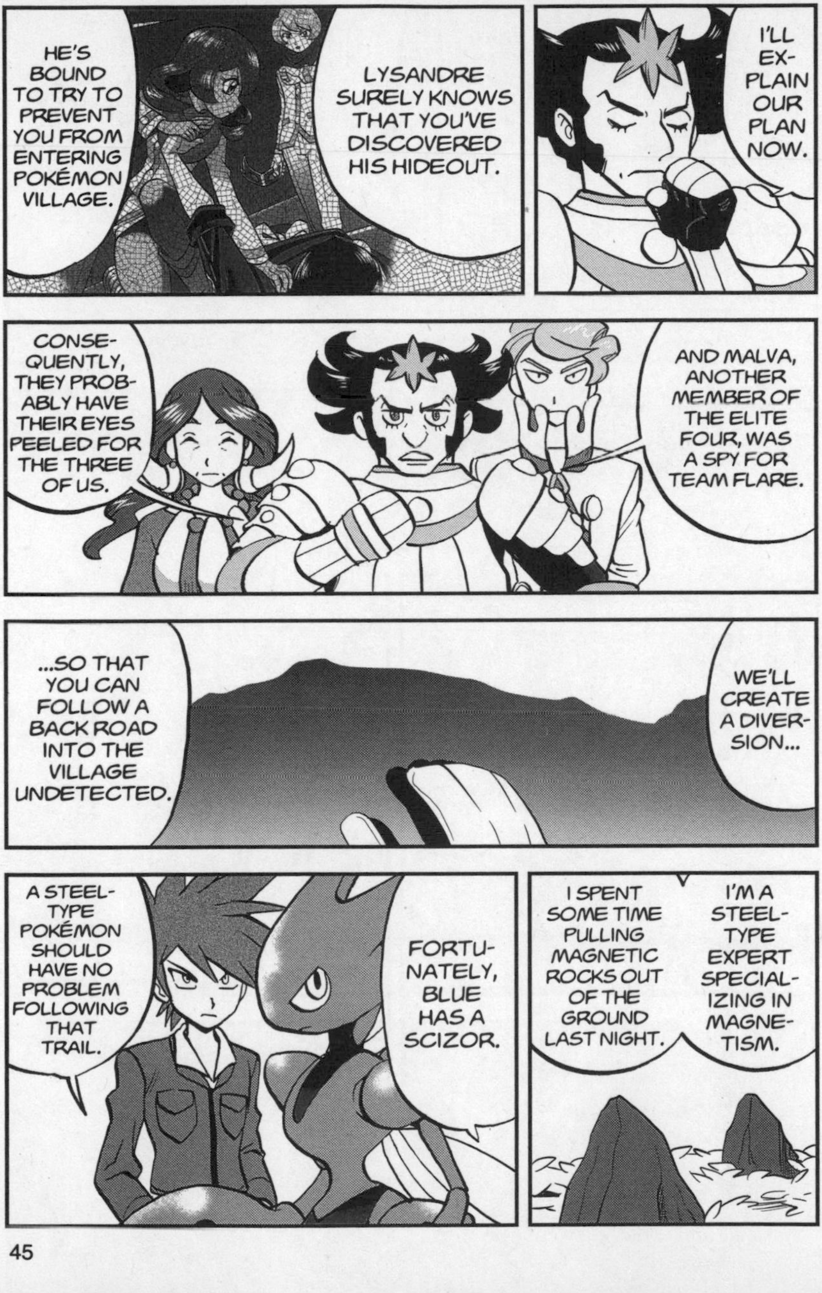
I'LL EXPLAIN OUR PLAN NOW.
LYSANDRE SURELY KNOWS THAT YOU'VE DISCOVERED HIS HIDEOUT.
HE'S BOUND TO TRY TO PREVENT YOU FROM ENTERING POKÉMON VILLAGE.
AND MALVA, ANOTHER MEMBER OF THE ELITE FOUR, WAS A SPY FOR TEAM FLARE.
CONSEQUENTLY, THEY PROBABLY HAVE THEIR EYES PEELED FOR THE THREE OF US.
WE'LL CREATE A DIVERSION...
...SO THAT YOU CAN FOLLOW A BACK ROAD INTO THE VILLAGE UNDETECTED.
I'M A STEEL-TYPE EXPERT SPECIALIZING IN MAGNETISM.
I SPENT SOME TIME PULLING MAGNETIC ROCKS OUT OF THE GROUND LAST NIGHT.
FORTUNATELY, BLUE HAS A SCIZOR.
A STEEL-TYPE POKÉMON SHOULD HAVE NO PROBLEM FOLLOWING THAT TRAIL.

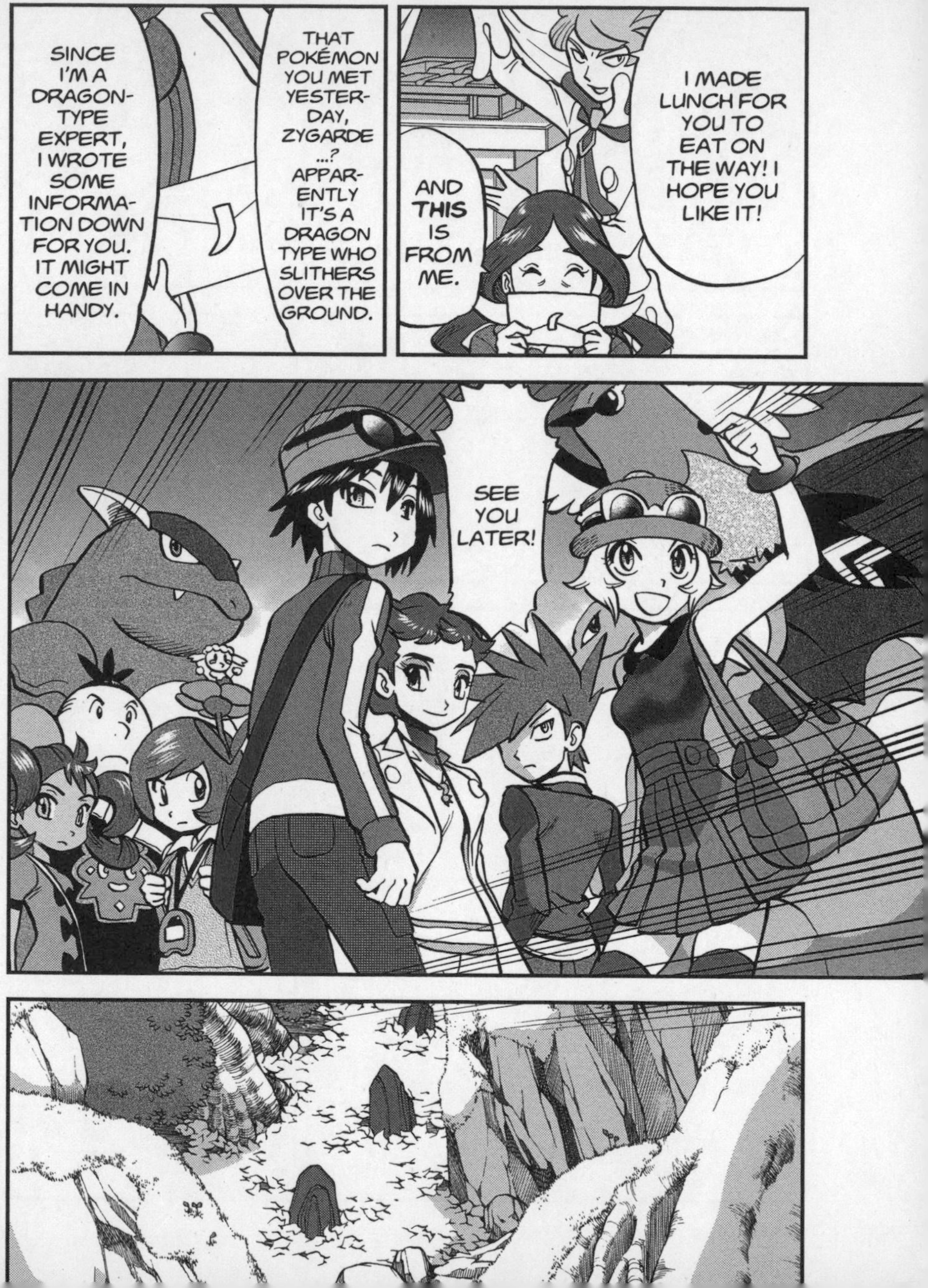
I MADE LUNCH FOR YOU TO EAT ON THE WAY! I HOPE YOU LIKE IT!
AND THIS IS FROM ME.
THAT POKÉMON YOU MET YESTERDAY, ZYGARDE...? APPARENTLY IT'S A DRAGON TYPE WHO SLITHERS OVER THE GROUND.
SINCE I'M A DRAGON-TYPE EXPERT, I WROTE SOME INFORMATION DOWN FOR YOU. IT MIGHT COME IN HANDY.
SEE YOU LATER!

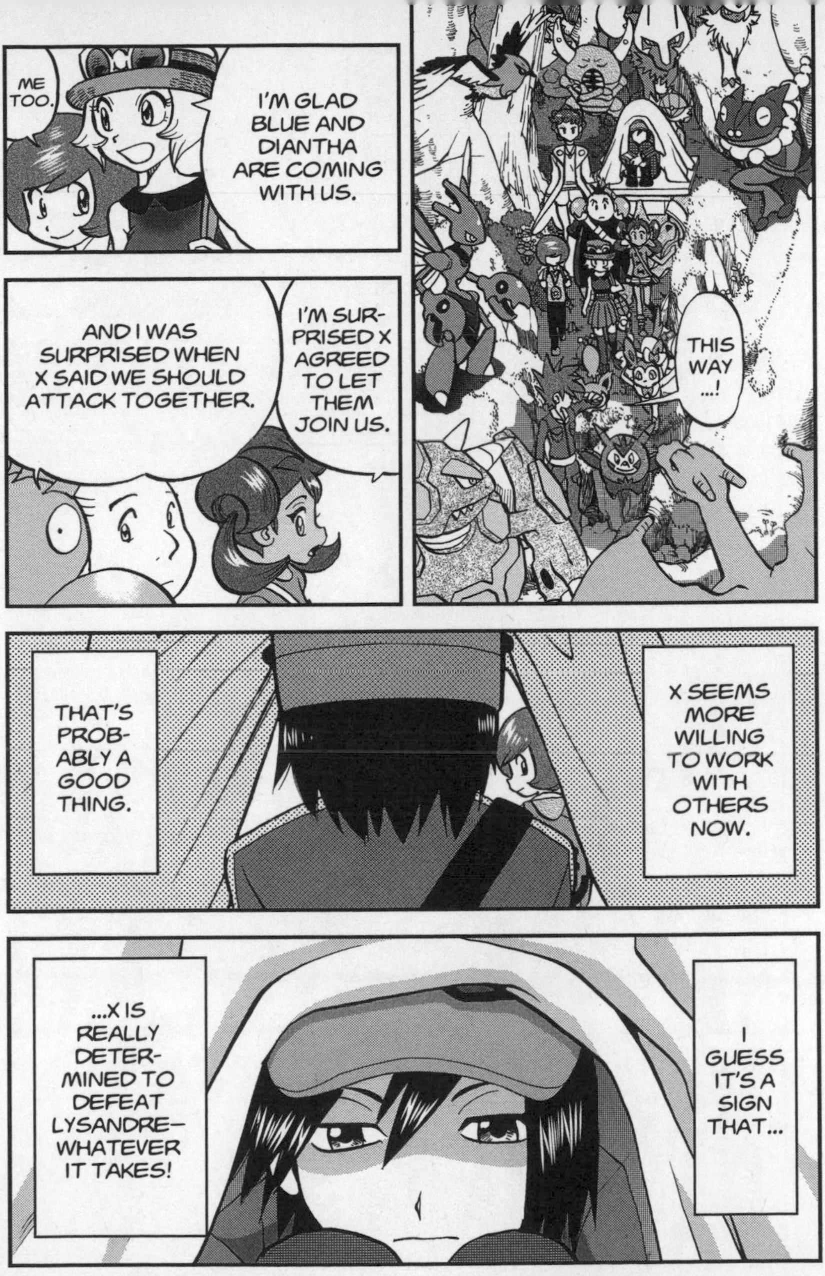
THIS WAY ...!
I'M GLAD BLUE AND DIANTHA ARE COMING WITH US.
ME TOO.
I'M SUR-PRISED X AGREED TO LET THEM JOIN US.
AND I WAS SURPRISED WHEN X SAID WE SHOULD ATTACK TOGETHER.
X SEEMS MORE WILLING TO WORK WITH OTHERS NOW.
THAT'S PROB-ABLY A GOOD THING.
I GUESS IT'S A SIGN THAT...
...X IS REALLY DETER-MINED TO DEFEAT LYSANDRE—WHATEVER IT TAKES!

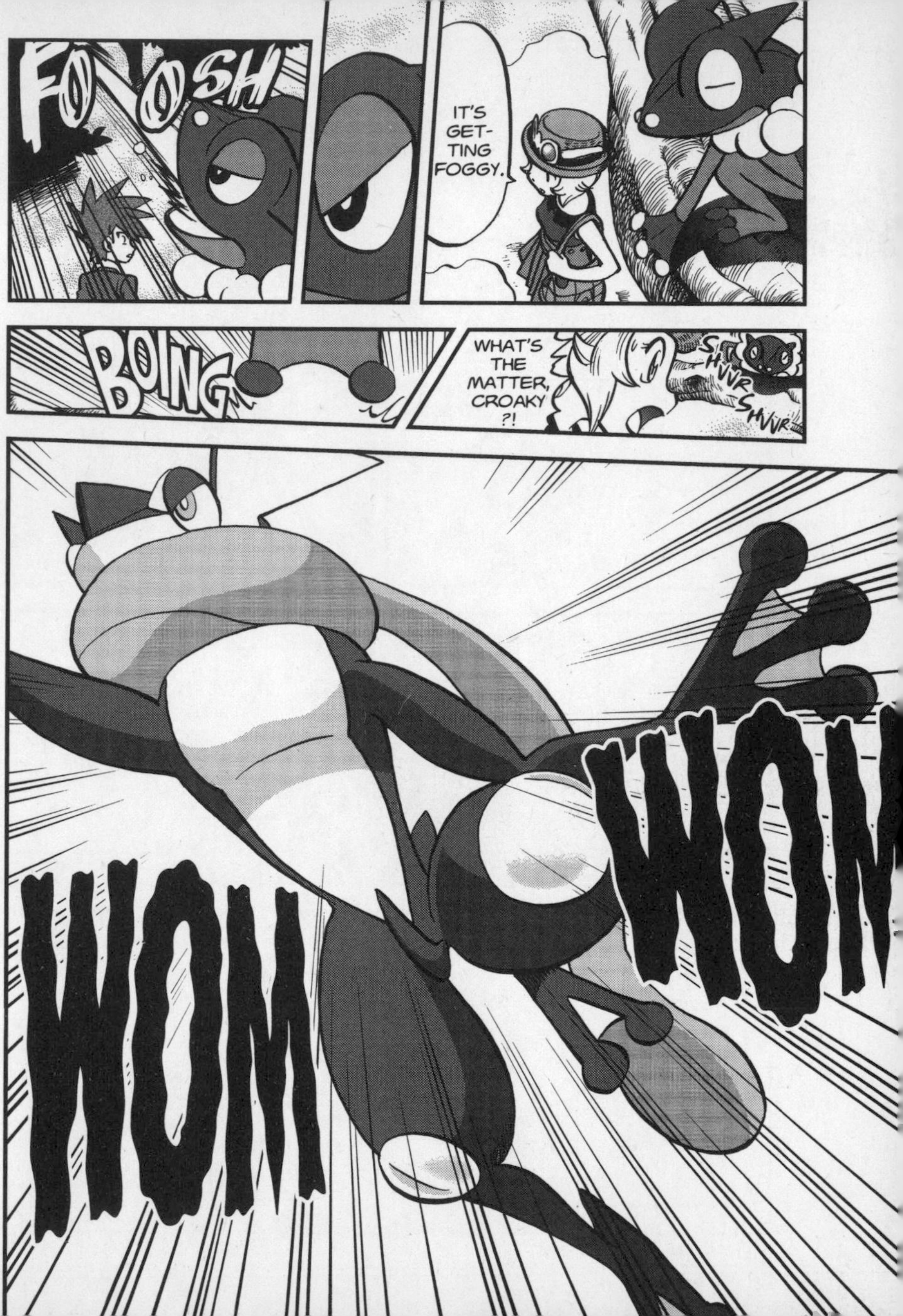
IT'S GET-TING FOGGY.
FOOSH
WHAT'S THE MATTER, CROAKY ?!
SHVVR
SHVVR
BOING
WOM
WOM

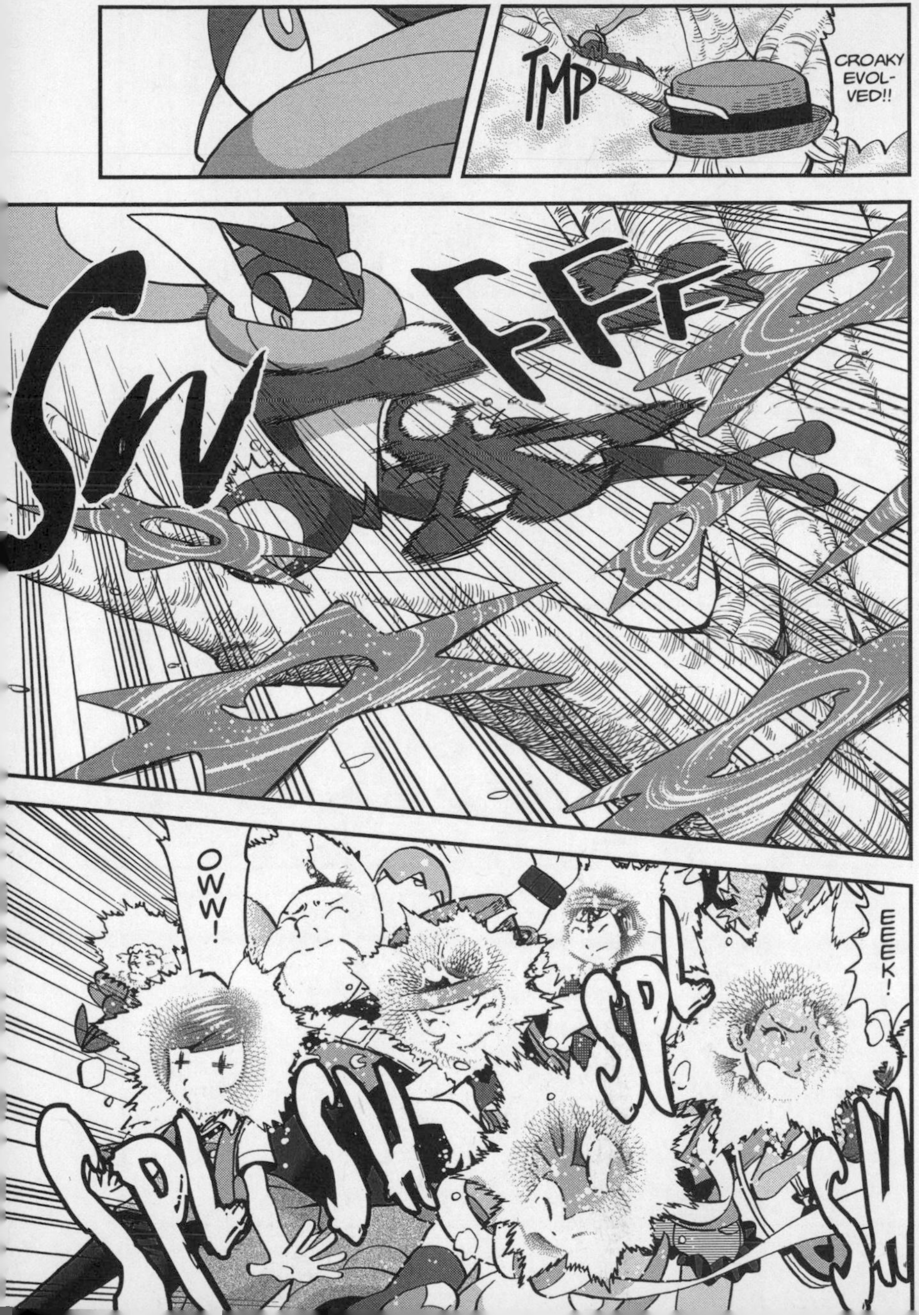
CROAKY EVOL-VED!!
TMP
SWFFF
EEEK!
SPLSH
OWW!
SPLSH

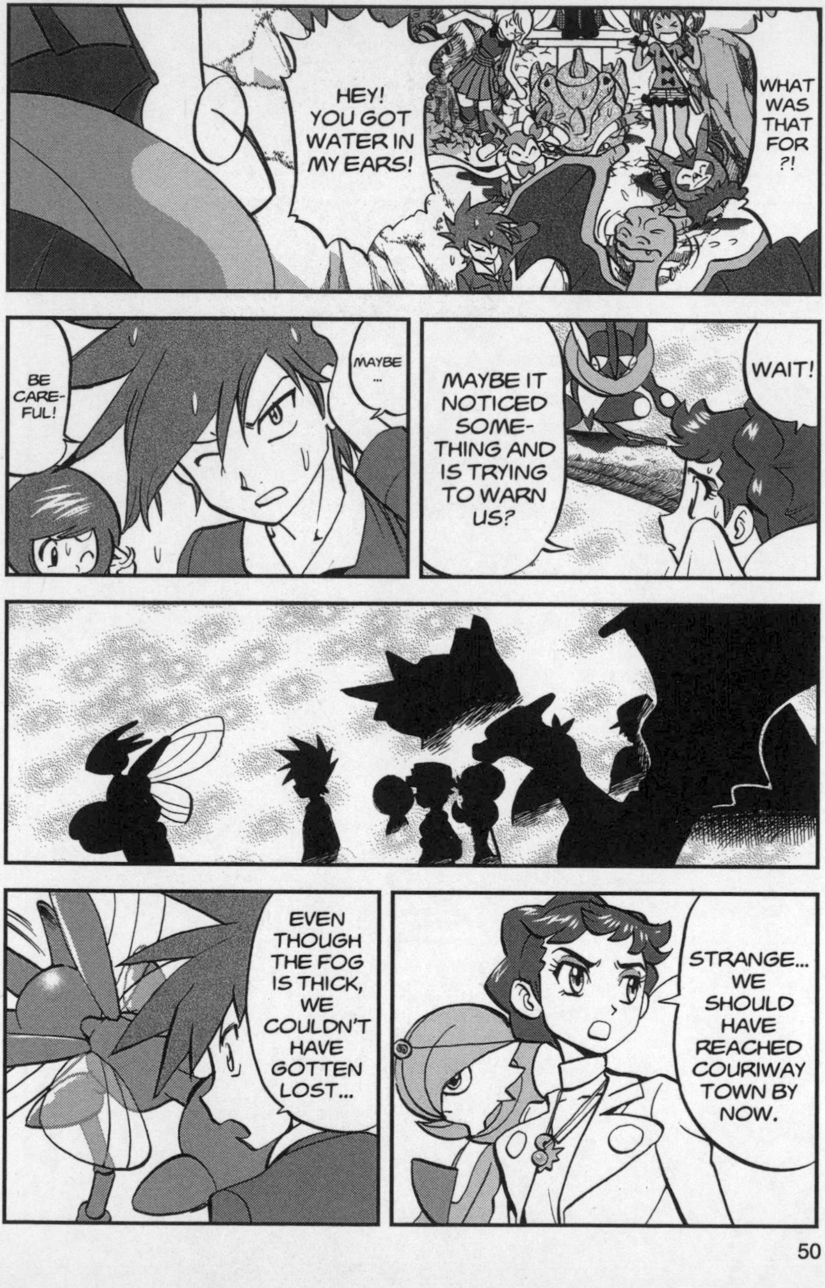
WHAT WAS THAT FOR ?!
HEY! YOU GOT WATER IN MY EARS!
WAIT!
MAYBE IT NOTICED SOME-THING AND IS TRYING TO WARN US?
MAYBE ...
BE CARE-FUL!
STRANGE... WE SHOULD HAVE REACHED COURIWAY TOWN BY NOW.
EVEN THOUGH THE FOG IS THICK, WE COULDN'T HAVE GOTTEN LOST...

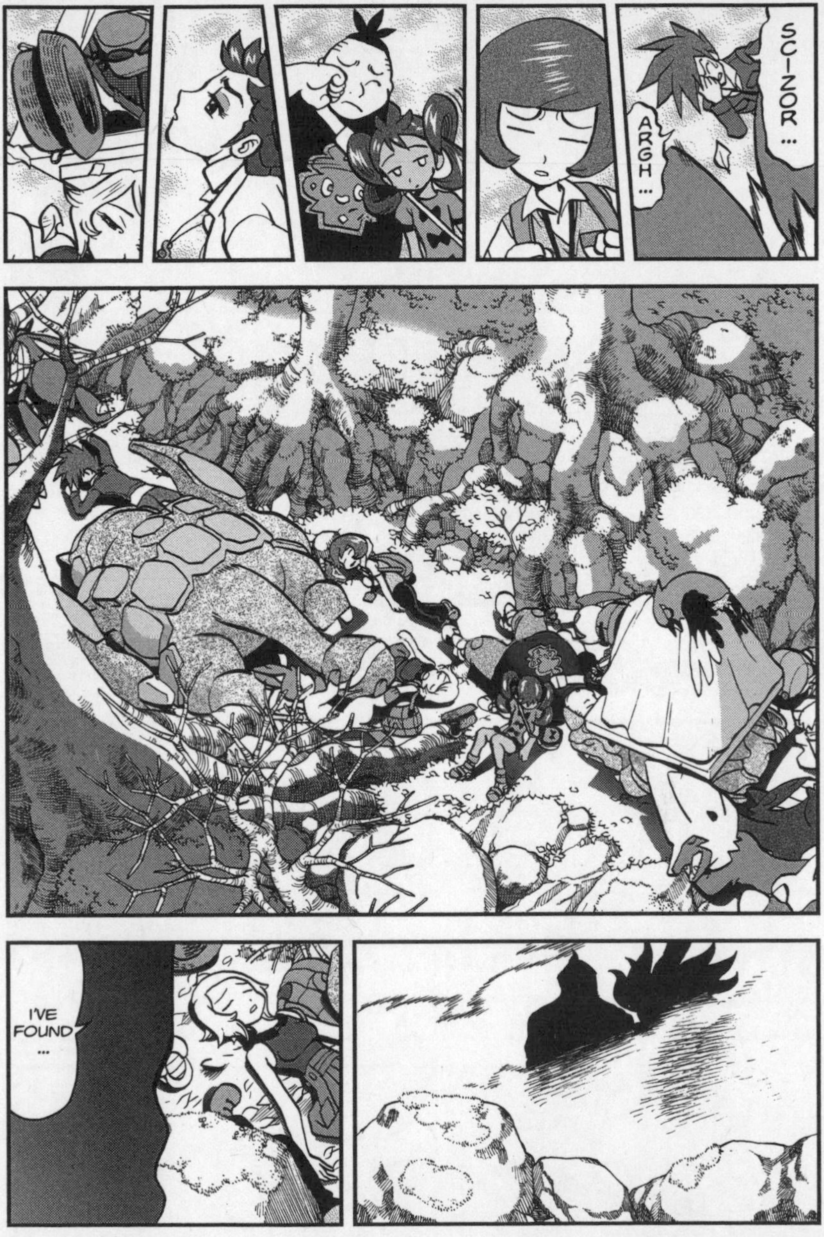
SCIZOR ...
ARGH ...
I'VE FOUND ...

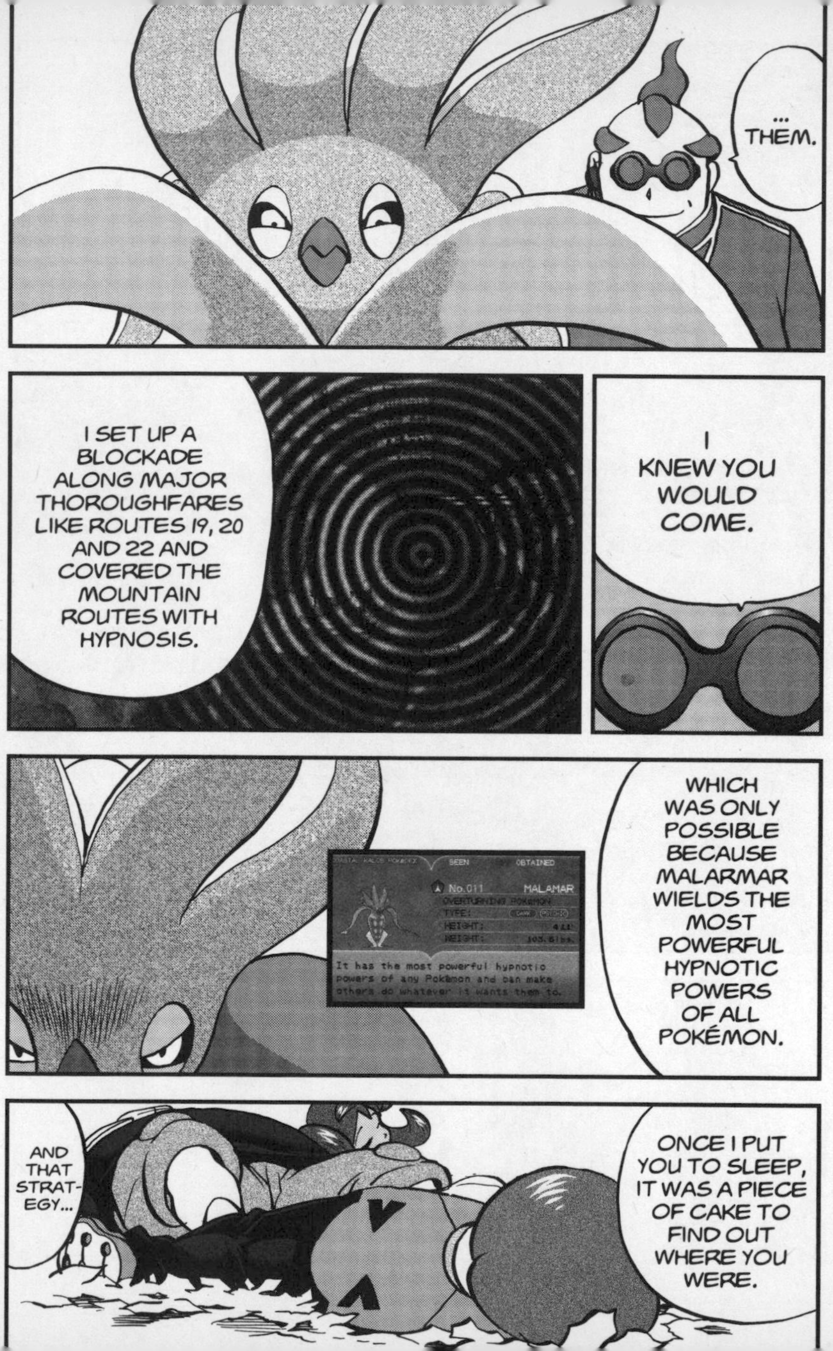
... THEM.
I KNEW YOU WOULD COME.
I SET UP A BLOCKADE ALONG MAJOR THOROUGHFARES LIKE ROUTES 19, 20 AND 22 AND COVERED THE MOUNTAIN ROUTES WITH HYPNOSIS.
WHICH WAS ONLY POSSIBLE BECAUSE MALARMAR WIELDS THE MOST POWERFUL HYPNOTIC POWERS OF ALL POKÉMON.
SEEN
OBTAINED
No.011 MALAMAR
TYPE:
HEIGHT:
WEIGHT:
It has the most powerful hypnotic powers of any Pokémon and can make others do whatever it wants them to.
ONCE I PUT YOU TO SLEEP, IT WAS A PIECE OF CAKE TO FIND OUT WHERE YOU WERE.
AND THAT STRAT-EGY...

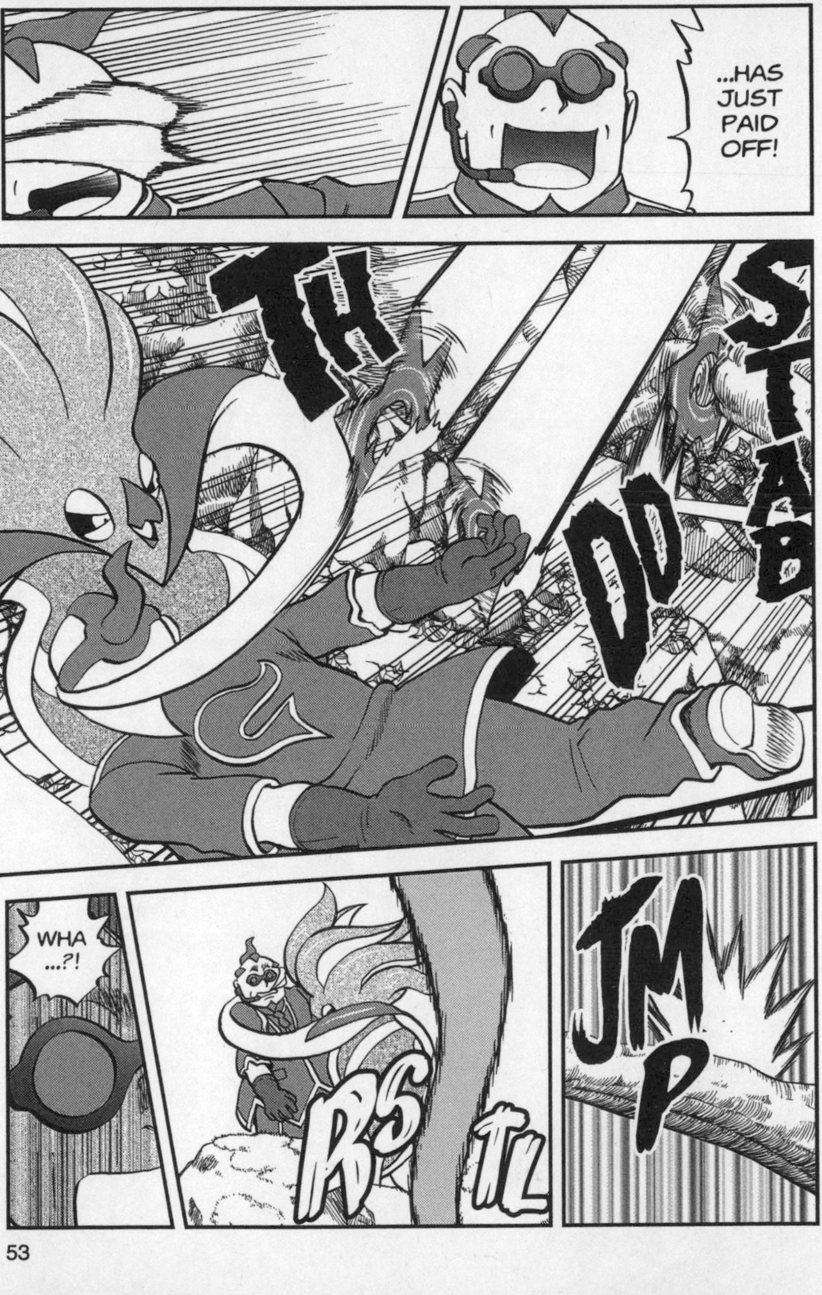
...HAS JUST PAID OFF!
STAB
DD
TH
JM P
RS TL
WHA ...?!

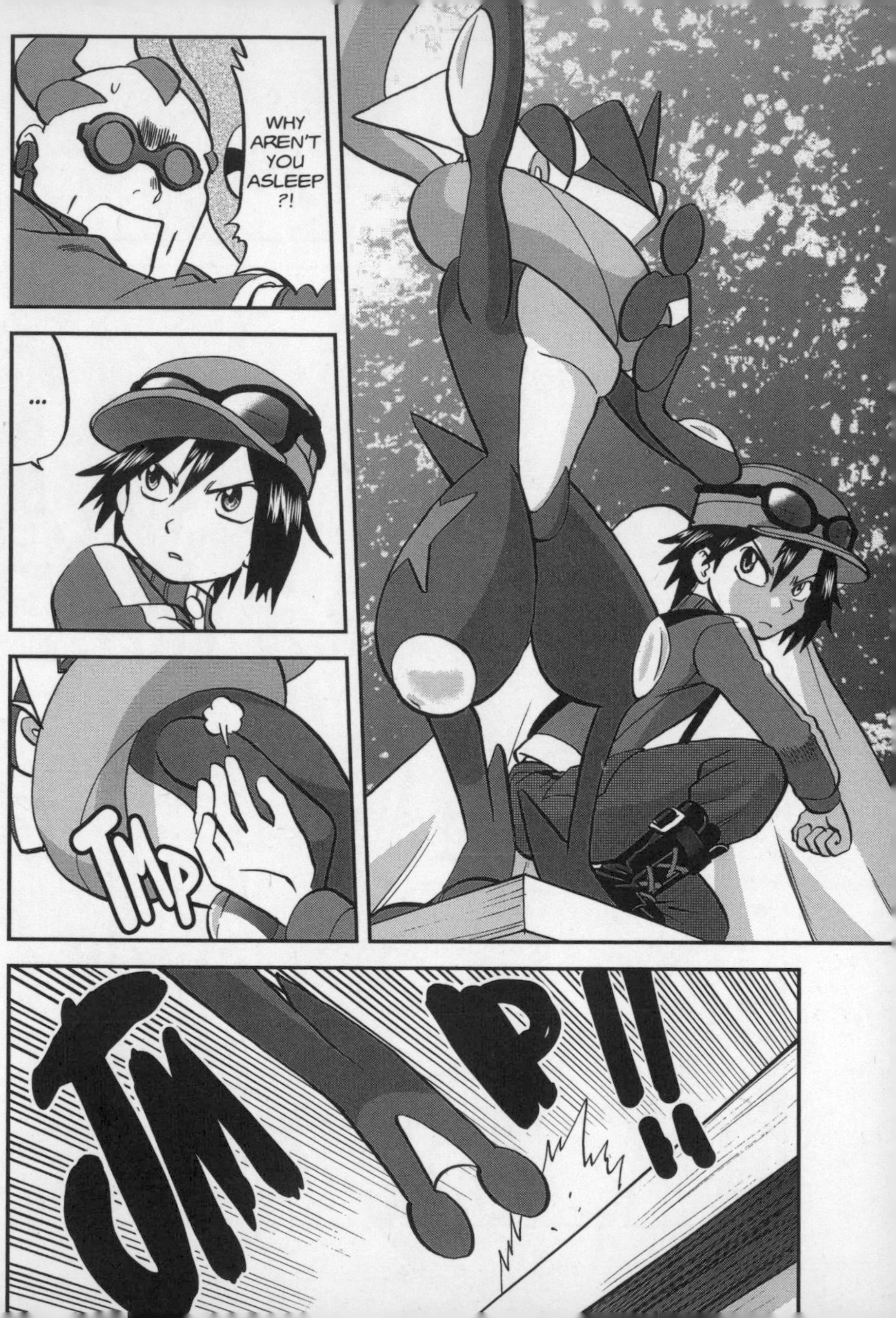
WHY AREN'T YOU ASLEEP ?!
...
TMP
TMP!!

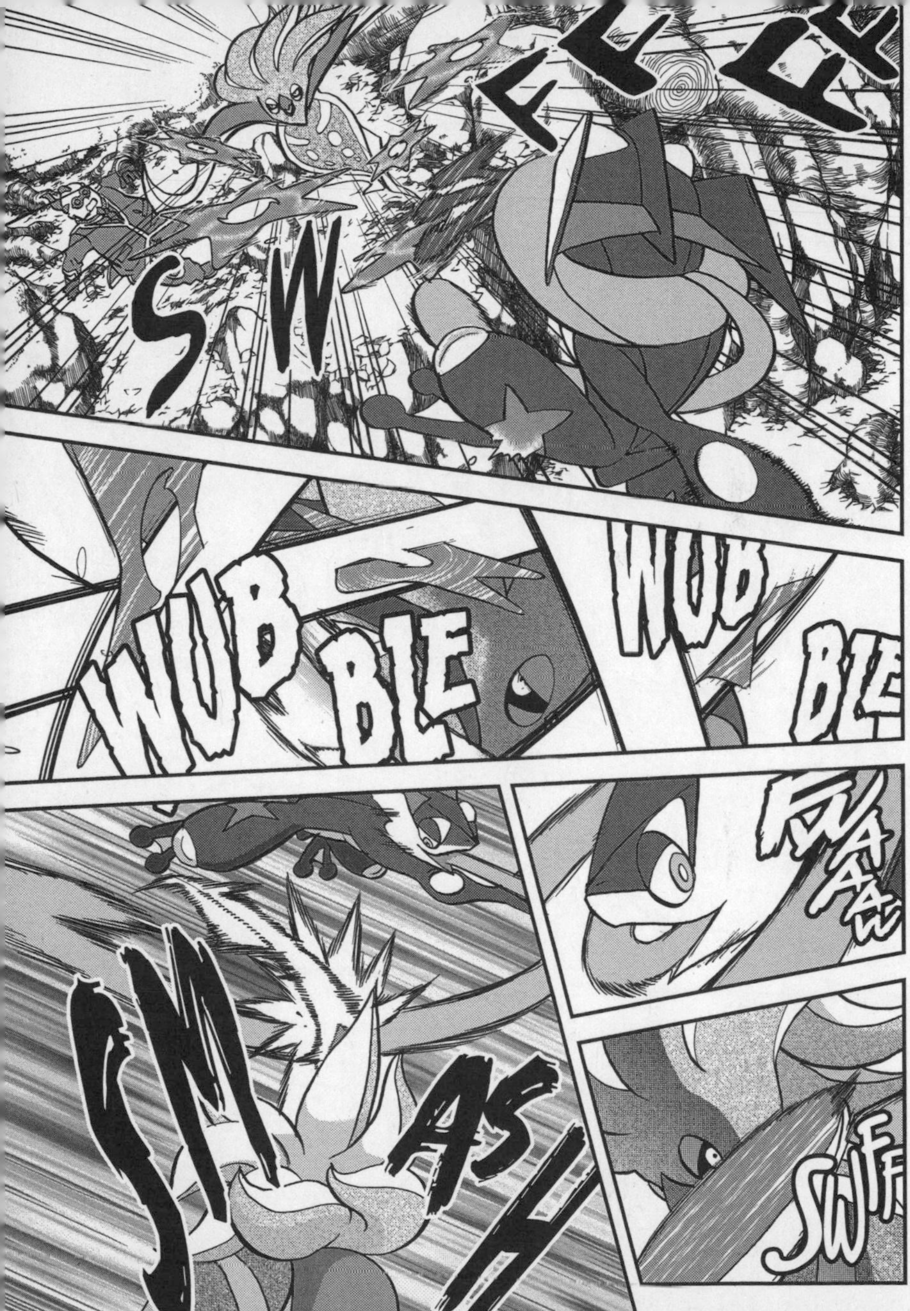
SW
WUB BLE
WUB BLE
FWAAW
SWFF
SMASH

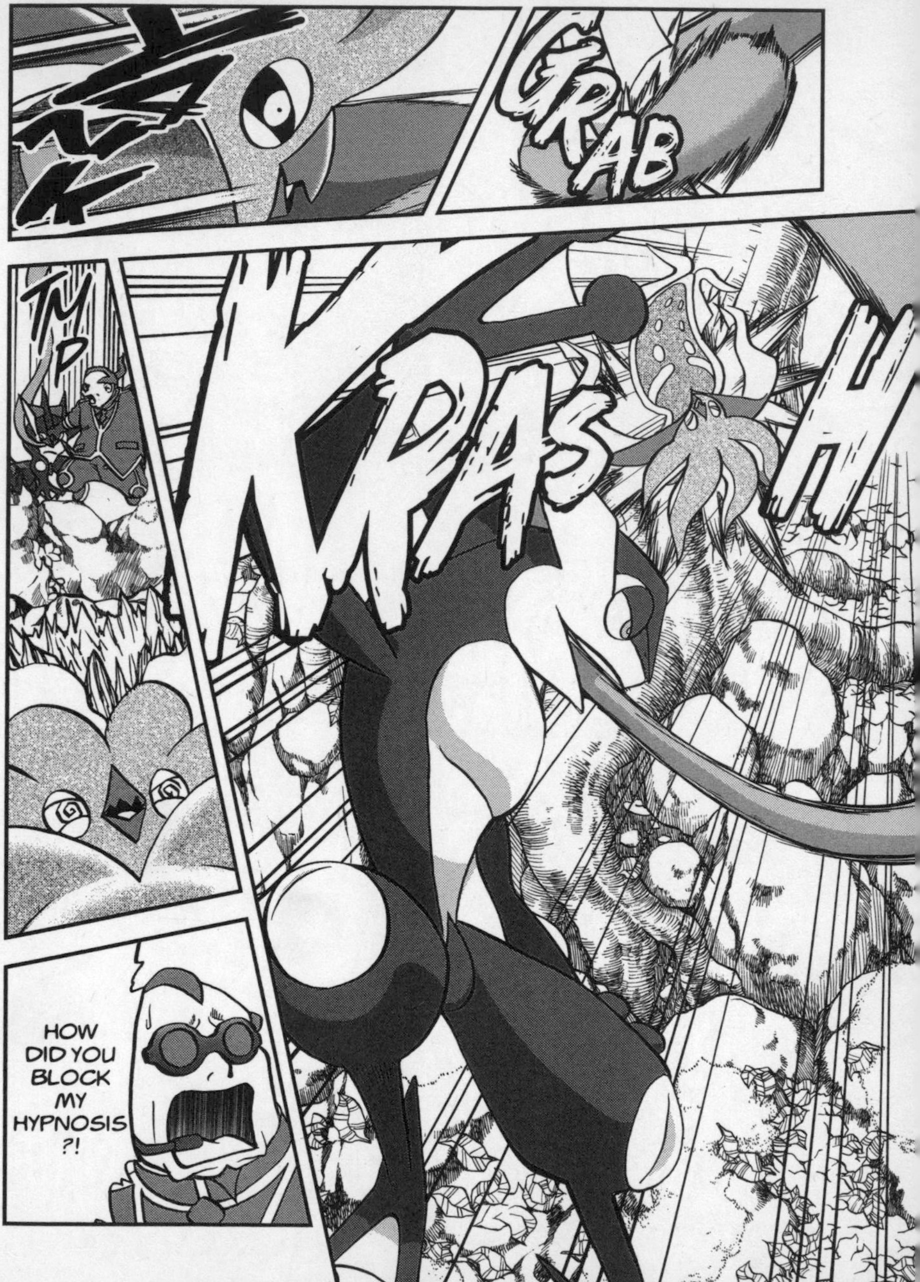
GRAB
KRASH
TMP
HOW DID YOU BLOCK MY HYPNOSIS ?!

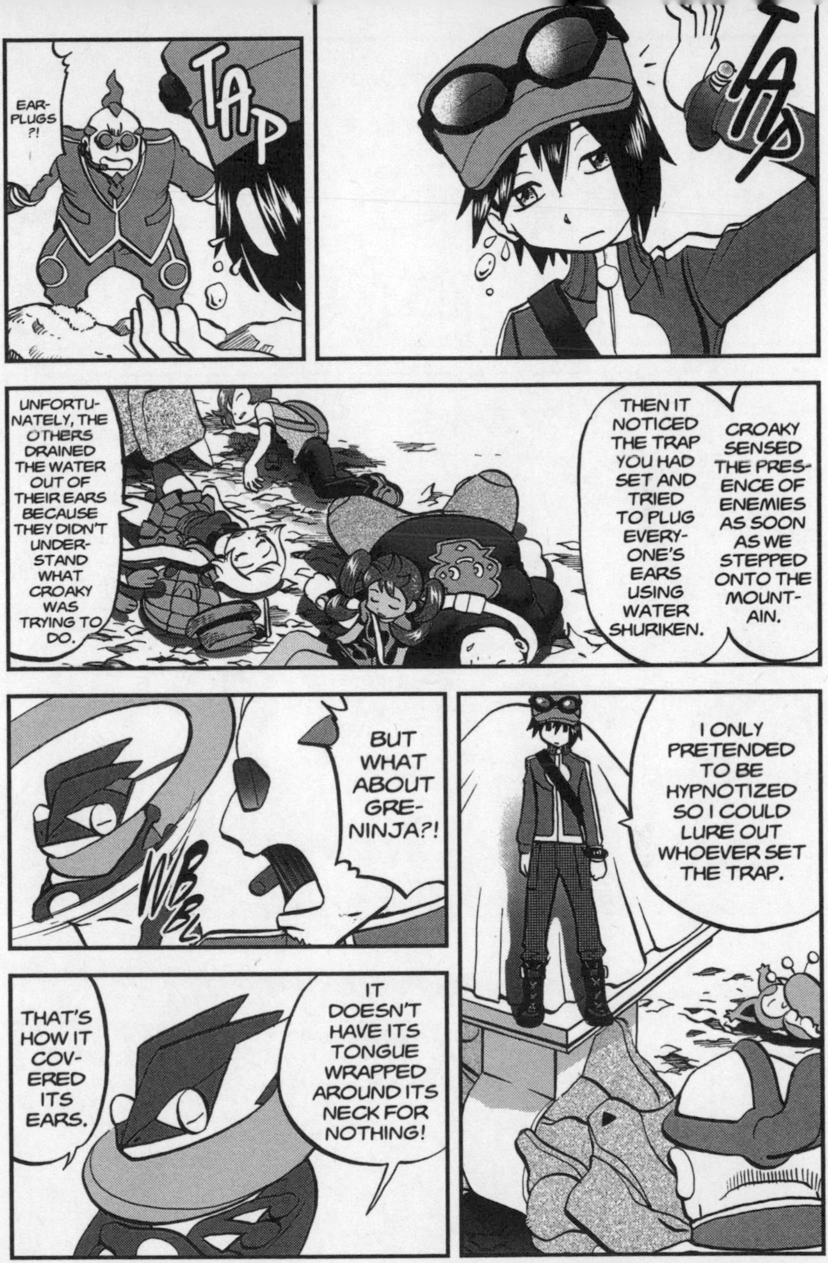
TAP TAP
TAP
EAR-PLUGS?!
CROAKY SENSED THE PRESENCE OF ENEMIES AS SOON AS WE STEPPED ONTO THE MOUNTAIN.
THEN IT NOTICED THE TRAP YOU HAD SET AND TRIED TO PLUG EVERYONE'S EARS USING WATER SHURIKEN.
UNFORTUNATELY, THE OTHERS DRAINED THE WATER OUT OF THEIR EARS BECAUSE THEY DIDN'T UNDERSTAND WHAT CROAKY WAS TRYING TO DO.
I ONLY PRETENDED TO BE HYPNOTIZED SO I COULD LURE OUT WHOEVER SET THE TRAP.
BUT WHAT ABOUT GRENINJA?!
IT DOESN'T HAVE ITS TONGUE WRAPPED AROUND ITS NECK FOR NOTHING!
THAT'S HOW IT COVERED ITS EARS.

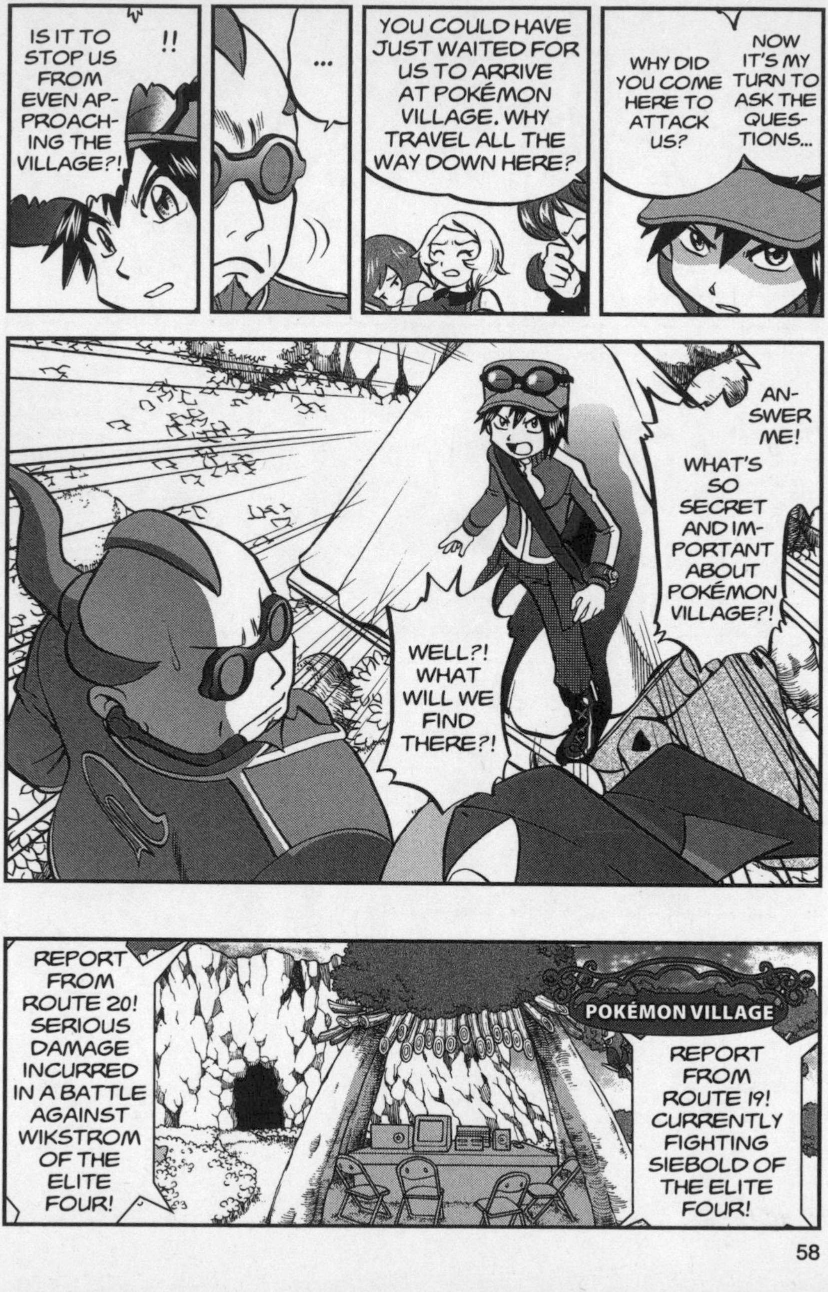
NOW IT'S MY TURN TO ASK THE QUESTIONS...
WHY DID YOU COME HERE TO ATTACK US?
YOU COULD HAVE JUST WAITED FOR US TO ARRIVE AT POKÉMON VILLAGE. WHY TRAVEL ALL THE WAY DOWN HERE?
...
!!
IS IT TO STOP US FROM EVEN APPROACHING THE VILLAGE?!
ANSWER ME!
WHAT'S SO SECRET AND IMPORTANT ABOUT POKÉMON VILLAGE?!
WELL?! WHAT WILL WE FIND THERE?!
POKÉMON VILLAGE
REPORT FROM ROUTE 19! CURRENTLY FIGHTING SIEBOLD OF THE ELITE FOUR!
REPORT FROM ROUTE 20! SERIOUS DAMAGE INCURRED IN A BATTLE AGAINST WIKSTROM OF THE ELITE FOUR!

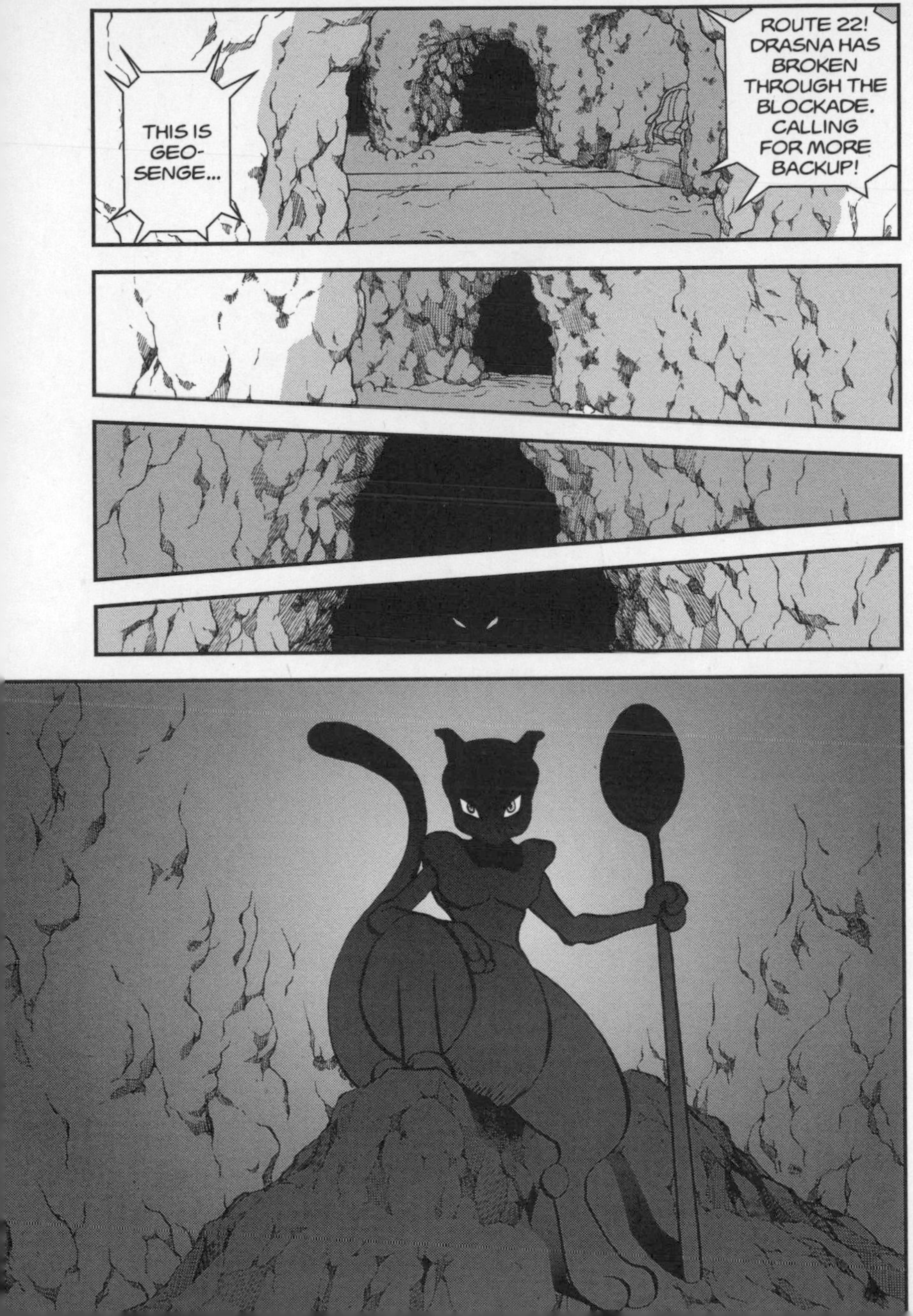
ROUTE 22! DRASNA HAS BROKEN THROUGH THE BLOCKADE. CALLING FOR MORE BACKUP!
THIS IS GEO-SENGE...

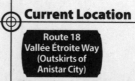

Current Location

**Route 18
Vallée Étroite Way
(Outskirts of
Anistar City)**

**This path is best known for its
trolley, once used for the coal
mine, and the curious Inverse
Battle house.**

Adventure 33 Chesnaught Protects

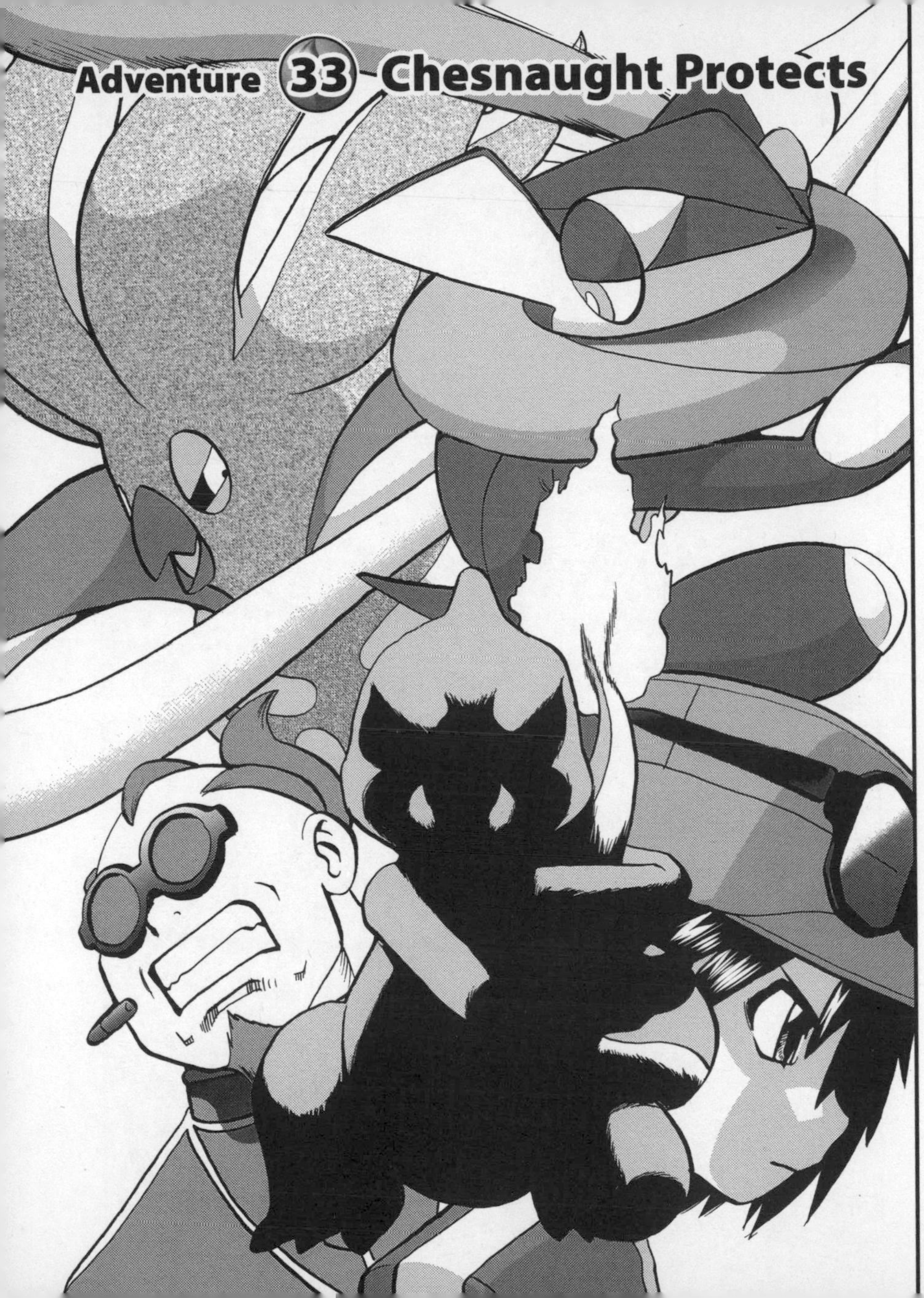

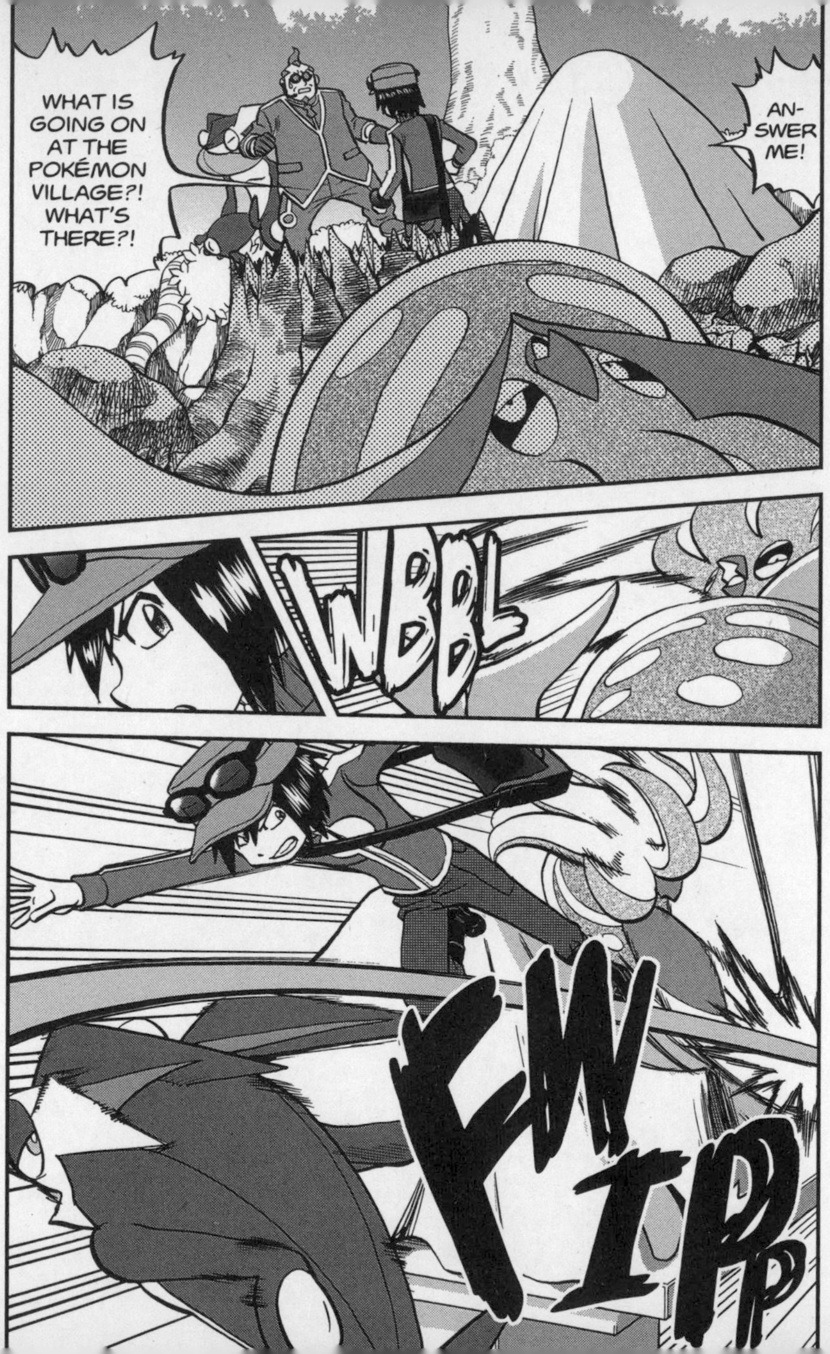
AN-SWER ME!
WHAT IS GOING ON AT THE POKÉMON VILLAGE?! WHAT'S THERE?!
WBBL
FWIPPP

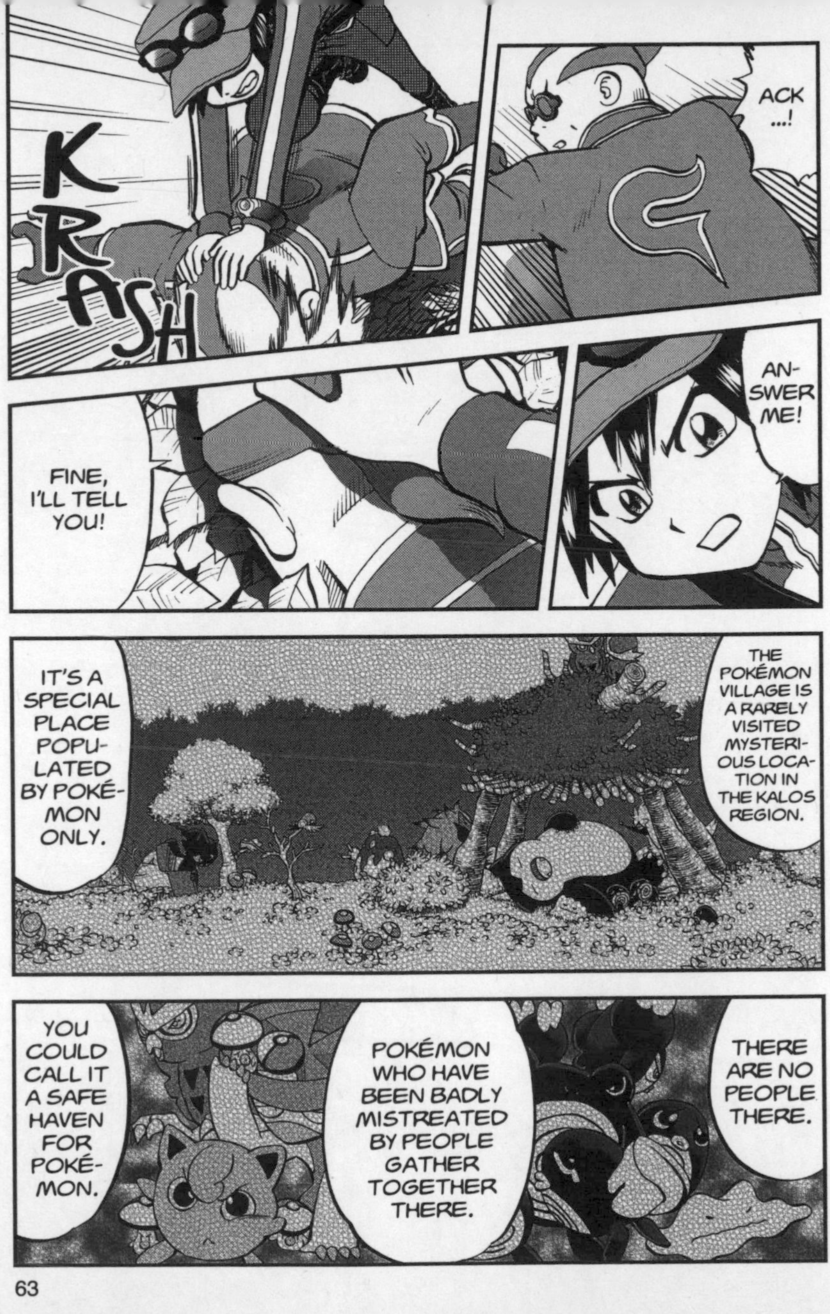
ACK ...!
KRASH
AN-SWER ME!
FINE, I'LL TELL YOU!
THE POKÉMON VILLAGE IS A RARELY VISITED MYSTERIOUS LOCATION IN THE KALOS REGION.
IT'S A SPECIAL PLACE POPULATED BY POKÉMON ONLY.
THERE ARE NO PEOPLE THERE.
POKÉMON WHO HAVE BEEN BADLY MISTREATED BY PEOPLE GATHER TOGETHER THERE.
YOU COULD CALL IT A SAFE HAVEN FOR POKÉMON.

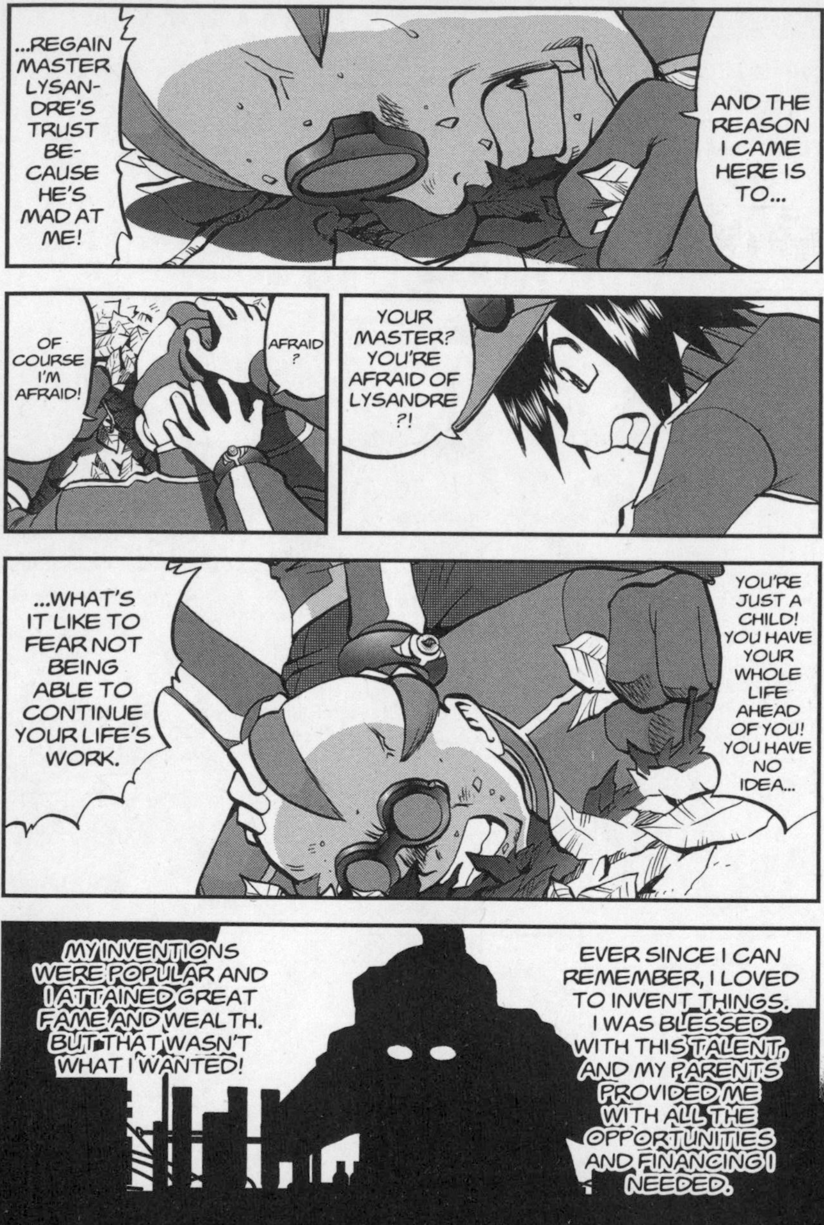
AND THE REASON I CAME HERE IS TO...
...REGAIN MASTER LYSAN-DRE'S TRUST BE-CAUSE HE'S MAD AT ME!
YOUR MASTER? YOU'RE AFRAID OF LYSANDRE?!
AFRAID?
OF COURSE I'M AFRAID!
YOU'RE JUST A CHILD! YOU HAVE YOUR WHOLE LIFE AHEAD OF YOU! YOU HAVE NO IDEA...
...WHAT'S IT LIKE TO FEAR NOT BEING ABLE TO CONTINUE YOUR LIFE'S WORK.
EVER SINCE I CAN REMEMBER, I LOVED TO INVENT THINGS. I WAS BLESSED WITH THIS TALENT, AND MY PARENTS PROVIDED ME WITH ALL THE OPPORTUNITIES AND FINANCING I NEEDED.
MY INVENTIONS WERE POPULAR AND I ATTAINED GREAT FAME AND WEALTH. BUT THAT WASN'T WHAT I WANTED!

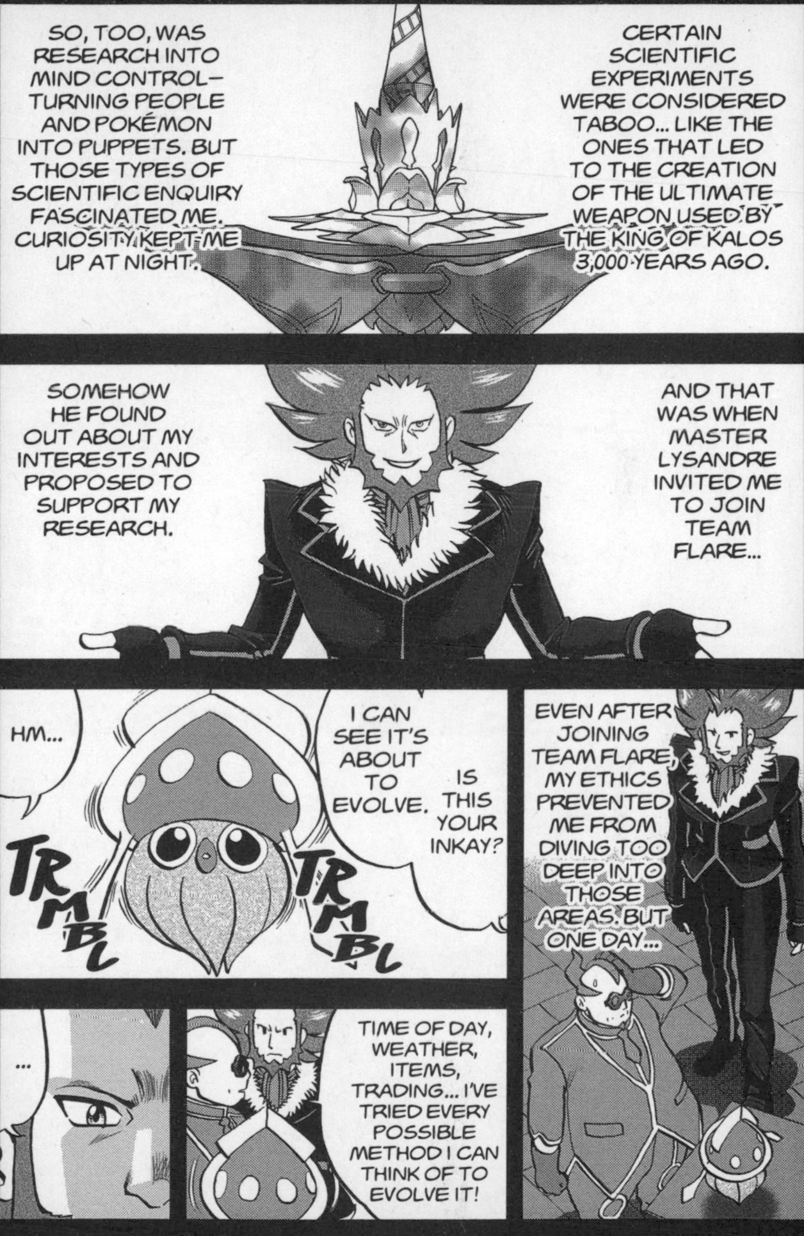
CERTAIN SCIENTIFIC EXPERIMENTS WERE CONSIDERED TABOO... LIKE THE ONES THAT LED TO THE CREATION OF THE ULTIMATE WEAPON USED BY THE KING OF KALOS 3,000 YEARS AGO.
SO, TOO, WAS RESEARCH INTO MIND CONTROL—TURNING PEOPLE AND POKÉMON INTO PUPPETS. BUT THOSE TYPES OF SCIENTIFIC ENQUIRY FASCINATED ME. CURIOSITY KEPT ME UP AT NIGHT.
AND THAT WAS WHEN MASTER LYSANDRE INVITED ME TO JOIN TEAM FLARE...
SOMEHOW HE FOUND OUT ABOUT MY INTERESTS AND PROPOSED TO SUPPORT MY RESEARCH.
EVEN AFTER JOINING TEAM FLARE, MY ETHICS PREVENTED ME FROM DIVING TOO DEEP INTO THOSE AREAS. BUT ONE DAY...
IS THIS YOUR INKAY?
I CAN SEE IT'S ABOUT TO EVOLVE.
TRMBL
TRMBL
HM...
TIME OF DAY, WEATHER, ITEMS, TRADING... I'VE TRIED EVERY POSSIBLE METHOD I CAN THINK OF TO EVOLVE IT!
...

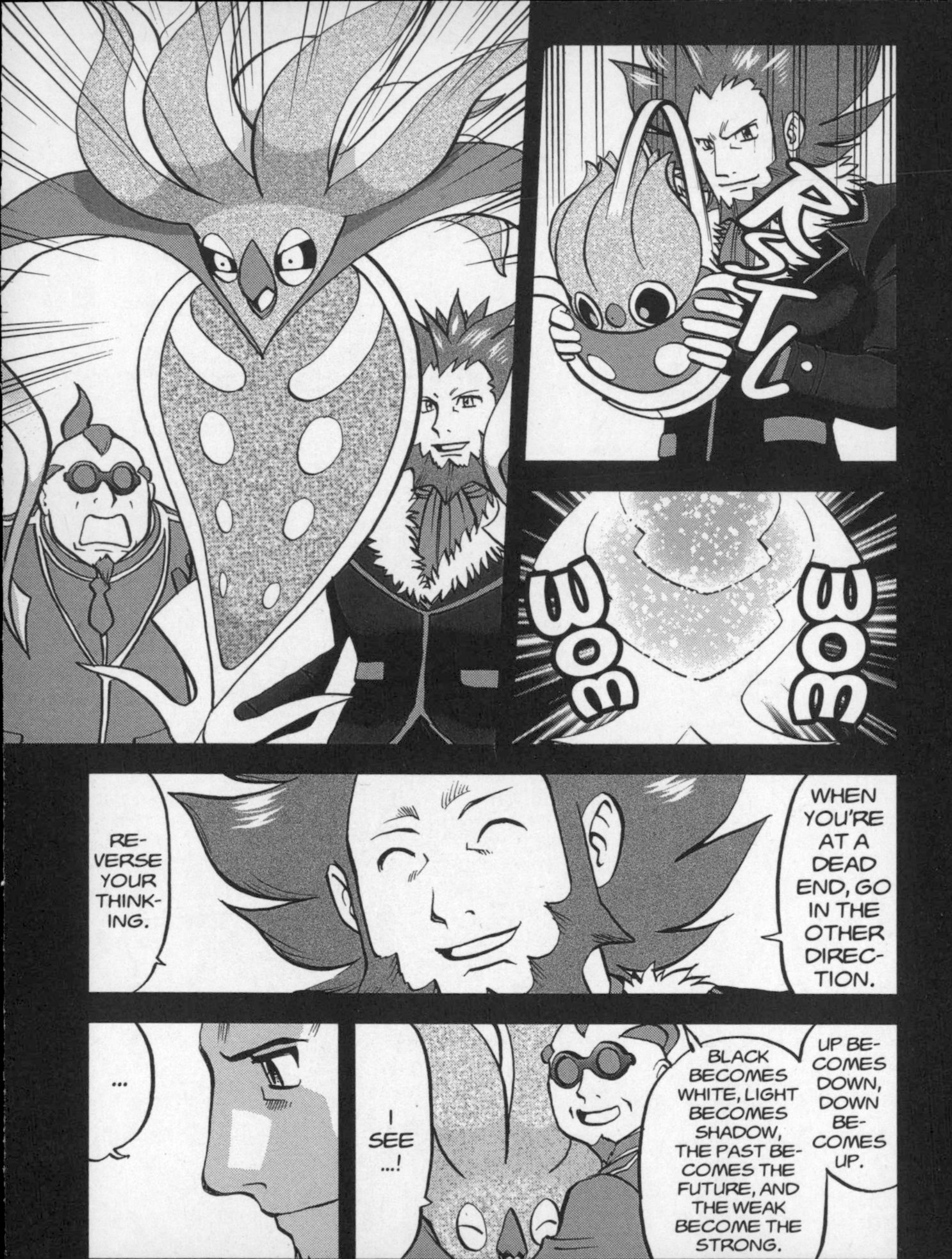
RSTL
BOOM
BOOM
WHEN YOU'RE AT A DEAD END, GO IN THE OTHER DIRECTION.
REVERSE YOUR THINKING.
UP BECOMES DOWN, DOWN BECOMES UP.
BLACK BECOMES WHITE, LIGHT BECOMES SHADOW, THE PAST BECOMES THE FUTURE, AND THE WEAK BECOME THE STRONG.
I SEE...!
...

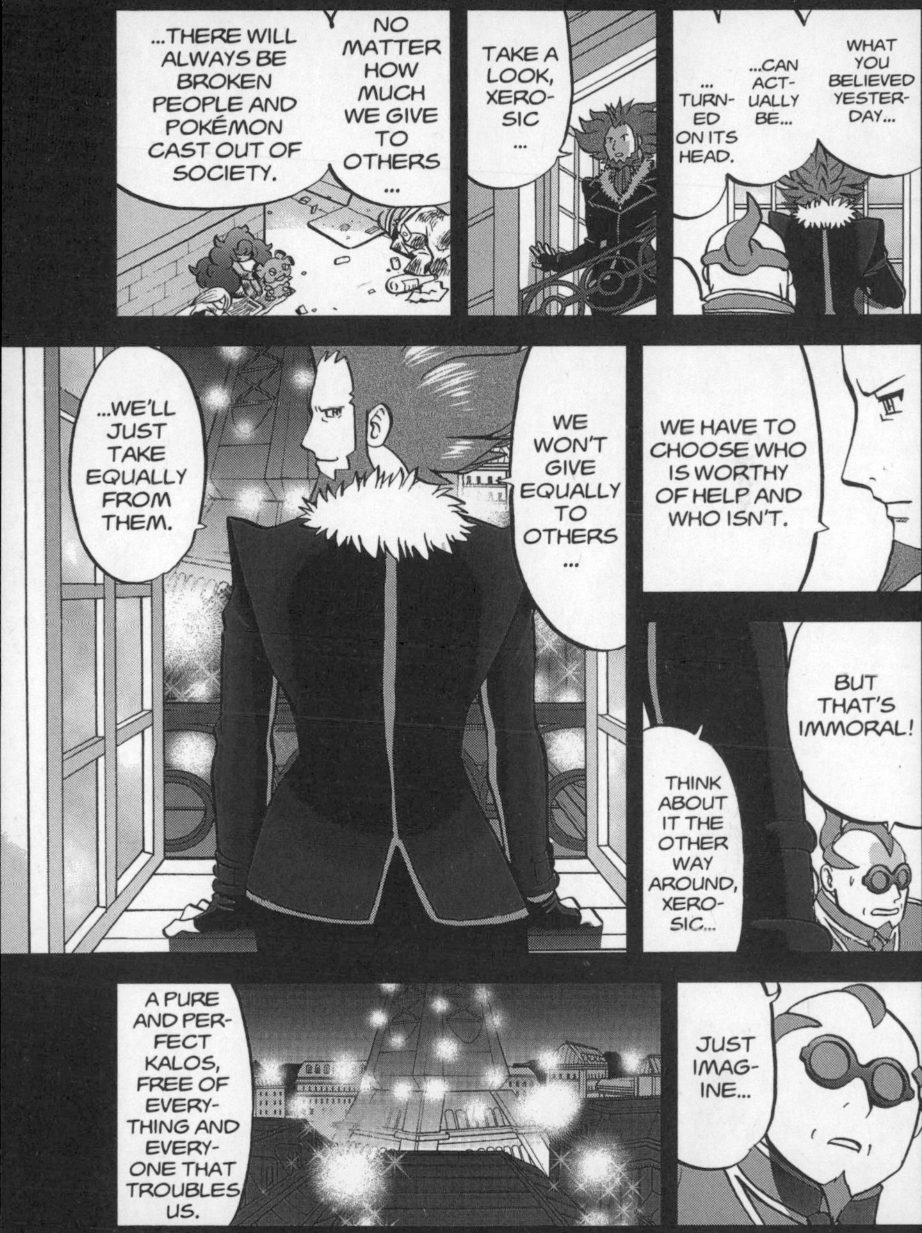
WHAT YOU BELIEVED YESTERDAY...
...CAN ACTUALLY BE...
...TURNED ON ITS HEAD.
TAKE A LOOK, XEROSIC...
NO MATTER HOW MUCH WE GIVE TO OTHERS...
...THERE WILL ALWAYS BE BROKEN PEOPLE AND POKÉMON CAST OUT OF SOCIETY.
WE HAVE TO CHOOSE WHO IS WORTHY OF HELP AND WHO ISN'T.
BUT THAT'S IMMORAL!
THINK ABOUT IT THE OTHER WAY AROUND, XEROSIC...
WE WON'T GIVE EQUALLY TO OTHERS...
...WE'LL JUST TAKE EQUALLY FROM THEM.
JUST IMAGINE...
A PURE AND PERFECT KALOS, FREE OF EVERYTHING AND EVERYONE THAT TROUBLES US.

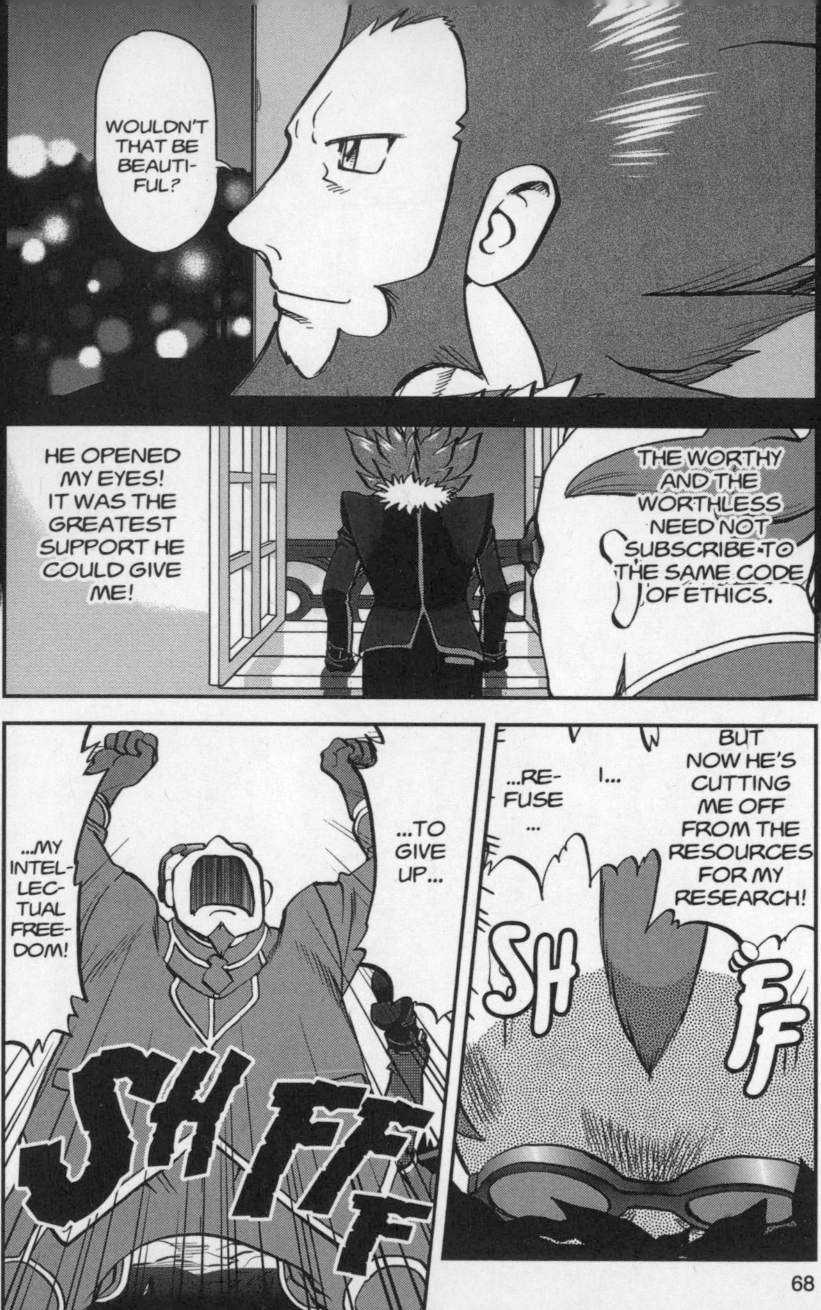
WOULDN'T THAT BE BEAUTI-FUL?
THE WORTHY AND THE WORTHLESS NEED NOT SUBSCRIBE TO THE SAME CODE OF ETHICS.
HE OPENED MY EYES! IT WAS THE GREATEST SUPPORT HE COULD GIVE ME!
BUT NOW HE'S CUTTING ME OFF FROM THE RESOURCES FOR MY RESEARCH!
I...
...RE-FUSE ...
SHFF
...TO GIVE UP...
...MY INTEL-LEC-TUAL FREE-DOM!
SHFFF

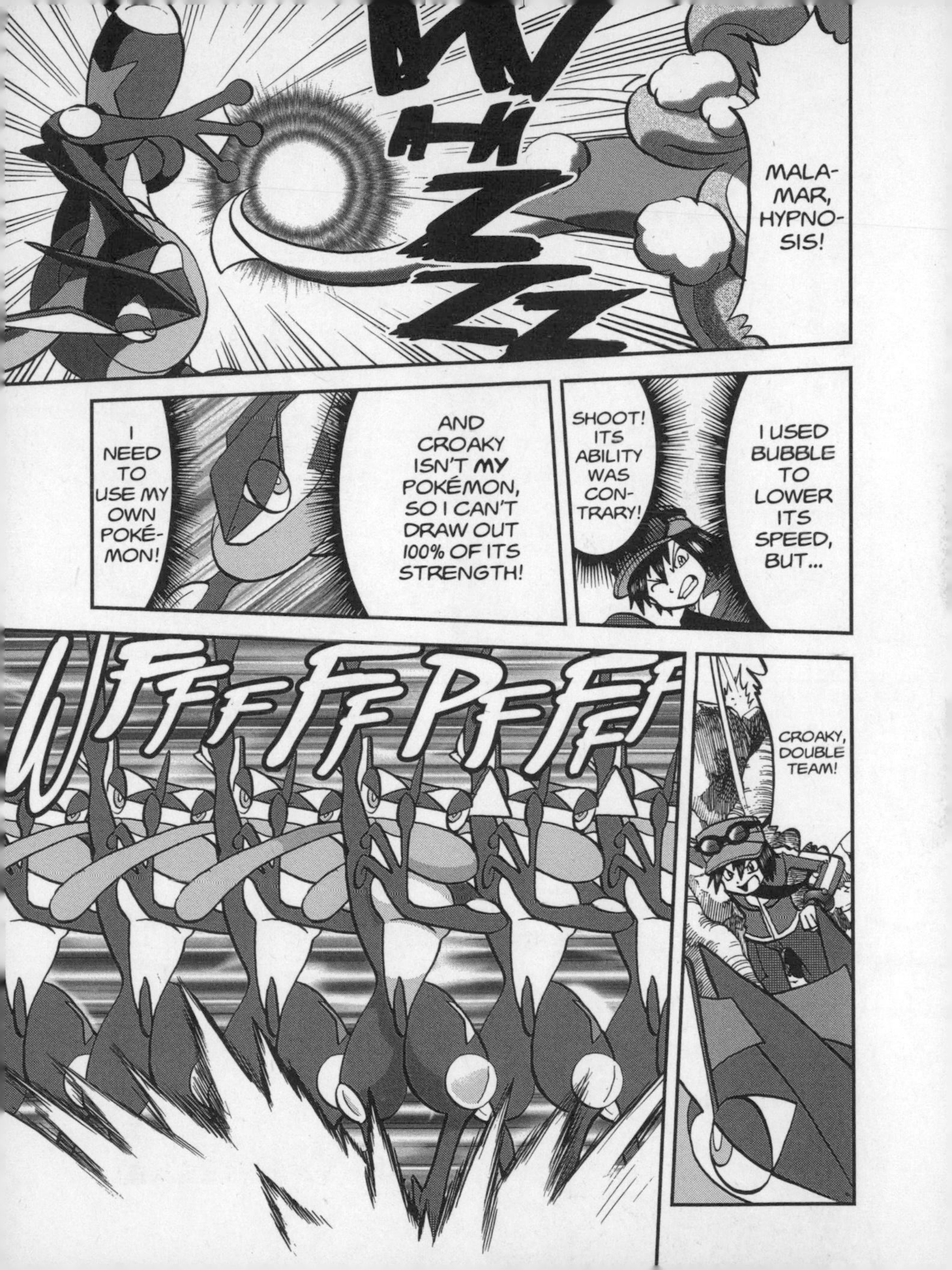
WHIZZZ
MALAMAR, HYPNOSIS!
I USED BUBBLE TO LOWER ITS SPEED, BUT...
SHOOT! ITS ABILITY WAS CONTRARY!
AND CROAKY ISN'T **MY** POKÉMON, SO I CAN'T DRAW OUT 100% OF ITS STRENGTH!
I NEED TO USE MY OWN POKÉMON!
CROAKY, DOUBLE TEAM!
WFFFFFPFFFF

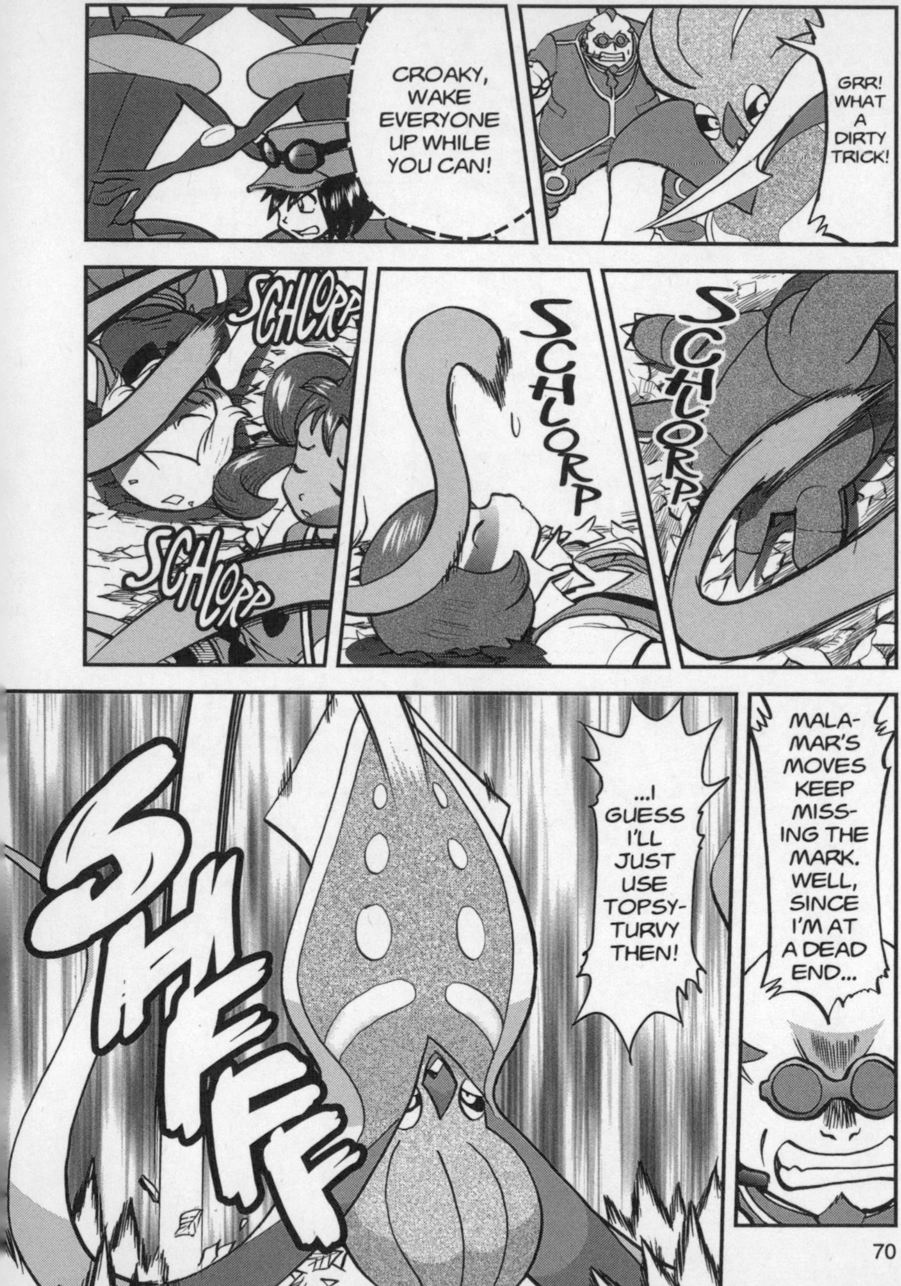
GRR! WHAT A DIRTY TRICK!
CROAKY, WAKE EVERYONE UP WHILE YOU CAN!
SCHLORP
SCHLORP
SCHLORP
SCHLORP
MALAMAR'S MOVES KEEP MISSING THE MARK. WELL, SINCE I'M AT A DEAD END...
...I GUESS I'LL JUST USE TOPSY-TURVY THEN!

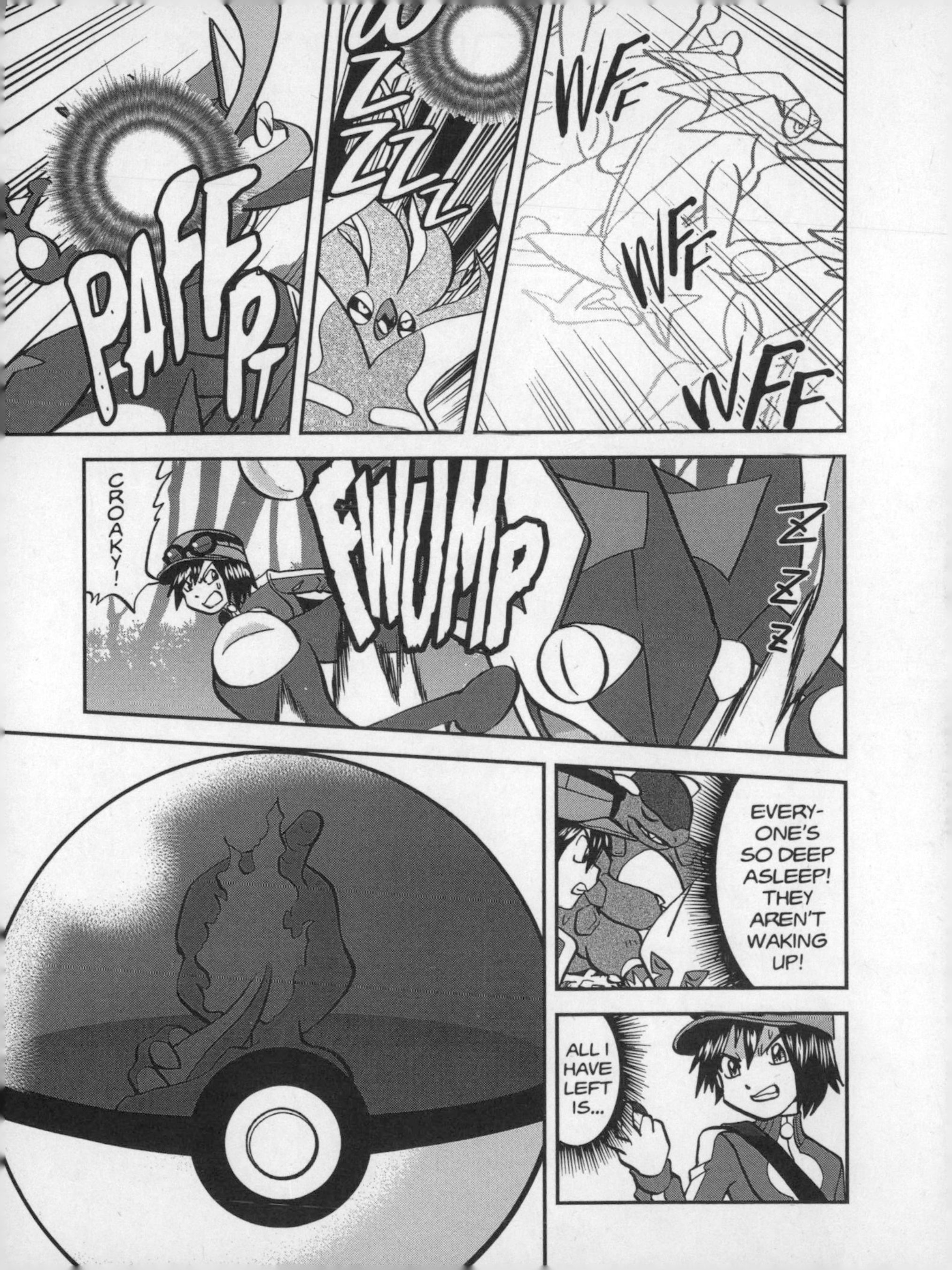
WFF
WFF
WFF
ZZZZZ
PAFF
PT
ZZZZ
FWUMP
CROAKY!
EVERY-ONE'S SO DEEP ASLEEP! THEY AREN'T WAKING UP!
ALL I HAVE LEFT IS...

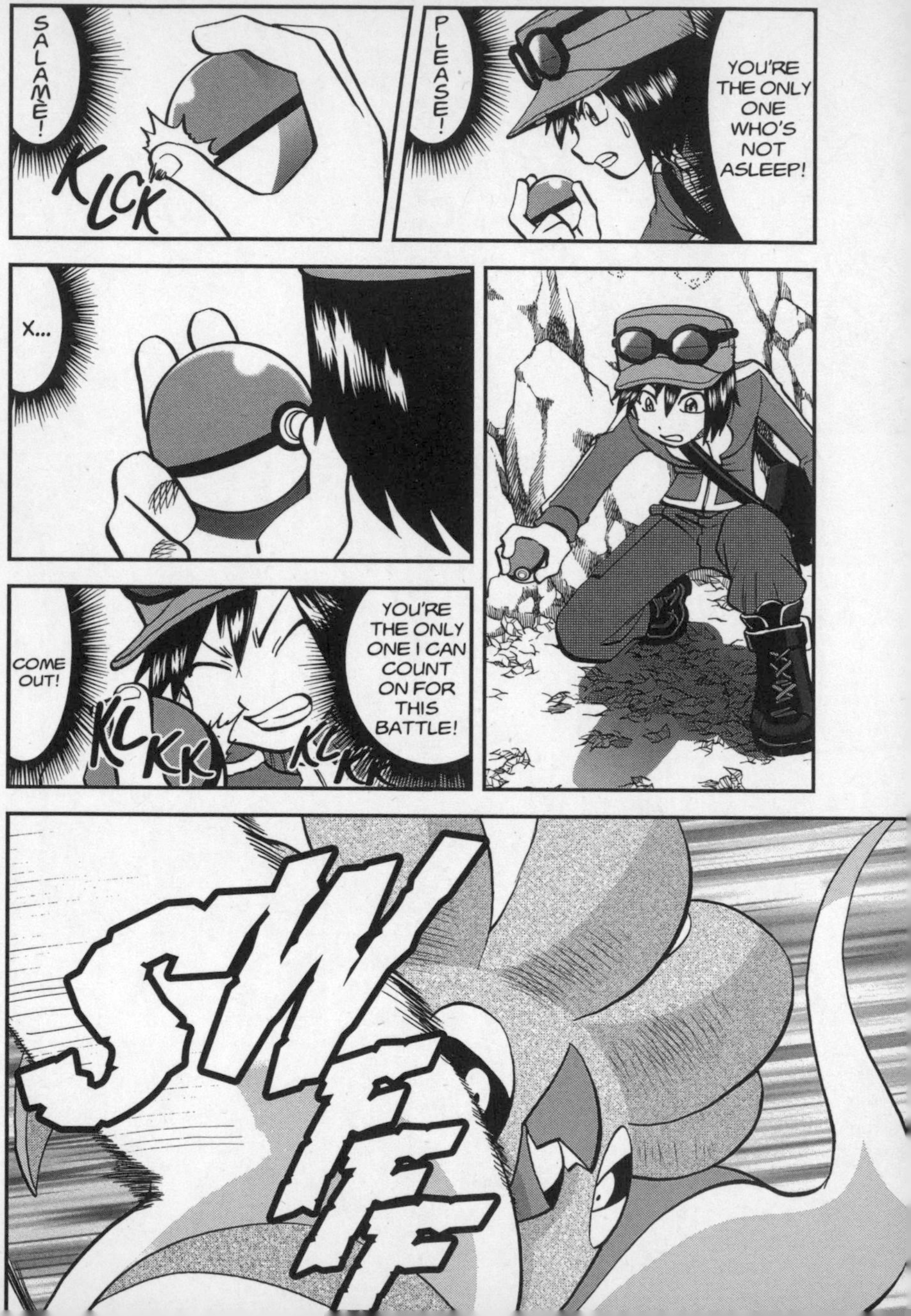
YOU'RE THE ONLY ONE WHO'S NOT ASLEEP!
PLEASE!
SALAMÈ!
KLCK
X...
YOU'RE THE ONLY ONE I CAN COUNT ON FOR THIS BATTLE!
COME OUT!
KLKK
KLCKK
SWFF

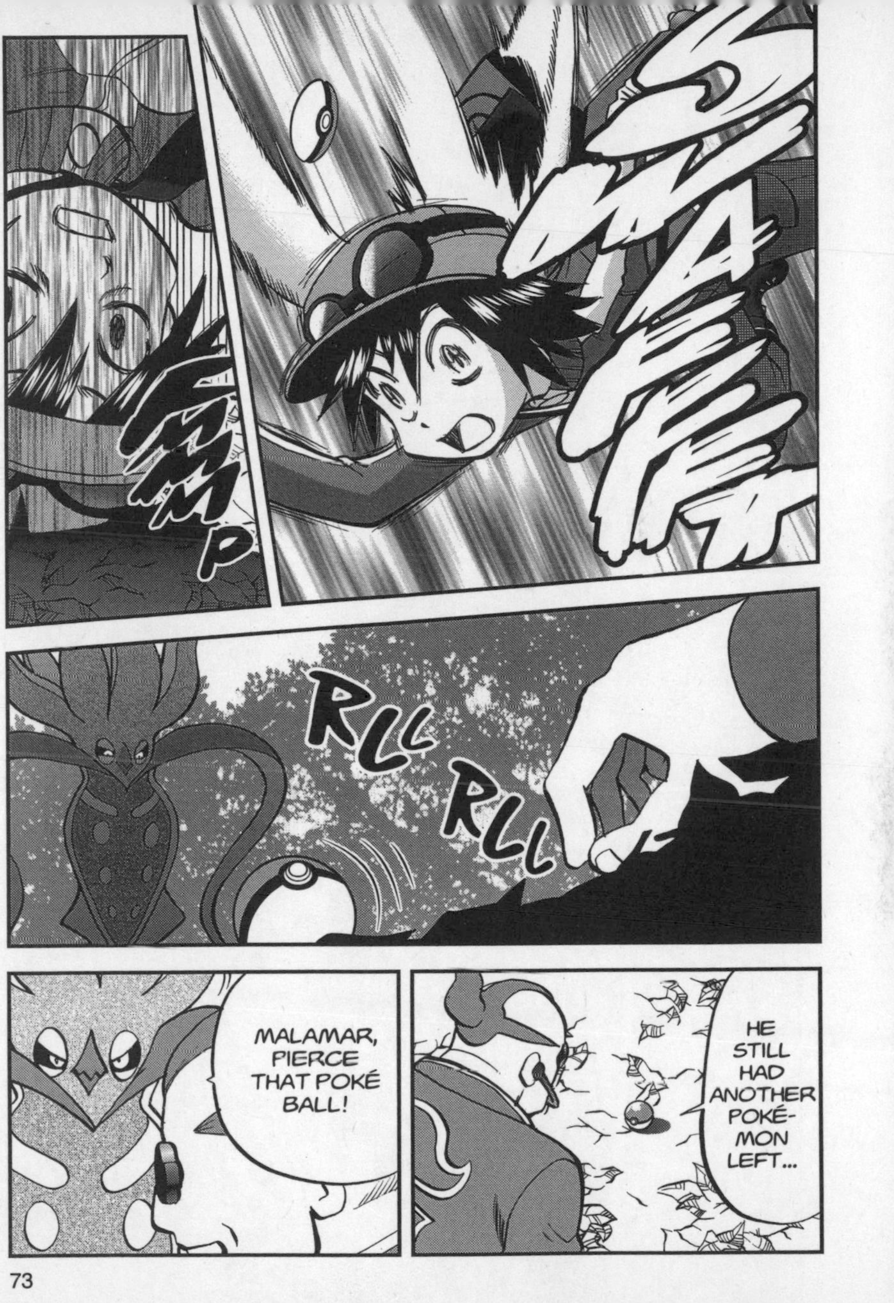
RLL
RLL
HE STILL HAD ANOTHER POKÉMON LEFT...
MALAMAR, PIERCE THAT POKÉ BALL!

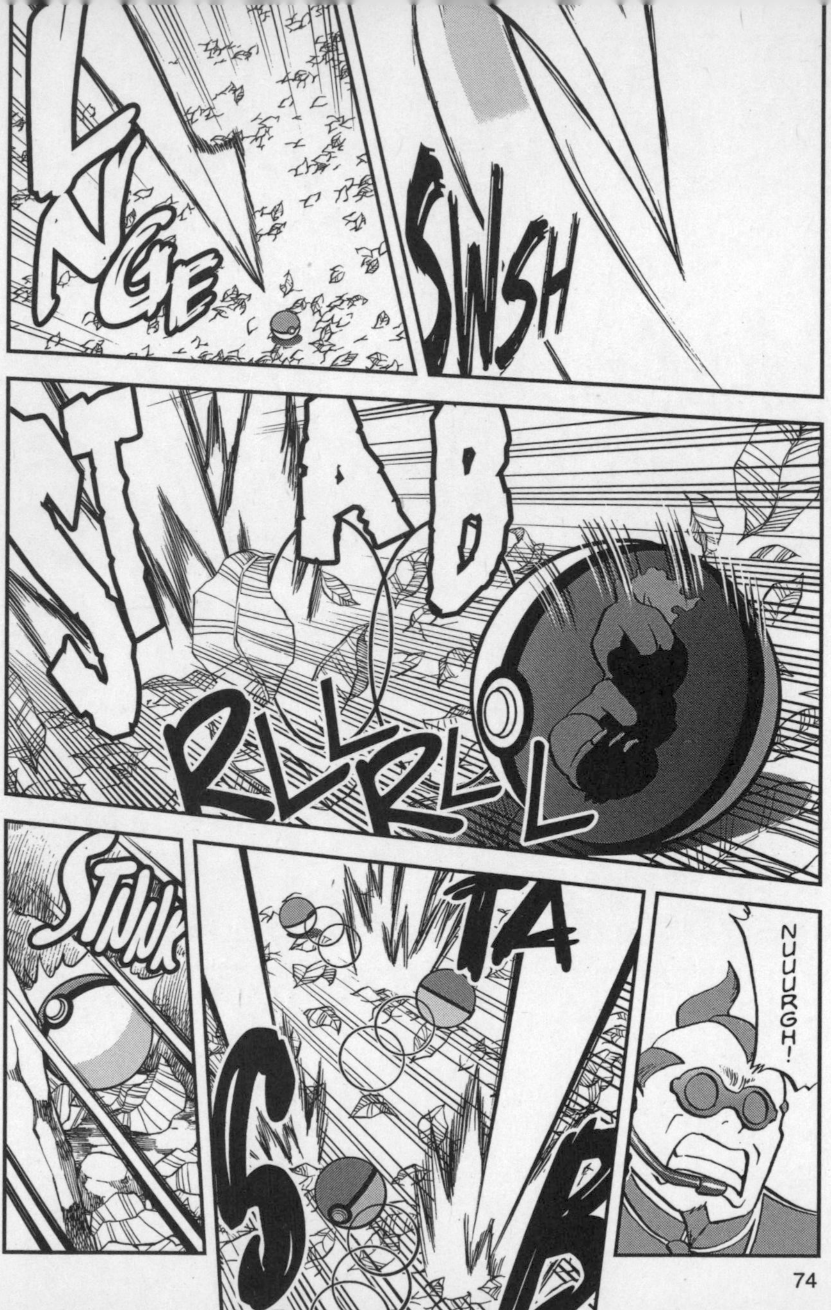
SWISH
NUUURGH!
STUNK

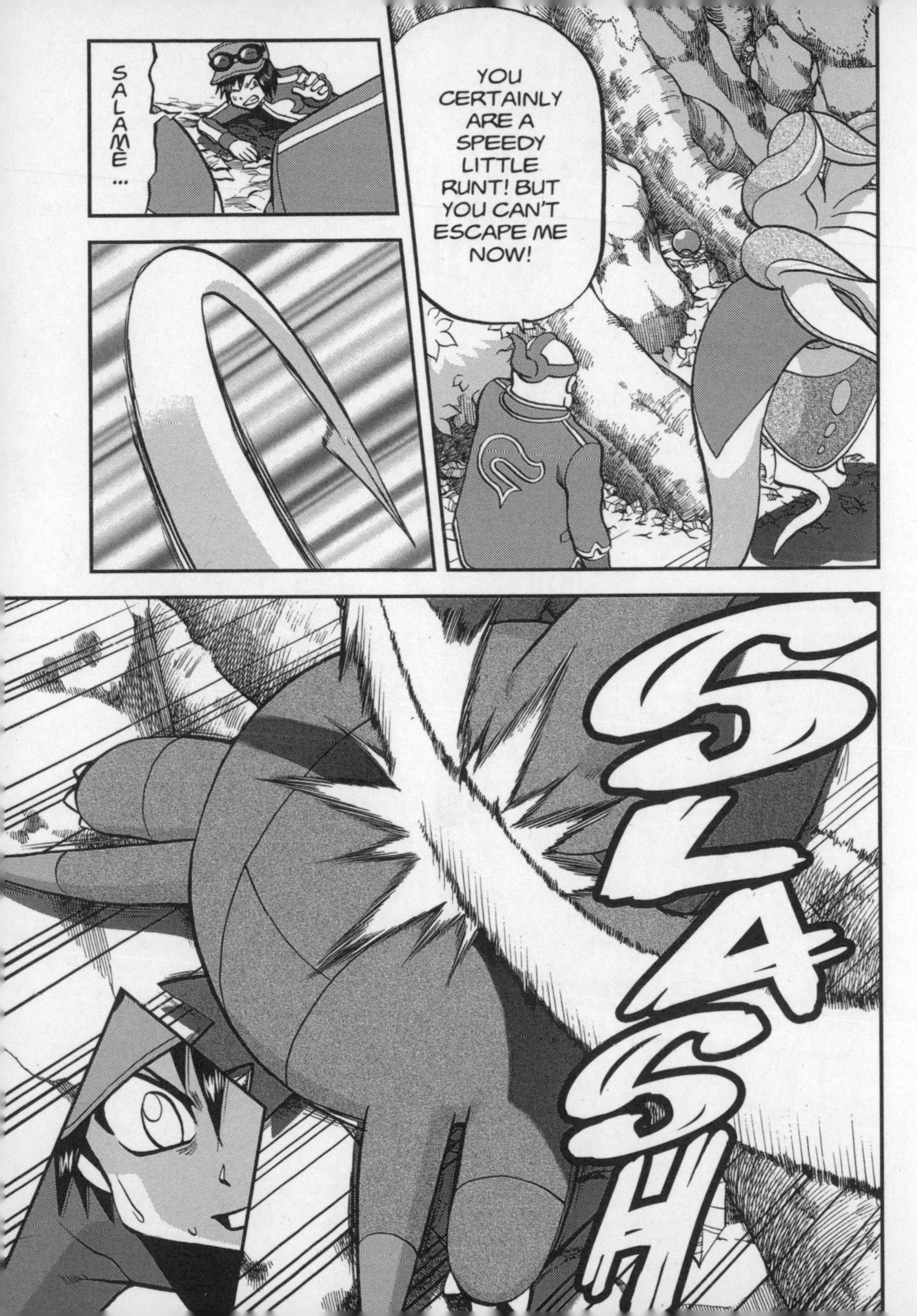
YOU CERTAINLY ARE A SPEEDY LITTLE RUNT! BUT YOU CAN'T ESCAPE ME NOW!
SALAME...
SLASH

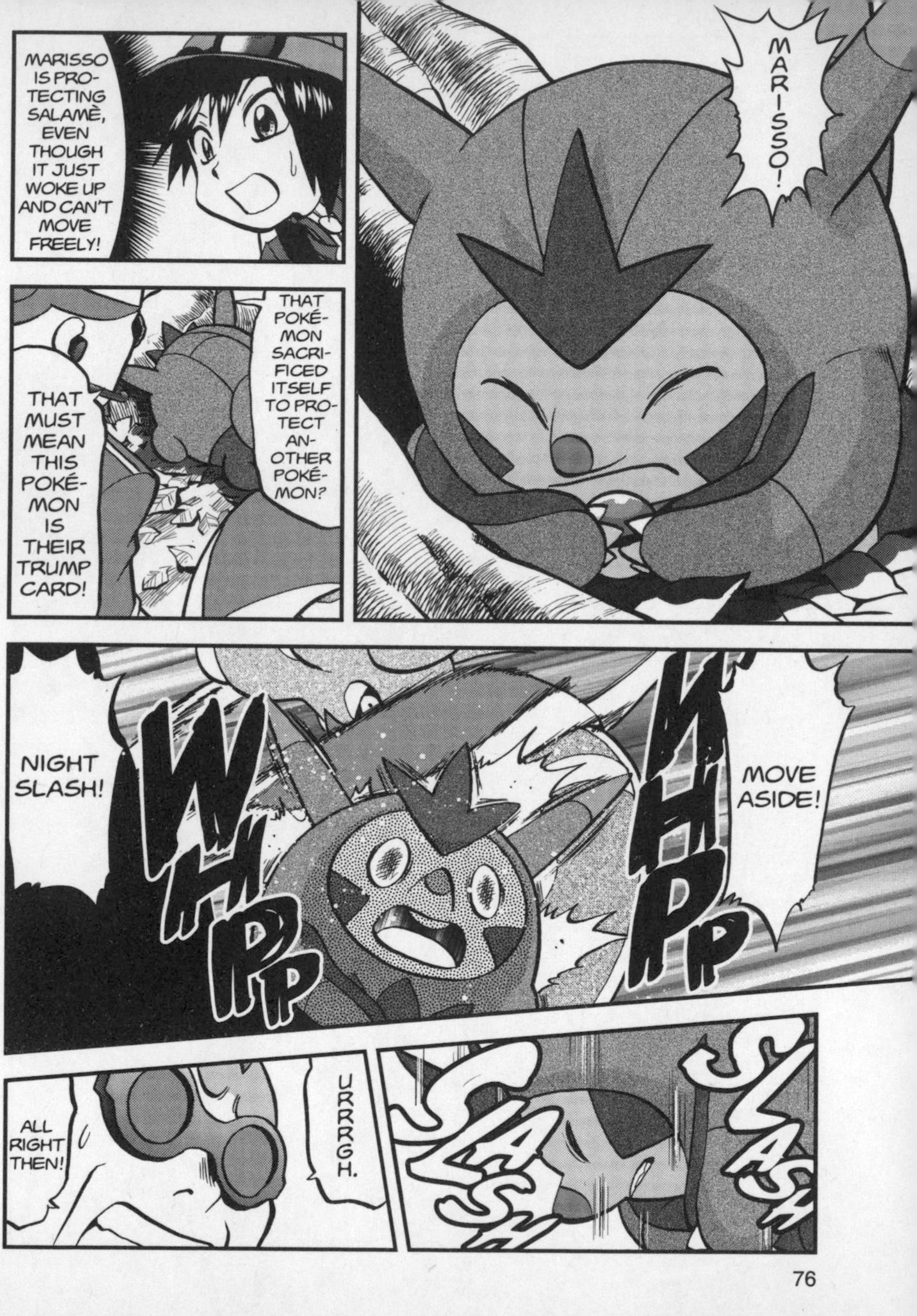
MARISSO!
MARISSO IS PROTECTING SALAMÈ, EVEN THOUGH IT JUST WOKE UP AND CAN'T MOVE FREELY!
THAT POKÉMON SACRIFICED ITSELF TO PROTECT ANOTHER POKÉMON?
THAT MUST MEAN THIS POKÉMON IS THEIR TRUMP CARD!
MOVE ASIDE!
WHIPP
WHIPP
NIGHT SLASH!
SLASH
SLASH
URRRGH.
ALL RIGHT THEN!

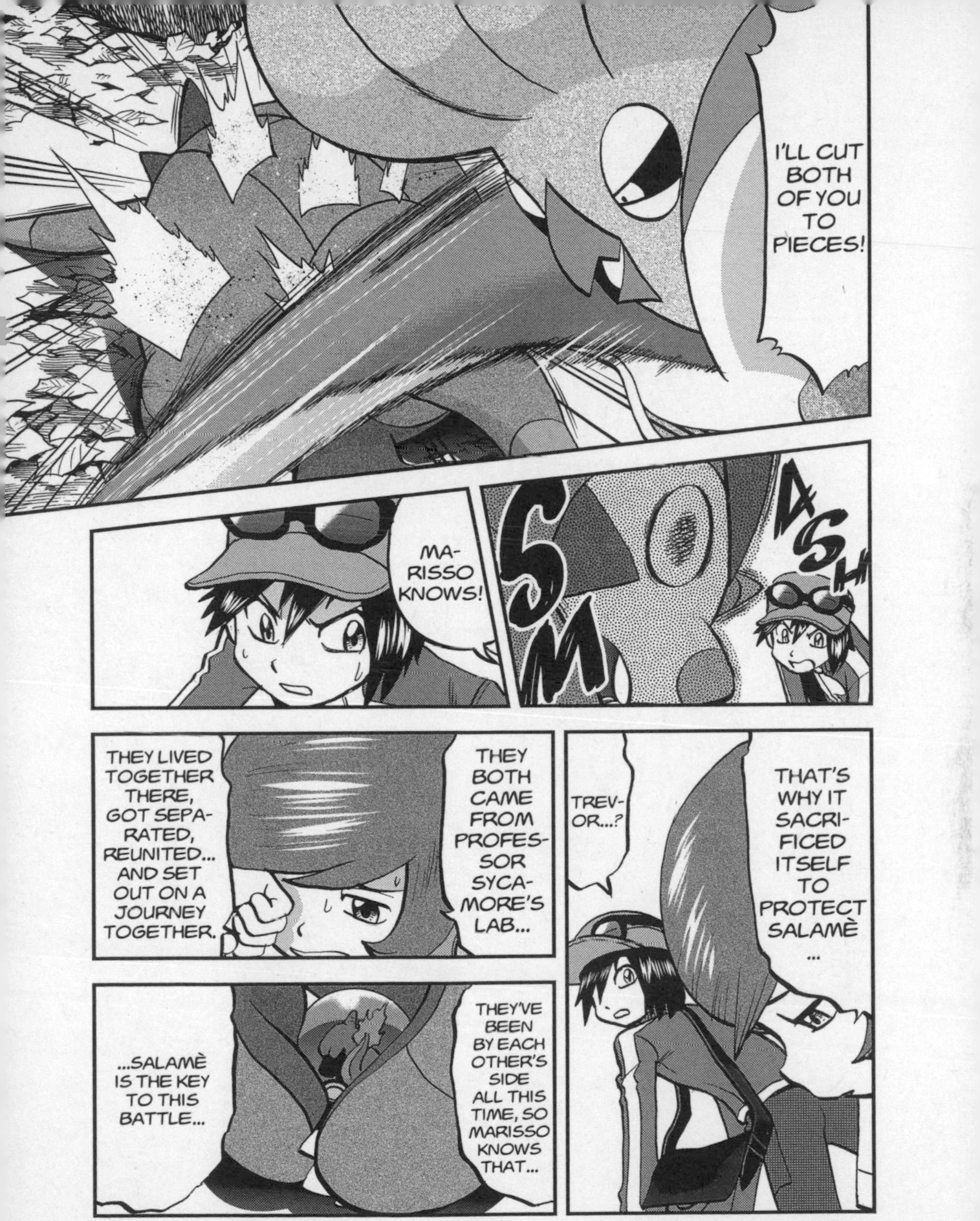
I'LL CUT BOTH OF YOU TO PIECES!
SMASH
MA-RISSO KNOWS!
THAT'S WHY IT SACRI-FICED ITSELF TO PROTECT SALAMÈ...
TREV-OR...?
THEY BOTH CAME FROM PROFES-SOR SYCA-MORE'S LAB...
THEY LIVED TOGETHER THERE, GOT SEPA-RATED, REUNITED... AND SET OUT ON A JOURNEY TOGETHER.
THEY'VE BEEN BY EACH OTHER'S SIDE ALL THIS TIME, SO MARISSO KNOWS THAT...
...SALAMÈ IS THE KEY TO THIS BATTLE...

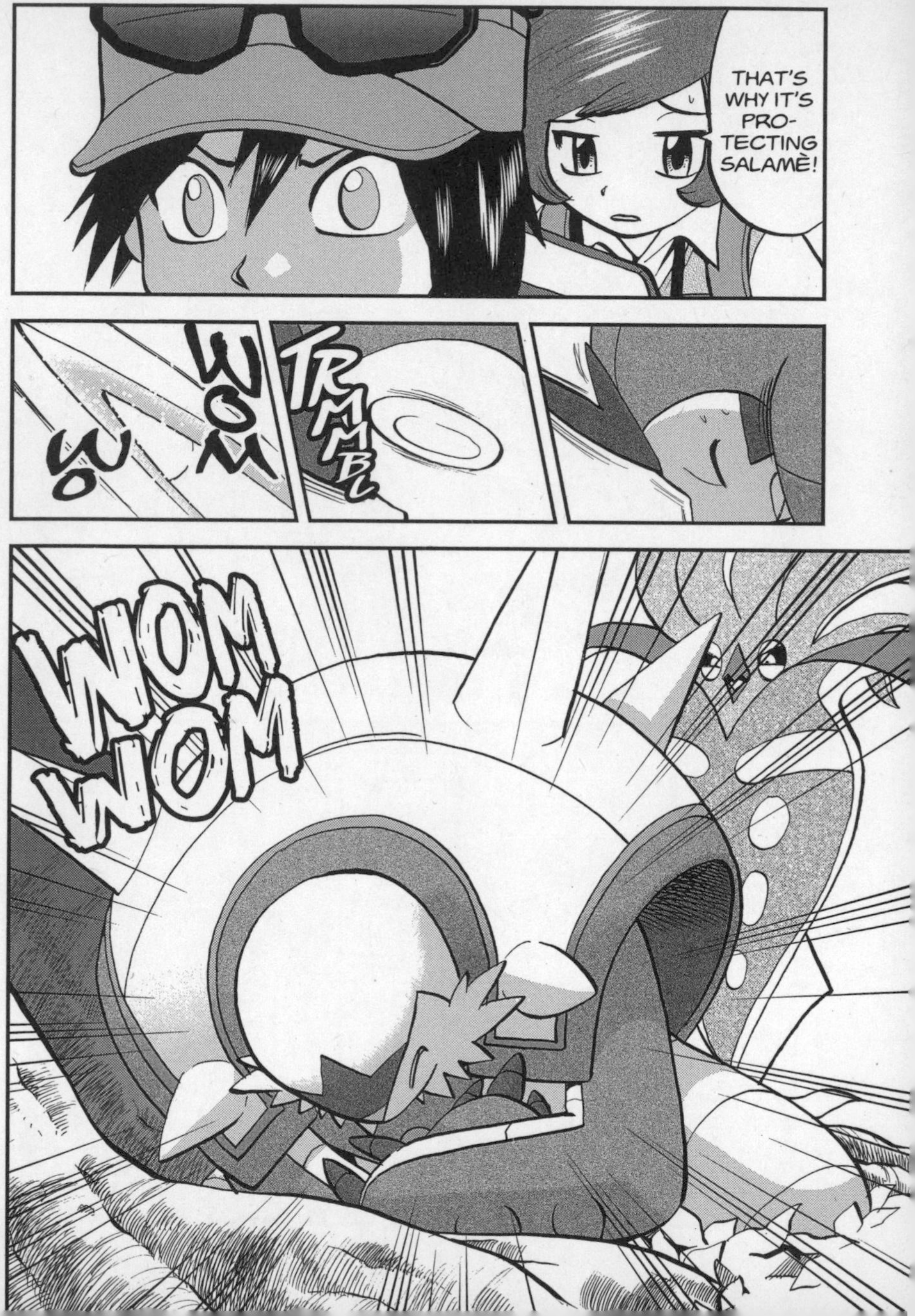
THAT'S WHY IT'S PRO-TECTING SALAMÈ!
TRMMBL
WOM
WO
WOM WOM

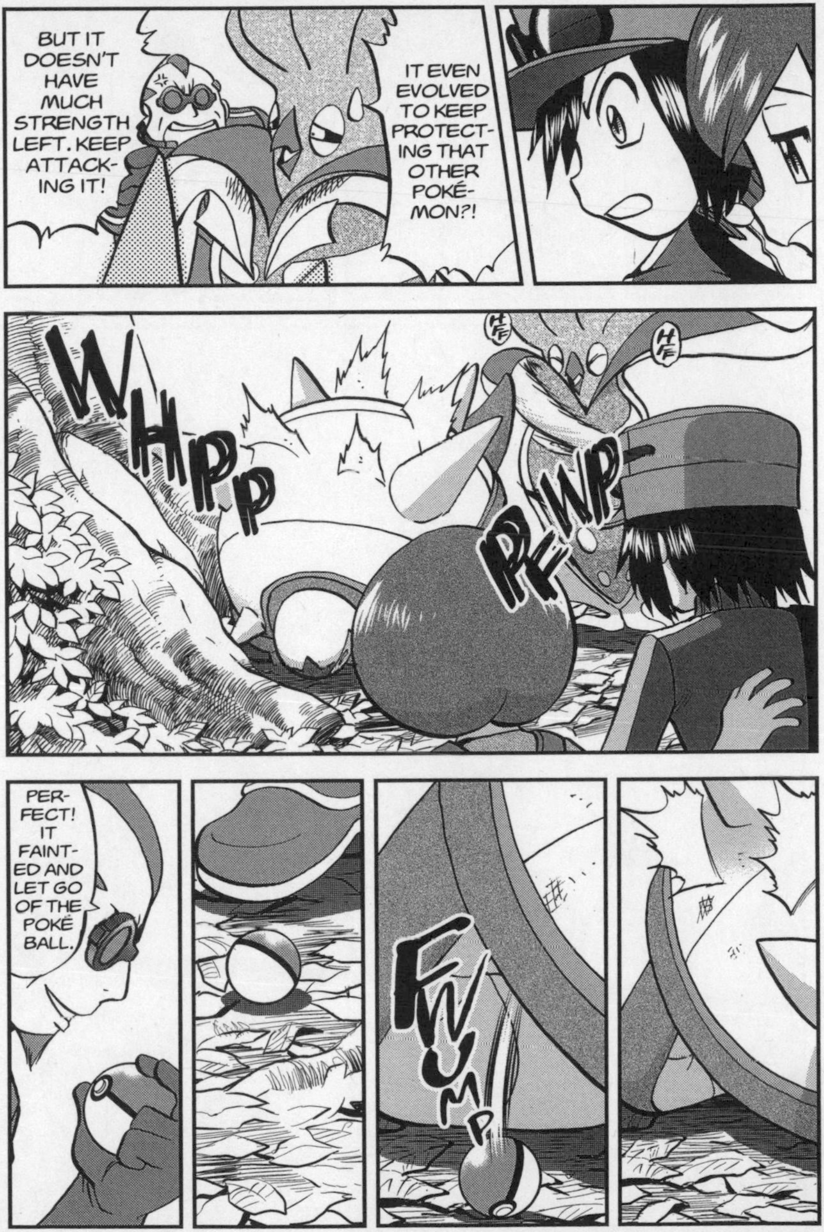
IT EVEN EVOLVED TO KEEP PROTECTING THAT OTHER POKÉMON?!
BUT IT DOESN'T HAVE MUCH STRENGTH LEFT. KEEP ATTACKING IT!
HF
HF
PFWP
WHPPP
FWUMP
PERFECT! IT FAINTED AND LET GO OF THE POKÉ BALL.

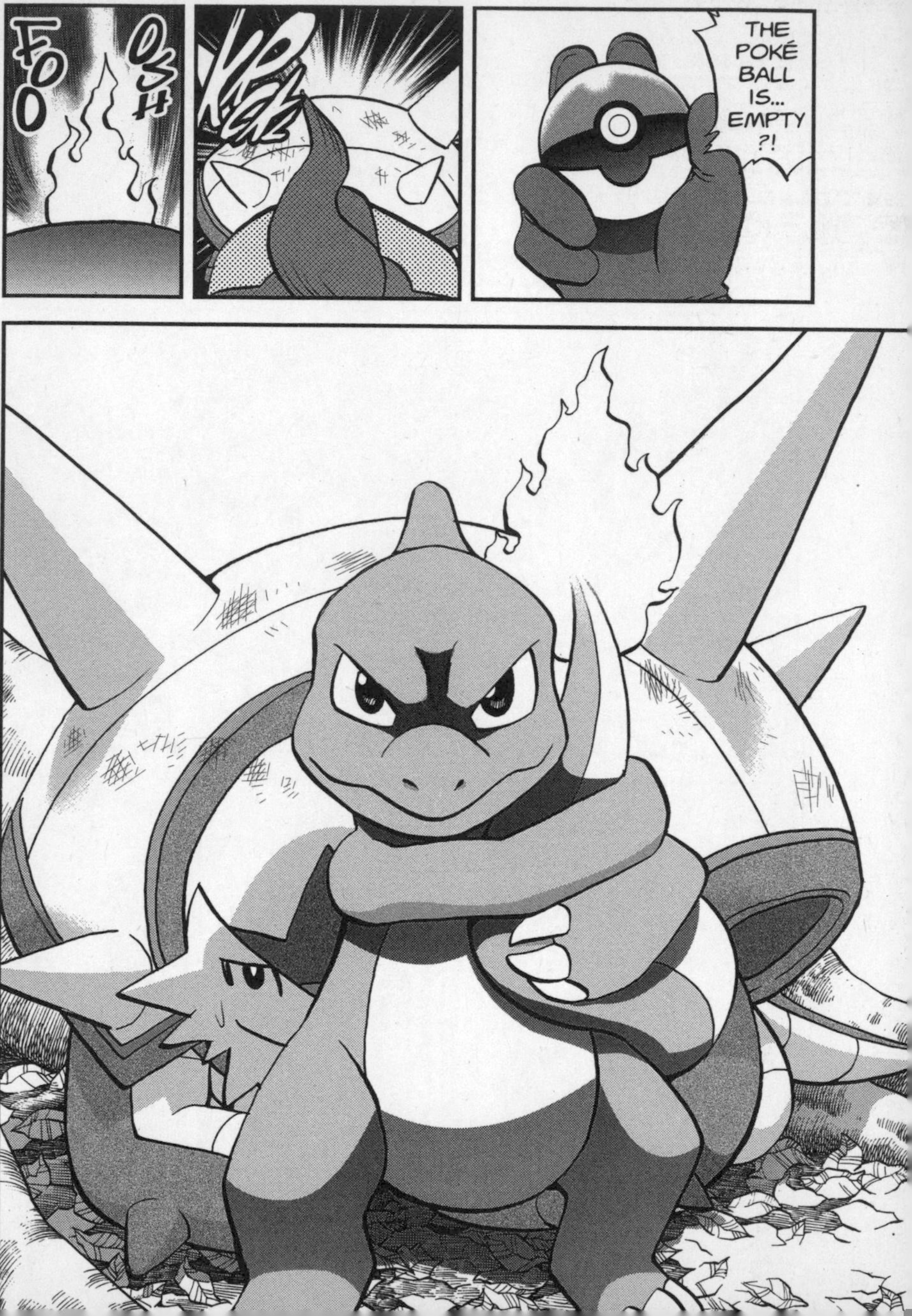
THE POKÉ BALL IS... EMPTY ?!
FOOOSH

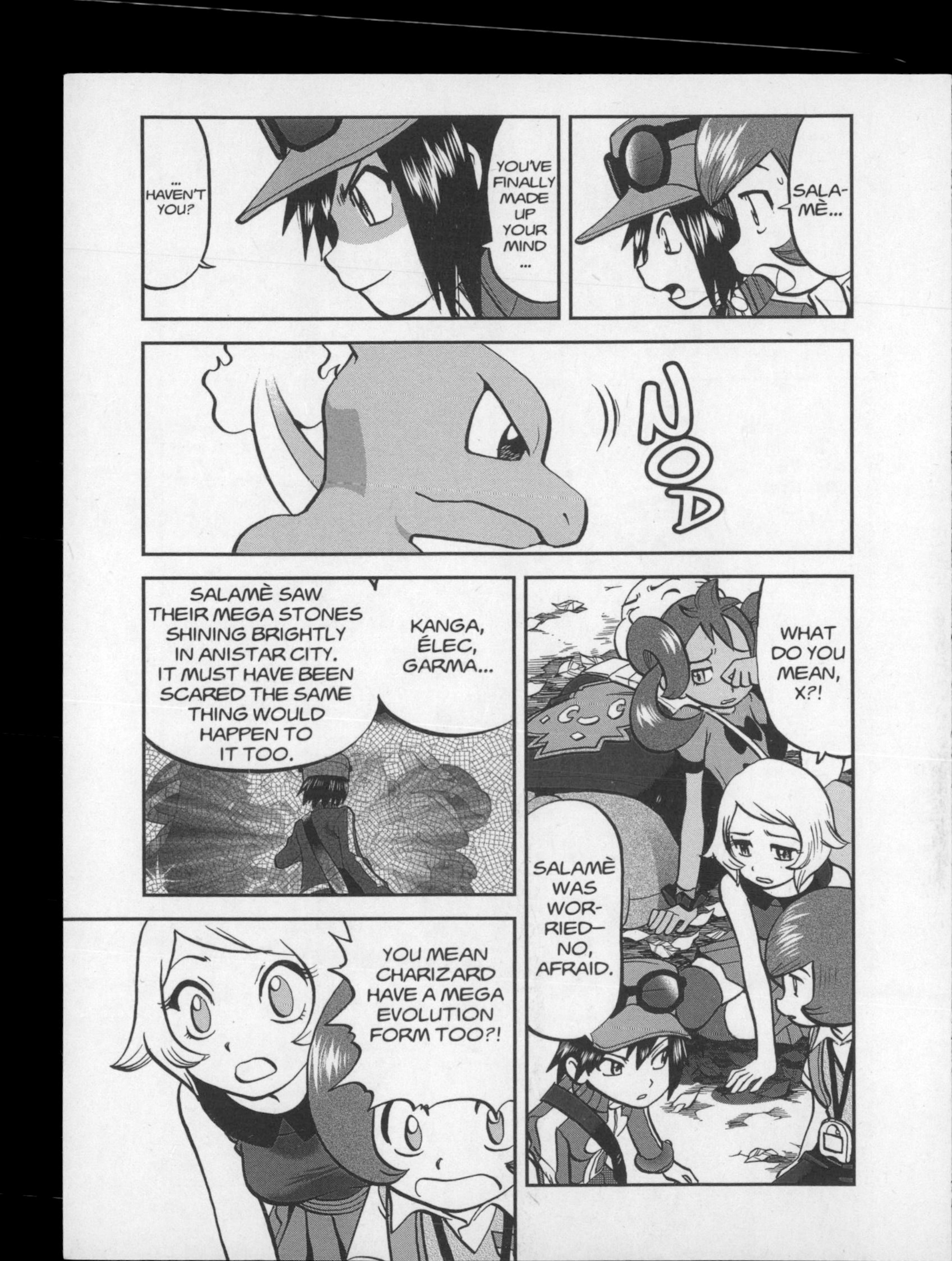
SALA-MÈ...
YOU'VE FINALLY MADE UP YOUR MIND ...
... HAVEN'T YOU?
ZOA
WHAT DO YOU MEAN, X?!
SALAMÈ WAS WOR-RIED— NO, AFRAID.
KANGA, ÉLEC, GARMA...
SALAMÈ SAW THEIR MEGA STONES SHINING BRIGHTLY IN ANISTAR CITY. IT MUST HAVE BEEN SCARED THE SAME THING WOULD HAPPEN TO IT TOO.
YOU MEAN CHARIZARD HAVE A MEGA EVOLUTION FORM TOO?!

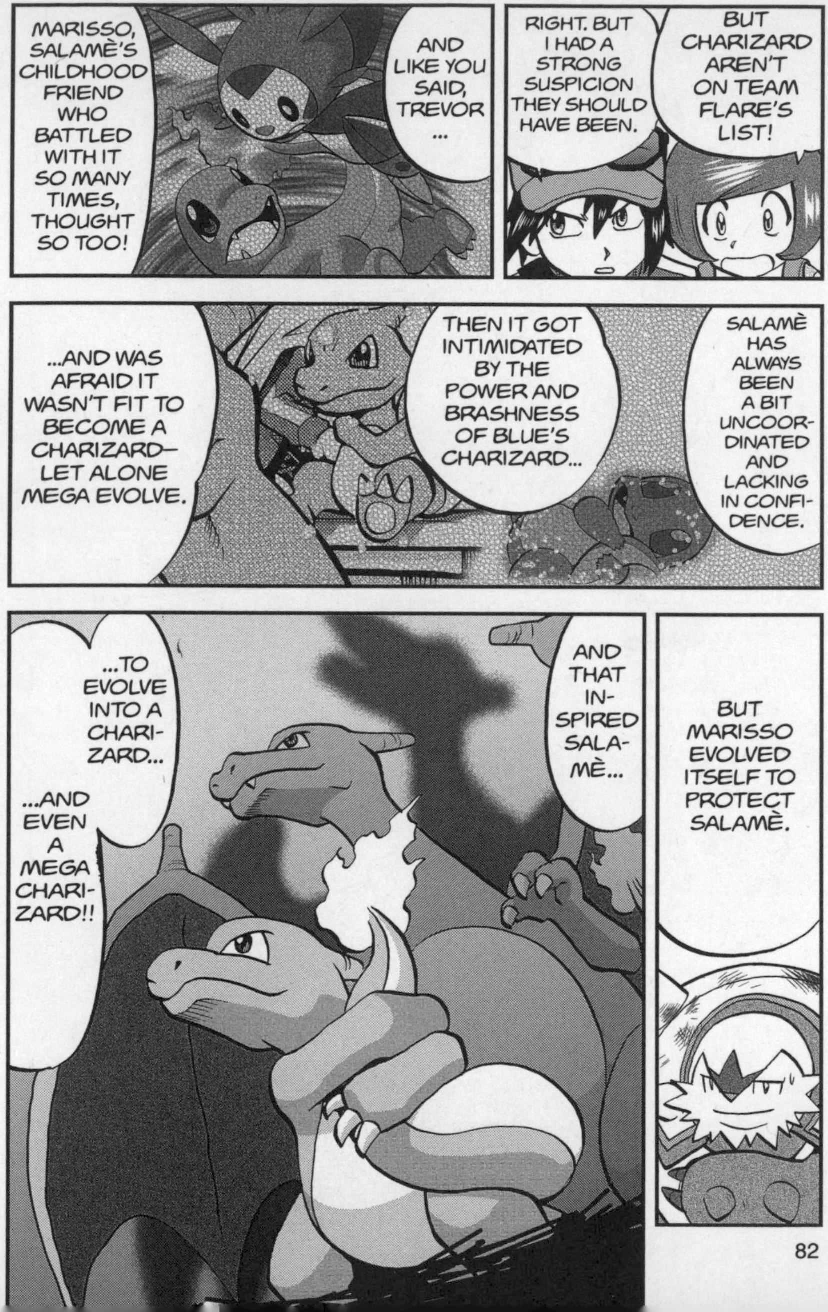
BUT CHARIZARD AREN'T ON TEAM FLARE'S LIST!
RIGHT. BUT I HAD A STRONG SUSPICION THEY SHOULD HAVE BEEN.
AND LIKE YOU SAID, TREVOR...
MARISSO, SALAMÈ'S CHILDHOOD FRIEND WHO BATTLED WITH IT SO MANY TIMES, THOUGHT SO TOO!
SALAMÈ HAS ALWAYS BEEN A BIT UNCOORDINATED AND LACKING IN CONFIDENCE.
THEN IT GOT INTIMIDATED BY THE POWER AND BRASHNESS OF BLUE'S CHARIZARD...
...AND WAS AFRAID IT WASN'T FIT TO BECOME A CHARIZARD—LET ALONE MEGA EVOLVE.
BUT MARISSO EVOLVED ITSELF TO PROTECT SALAMÈ.
AND THAT INSPIRED SALAMÈ...
...TO EVOLVE INTO A CHARIZARD...
...AND EVEN A MEGA CHARIZARD!!

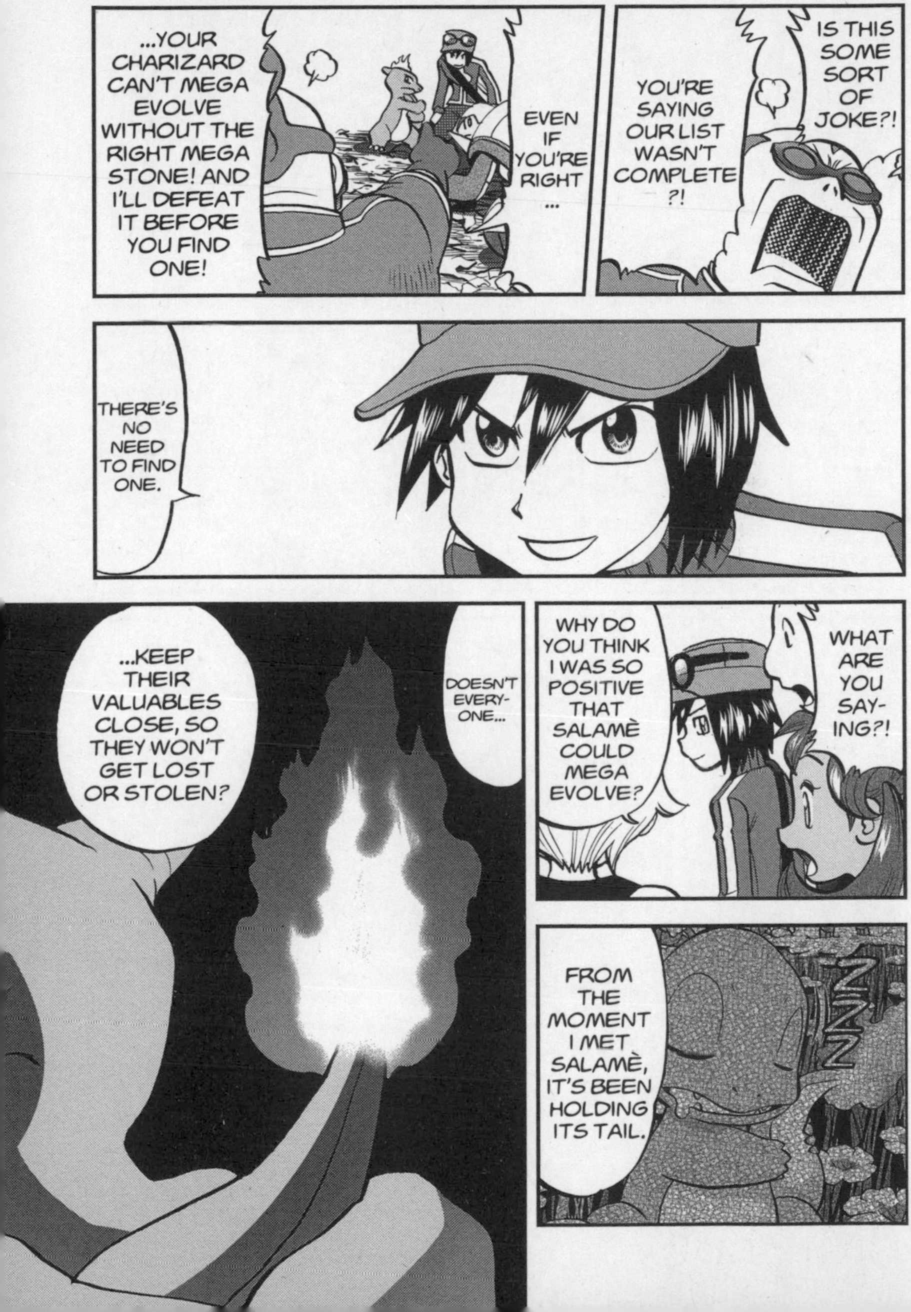
IS THIS SOME SORT OF JOKE?!
YOU'RE SAYING OUR LIST WASN'T COMPLETE?!
EVEN IF YOU'RE RIGHT...
...YOUR CHARIZARD CAN'T MEGA EVOLVE WITHOUT THE RIGHT MEGA STONE! AND I'LL DEFEAT IT BEFORE YOU FIND ONE!
THERE'S NO NEED TO FIND ONE.
WHAT ARE YOU SAYING?!
WHY DO YOU THINK I WAS SO POSITIVE THAT SALAMÈ COULD MEGA EVOLVE?
FROM THE MOMENT I MET SALAMÈ, IT'S BEEN HOLDING ITS TAIL.
ZZZ
DOESN'T EVERYONE...
...KEEP THEIR VALUABLES CLOSE, SO THEY WON'T GET LOST OR STOLEN?

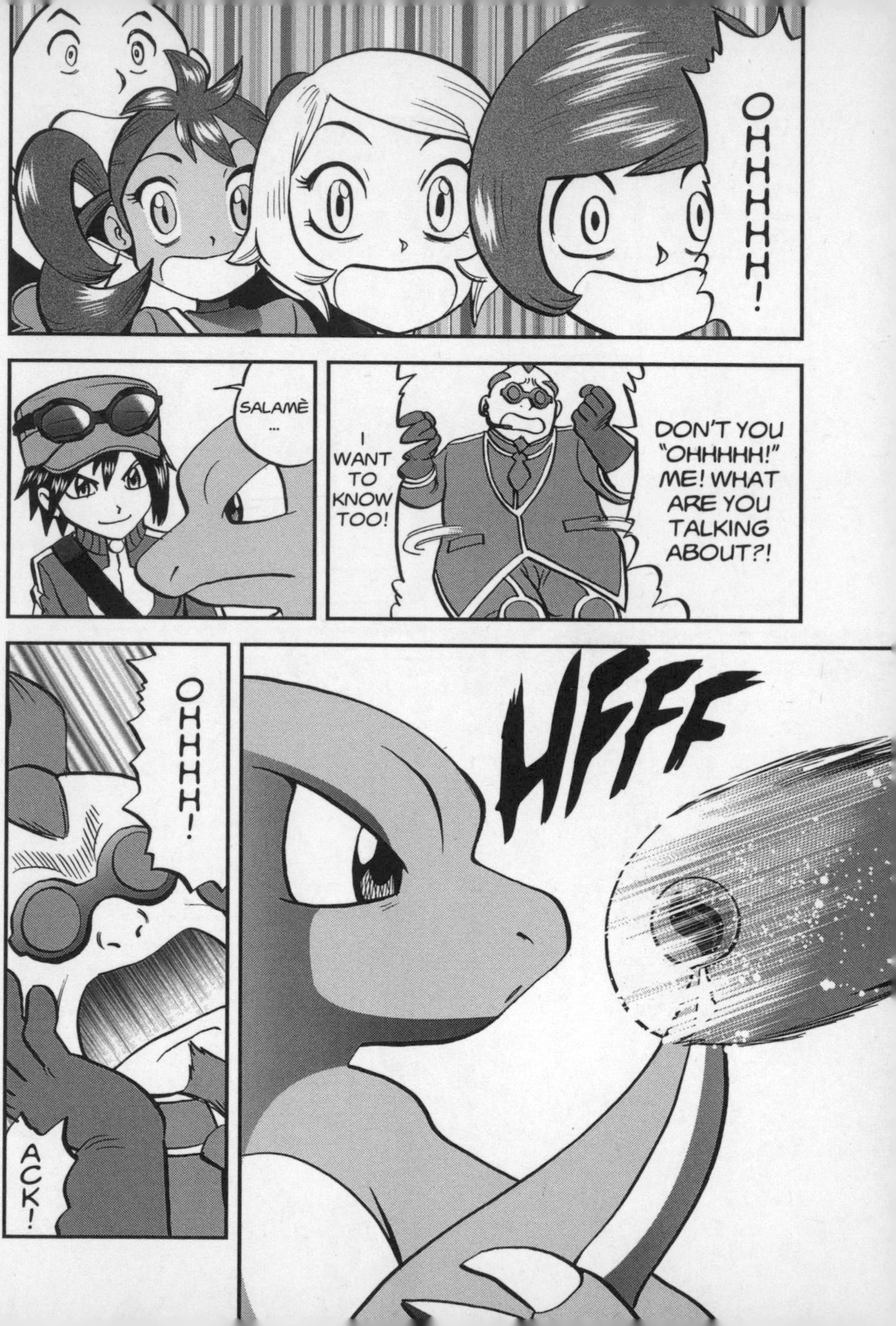
OHHHHH!
DON'T YOU "OHHHHH!" ME! WHAT ARE YOU TALKING ABOUT?!
I WANT TO KNOW TOO!
SALAMÈ ...
HFFF
OHHHHH!
ACK!

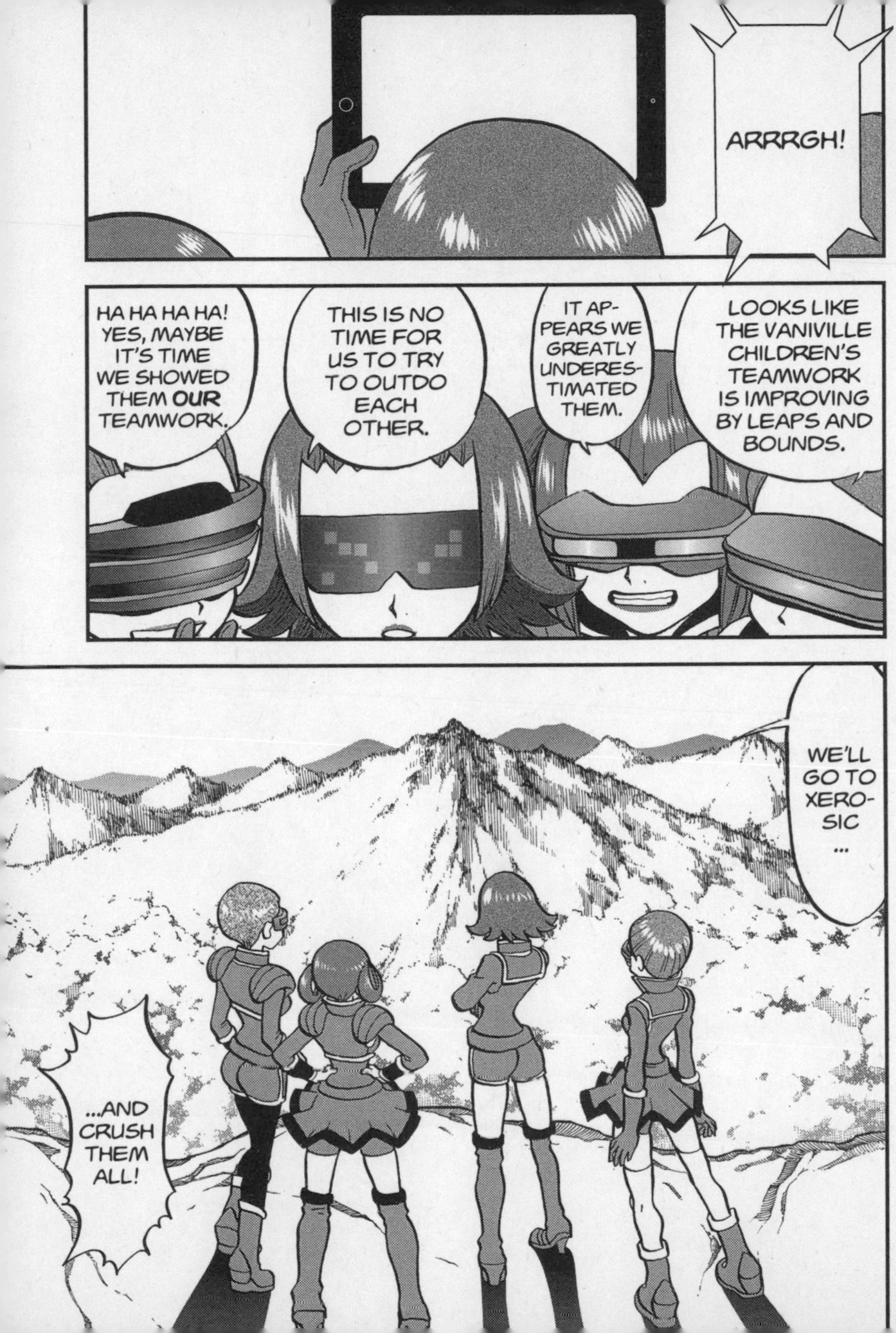
ARRRGH!
LOOKS LIKE THE VANIVILLE CHILDREN'S TEAMWORK IS IMPROVING BY LEAPS AND BOUNDS.
IT APPEARS WE GREATLY UNDERESTIMATED THEM.
THIS IS NO TIME FOR US TO TRY TO OUTDO EACH OTHER.
HA HA HA HA! YES, MAYBE IT'S TIME WE SHOWED THEM **OUR** TEAMWORK.
WE'LL GO TO XEROSIC...
...AND CRUSH THEM ALL!

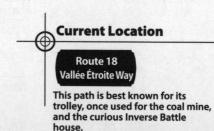

Current Location

Route 18
Vallée Étroite Way

This path is best known for its
trolley, once used for the coal mine,
and the curious Inverse Battle
house.

No.
Date

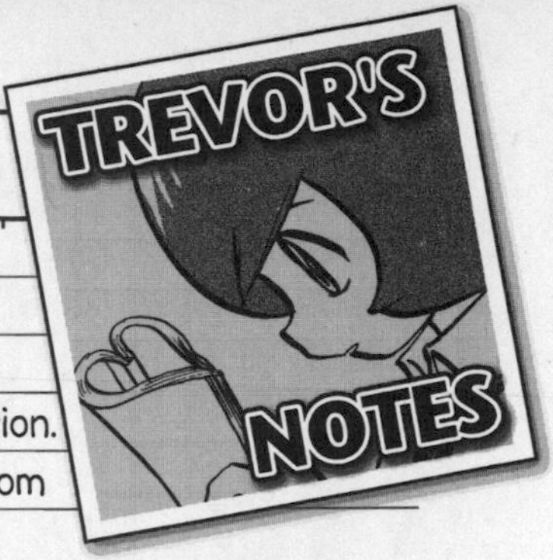
TREVOR'S
NOTES

◆ CURRENT DATA ◆

- Professor Sycamore hypothesized that the sundial at Anistar City was somehow connected with Mega Evolution. Research revealed that the energy from the sundial synchronizes with the Key Stones to power up the Mega Ring. The enhanced Mega Ring then makes Mega Stones hidden in tall grass and under water shine brightly.

- Now we have a way to locate hidden Mega Stones—but it's only possible during the one hour between 8 and 9 o'clock while the sundial is shining.

- More about the shining Mega Stones.
Enhanced Mega Rings make all Mega Stones shine from 8 to 9 o'clock. This includes Mega Stones that Pokémon already have on them, as well as Mega Stones inside bags. The only time they won't shine is when they are inside a Poké Ball with a Pokémon. We discovered this after we learned about Salamè's secret.

- Anyone holding a Mega Ring (in other words, it doesn't have to be a Mega Evolution successor) can find Mega Stones during the one hour when the sundial is shining. And one doesn't need to bring along the Pokémon who needs this particular Mega Stone either.

- We have discovered that Salamè is a Mega Evolving Pokémon. Since it wasn't included on the list, it appears the list isn't comprehensive. How many other Mega Evolving Pokémon are there that we don't know about...?

MOUNTAIN KALOS POKÉDEX

NUMBER 150

LEGENDARY POKÉMON ZYGARDE

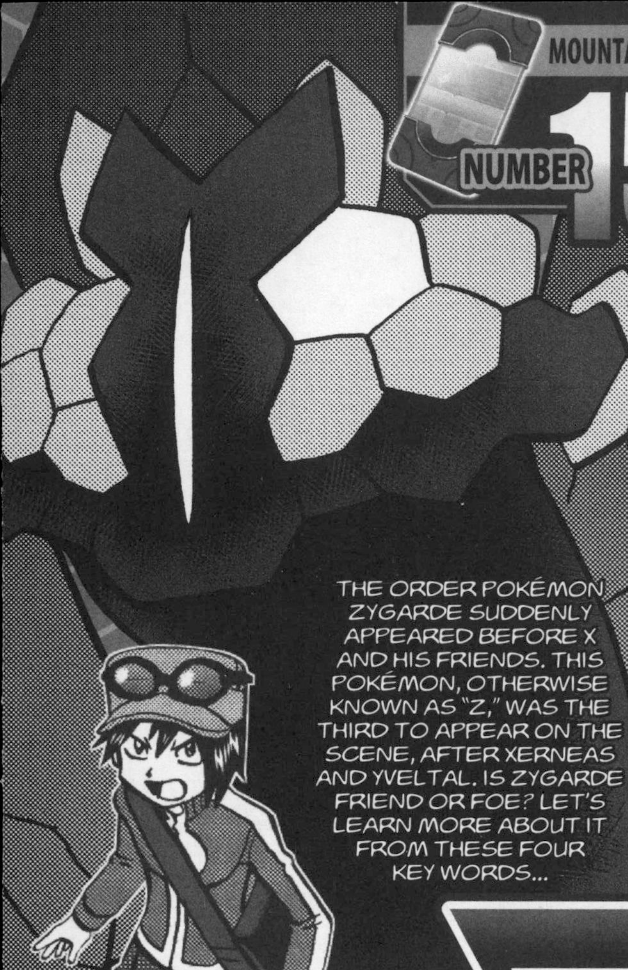

THE ORDER POKÉMON ZYGARDE SUDDENLY APPEARED BEFORE X AND HIS FRIENDS. THIS POKÉMON, OTHERWISE KNOWN AS "Z," WAS THE THIRD TO APPEAR ON THE SCENE, AFTER XERNEAS AND YVELTAL. IS ZYGARDE FRIEND OR FOE? LET'S LEARN MORE ABOUT IT FROM THESE FOUR KEY WORDS...

- 16'05"
- 672.4 lbs.
- Order Pokémon
- Unknown
- Dragon, Ground
- Aura Break (An ability that weakens the effects of Fairy Aura and Dark Aura)

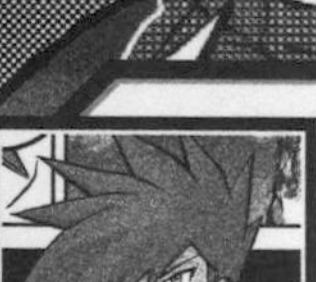

▲RUMORS ABOUT THE EXISTENCE OF MYSTERIOUS Z WERE HEARD IN OTHER REGIONS AS WELL. BLUE TRAVELLED TO KALOS FROM THE KANTO REGION AFTER HE HEARD ABOUT ITS EXISTENCE FROM PROFESSOR ROWAN AND PROFESSOR OAK.

KEYWORD 1

【OVERSEER】

ZYGARDE IS SAID TO LIVE DEEP INSIDE THE TERMINUS CAVE, KEEPING A WATCHFUL EYE OUT FOR THOSE WHO WOULD DESTROY THE ECOSYSTEM. ITS ABILITY GIVES IT AN ADVANTAGE OVER XERNEAS AND YVELTAL. IT SEEMS LIKELY THAT ZYGARDE CONSIDERS BATTLES BETWEEN THE OTHER TWO AS A THREAT TO THE BALANCE OF NATURE.

...THE OVER-SEER ...
...Z.

▲▶ THIS 3,000-YEAR-OLD MAN REVEALED THE EXISTENCE OF ZYGARDE TO TEAM FLARE.

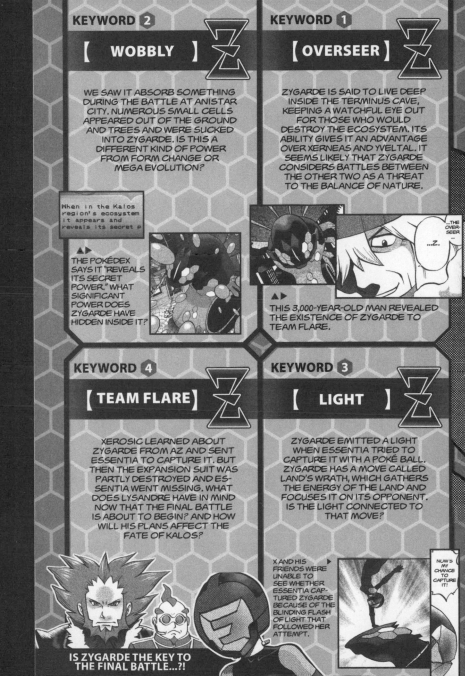

KEYWORD 2

【WOBBLY】

WE SAW IT ABSORB SOMETHING DURING THE BATTLE AT ANISTAR CITY. NUMEROUS SMALL CELLS APPEARED OUT OF THE GROUND AND TREES AND WERE SUCKED INTO ZYGARDE. IS THIS A DIFFERENT KIND OF POWER FROM FORM CHANGE OR MEGA EVOLUTION?

When in the Kalos
region's ecosystem
it appears and
reveals its secret p

▲▶ THE POKÉDEX SAYS IT "REVEALS ITS SECRET POWER." WHAT SIGNIFICANT POWER DOES ZYGARDE HAVE HIDDEN INSIDE IT?

KEYWORD 3

【LIGHT】

ZYGARDE EMITTED A LIGHT WHEN ESSENTIA TRIED TO CAPTURE IT WITH A POKÉ BALL. ZYGARDE HAS A MOVE CALLED LAND'S WRATH, WHICH GATHERS THE ENERGY OF THE LAND AND FOCUSES IT ON ITS OPPONENT. IS THE LIGHT CONNECTED TO THAT MOVE?

NOW'S MY CHANCE TO CAPTURE IT!

X AND HIS FRIENDS WERE UNABLE TO SEE WHETHER ESSENTIA CAPTURED ZYGARDE BECAUSE OF THE BLINDING FLASH OF LIGHT THAT FOLLOWED HER ATTEMPT. ▶

KEYWORD 4

【TEAM FLARE】

XEROSIC LEARNED ABOUT ZYGARDE FROM AZ AND SENT ESSENTIA TO CAPTURE IT. BUT THEN THE EXPANSION SUIT WAS PARTLY DESTROYED AND ESSENTIA WENT MISSING. WHAT DOES LYSANDRE HAVE IN MIND NOW THAT THE FINAL BATTLE IS ABOUT TO BEGIN? AND HOW WILL HIS PLANS AFFECT THE FATE OF KALOS?

IS ZYGARDE THE KEY TO THE FINAL BATTLE...?!

**Pokémon X • Y
Volume 10
Perfect Square Edition**

Story by HIDENORI KUSAKA
Art by SATOSHI YAMAMOTO

©2017 The Pokémon Company International.
©1995–2016 Nintendo / Creatures Inc. / GAME FREAK inc.
TM, ®, and character names are trademarks of Nintendo.
POCKET MONSTERS SPECIAL X•Y Vol. 5
by Hidenori KUSAKA, Satoshi YAMAMOTO
© 2014 Hidenori KUSAKA, Satoshi YAMAMOTO
All rights reserved.
Original Japanese edition published by SHOGAKUKAN.
English translation rights in the United States of America, Canada, the United Kingdom,
Ireland, Australia, New Zealand and India arranged with SHOGAKUKAN.

English Adaptation—Bryant Turnage
Translation—Tetsuichiro Miyaki
Touch-up & Lettering—Annaliese Christman
Design—Alice Lewis
Editor—Annette Roman

The stories, characters and incidents mentioned
in this publication are entirely fictional.

No portion of this book may be reproduced or transmitted
in any form or by any means without written permission
from the copyright holders.

Printed in the U.S.A.

Published by
VIZ Media, LLC
P.O. Box 77010
San Francisco, CA 94107

10 9 8 7 6 5 4 3
First printing, April 2017
Third printing, January 2018

PARENTAL ADVISORY
POKÉMON ADVENTURES
is rated A and is suitable
for readers of all ages.
ratings.viz.com

www.perfectsquare.com   www.viz.com

THE SERIES

X Y

A NEW MEGA ADVENTURE!

Ash Ketchum's journey continues in
Pokémon the Series: XY
as he arrives in the Kalos region,
a land bursting with beauty, full of
new Pokémon to be discovered!

24
ACTION-PACKED
EPISODES!

Pick up **Pokémon the Series: XY** today!

IN STORES NATIONWIDE

visit **viz.com** for more information

TV Y7 FV

DVD VIDEO

©2015 Pokémon.
©1997-2014 Nintendo, Creatures, GAME FREAK, TV Tokyo, ShoPro, JR Kikaku. TM, ® Nintendo.

viz media

The Pokémon Company
INTERNATIONAL

The adventure continues in the Johto region!

POKÉMON

ADVENTURES ™

GOLD & SILVER BOX SET

Includes
**POKÉMON
ADVENTURES**
Vols. 8-14
and a collectible
poster!

Story by
HIDENORI KUSAKA

Art by
**MATO,
SATOSHI YAMAMOTO**

More exciting Pokémon adventures starring Gold and his rival Silver! First someone steals Gold's backpack full of Poké Balls (and Pokémon!). Then someone steals Prof. Elm's Totodile. Can Gold catch the thief—or thieves?!

Keep an eye on Team Rocket, Gold... Could they be behind this crime wave?

© 2010-2012 Pokémon
© 1995-2011 Nintendo/Creatures Inc./GAME FREAK Inc.
TM, ®, and character names are trademarks of Nintendo.
POCKET MONSTERS SPECIAL © 1997 Hidenori KUSAKA, MATO/SHOGAKUKAN
POCKET MONSTERS SPECIAL © 1997 Hidenori KUSAKA, Satoshi YAMAMOTO/SHOGAKUKAN

VIZ media
www.viz.com

PERFECT SQUARE

RATED A
ALL AGES
ratings.viz.com

Begin your Pokémon Adventure here in the Kanto region!

RED & BLUE BOX SET

Story by HIDENORI KUSAKA   Art by MATO

Includes
POKÉMON ADVENTURES
Vols. 1-7
and a collectible poster!

All your favorite Pokémon game characters jump out of the screen into the pages of this action-packed manga!

Red doesn't just want to train Pokémon, he wants to be their friend too. Bulbasaur and Poliwhirl seem game. But independent Pikachu won't be so easy to win over!

And watch out for Team Rocket, Red... They only want to be your enemy!

Start the adventure today!

© 2009-2012 Pokémon
© 1995-2010 Nintendo/Creatures Inc./GAME FREAK inc.
TM, ®, and character names are trademarks of Nintendo.
POCKET MONSTERS SPECIAL © 1997 Hidenori Kusaka, MATO/SHOGAKUKAN

VIZ media
www.viz.com

PERFECT SQUARE

Pokémon ADVENTURES™

HEARTGOLD & SOULSILVER

story by **HIDENORI KUSAKA**
art by **SATOSHI YAMAMOTO**

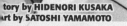

In this **two-volume** thriller, troublemaker Gold and feisty Silver must team up again to find their old enemy Lance and the Legendary Pokémon Arceus!

Available now!

© 2013 Pokémon.
© 1995-2013 Nintendo/Creatures Inc./GAME FREAK inc.
TM and ® and character names are trademarks of Nintendo.
POCKET MONSTERS SPECIAL © 1997 Hidenori KUSAKA, Satoshi YAMAMOTO/SHOGAKUKAN

POKéMON
POCKET COMICS

STORY & ART BY **SANTA HARUKAZE**

BLACK & WHITE

LEGENDARY POKÉMON

X•Y

A Pokémon pocket-sized book chock-full of four-panel gags, Pokémon trivia and fun quizzes based on the characters you know and love!

©2016 Pokémon.
©1995-2016 Nintendo/Creatures Inc./GAME FREAK inc. TM, ®, and character names are trademarks of Nintendo.
POKÉMON BW (Black • White) BAKUSHO 4KOMA MANGA ZENSHU © 2011 Santa HARUKAZE/SHOGAKUKAN
BAKUSHO 4KOMA DENSETSU NO POKÉMON O SAGASE!! © 2013 Santa HARUKAZE/SHOGAKUKAN
POKÉMON X•Y BAKUSHO 4KOMA MANGA ZENSHU © 2014 Santa HARUKAZE/SHOGAKUKAN

www.viz.com

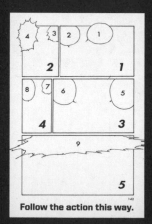

⟨⟨⟨ READ THIS WAY!

THIS IS THE END OF THIS GRAPHIC NOVEL!

To properly enjoy this VIZ Media graphic novel, please turn it around and begin reading from right to left.

This book has been printed in the original Japanese format in order to preserve the orientation of the original artwork. Have fun with it!

Follow the action this way.